THE

Volume I

A Merry Heart Doeth Good...

Joan Rossiter Burney

Library of Congress
Catalog Card No. 96-96835

ISBN 1-57579-021-1

4th Printing 1996

Printed in United States of America

PINE HILL PRESS, INC.
Freeman, S. Dak. 57029

Dedication

I dedicate this book to my beloved and sometimes crabby husband, Howard Keith Burney, better known as Kip, who insisted it be written, and made it possible for me to write it. I also dedicate it to my family, who have provided me with an endless source of material and encouragement, and to my friends, for the same reason. It is not easy to be an endless source of material, and I don't know what I'd have done without their constant support.

In addition, I dedicate it to the readers who've become an extended family, and who have had much to say about the contents of this book.

And lastly, I dedicate it to the editors who've put up with me all these years. My enthusiasm for writing is only matched by my lack of enthusiasm for spelling and the intricacies of grammar.

Thank you all and God bless. This is truly your book.

The essays in this book were selected from a multitude of columns written by Joan R. Burney from 1968 to 1987. They were printed under the following column titles:
At Random, Joan Burney, and Offer It Up.

Illustrator: Mary Burney Sandberg

Photo Credits:
Jim Denny, Omaha World Herald
WOWT Channel 6 in Omaha

Preface

Dear Reader:

This is a book meant to be read in bits and pieces. It is my fond hope that it will be the kind of book you will want to pick up now and then, and read a little here and there. You can go straight for the subjects that interest you, so the people who don't like cats will never need to read Chapter Four, if they don't want to. (And they won't want to.) Maybe you will even find a column where you will turn down a corner of the page so you can return to it again and again.

There has been tremendous pressure on me to compile my columns and put them in a book from both inside my house and outside of it. The external pressure comes when I'm on one of my speaking or teaching jaunts. People always assume, because I am a writer and a speaker, that I will have a book for them. And for years I've been promising one, saying sincerely, probably "next year."

The teacher in me liked the idea of having my own personal book, because people could take it home with them, and they'd have homework. So occasionally, I'd get excited about it. But then I would contemplate the necessity for going through piles of newspapers which had been gathering for years. And I would put it off again: I'd get at it someday. Surely — **next** year.

As I added more columns, the accumulation of piles accelerated. I started writing "At Random" in 1968, which means it will be twenty years old in '88. The Maverick Media newspapers picked up that column. And in 1974, I started writing "Offer It Up" for The Catholic Voice. In 1975, I started the "Joan Burney" column for the Norfolk Daily News. Other papers decided to use the columns, such as The Sioux City Journal, The Hastings Tribune, and The Missouri Valley Observer. That gets to be a lot of columns.

I liked to keep them all because different papers had different ways of printing them, which made it interesting. So the piles kept growing and growing. In later years I added to them with "Over the Feeder's Fence" for the Nebraska Cattleman and an advice column called "Comes the Dawn" for the Nebraska Farmer and The Colorado Farmer Rancher, among others. Along the way I've written an occasional "Aging Alumna" for the Trojan Newsletter, and for a few years

I wrote a column appropriately called "Udder Nonsense" for the Neu Cheese Company. These weren't all prize winners, of course, but a goodly number of them were, and for that I say alleluia.

As the accumulation of columns mounted, so did the pressure within the house. The fear of being pushed out of his home by piles of papers turned Kip testy, and the usually friendly cattlefeeder announced that he'd had it with my procrastination. He proclaimed the year 1987 "Next Year." He insisted I needed to compile the columns for the family, if for no other reason. Put the prize winners in a book, he said, get rid of the dogs, and get on with life. He was so determined that he gathered up my columns, gleaning missing ones from old newspaper archives, and with the aid of our young high school helper and friend, Laura Kuehler, he compiled them in eight huge spiral books. He took a deep breath, and then he began organizing them into categories. I helped some, but not much. This project did not interest me. It was just too much work.

Apparently I am not only a prodigious writer, I am an eclectic one, picking column topics from anywhere and everywhere. We ended up with eighteen categories. Good lord! And now we were down to choosing which categories got to be in the book, and which columns from those categories. Only I could make these choices.

That's when I had this brilliant idea. Why not let my readers choose? So I asked the dear readers to send me their favorite column, and then I would find my copy of same, autograph their's (if they gave a hoot about that) and send it back. Well, they gave a hoot, and it turned out to be a glorious, but time-consuming adventure. The bonus was that the inspirational comments that came with the columns engendered in the depths of my bosom the beginnings of enthusiasm for this project.

Many of the readers said that I wrote as if I'd been looking in their windows. They would say, "This column made me laugh out loud," or "This column made me cry," or "This column touched my heart and I copied it and sent it to everyone I knew." I was mightily energized. If the columns had touched people once, perhaps they'd touch even more people via the book. The very thought warmed my writer's heart.

In all, I've ended up with over three hundred and fifty columns which, according to my readers, should be in my book. Then I had a problem, happy though it was. This would be too many columns for the kind of a handy, low-budget, high quality paperback I had in mind. Hence the idea to start with half of them was born. So that's why this is "The Keepers" Volume One. Volume Two is already all sorted out, and I will get to it — perhaps next year.

In each chapter, the columns will be in chronological order, just as they were written, evolving even as I did through the years. I was most pleased to have some of my early columns show up. They came in yellowed and worn, and often pasted to pages out of scrapbooks. Because I'm using some of them, I need to warn you that in the early days I sometimes called Kip (with affectionate amusement) "The Old Bull-Shipper" because he did a lot of shipping of old bulls. There were people who were offended by that, and let me know (as readers tend to do), but I thought it suited him and hung on to it. Until one mind-expanding night when a lovely lady in Wynot introduced me to a gathered group of teachers as the wife of the "Old Bull-Shipper." Well, she meant to say "old bull-shipper" but she said, as plain as could be, what the people who objected to it thought I meant all along. So I quit using it. But for the sake of historical accuracy, I have left it in the early columns. I want you to know, however, that I really meant — shipper of old bulls.

I realize, as I prepare these columns for printing, that herein lies the story of my life, and of the lives of a lot of people whom I love. Although I didn't feel that way about each individual column, I feel that the accumulated ones are almost too intimate a portrait. It's a little scary. But over the years my columns have brought me close to any number of readers whom I now call friends.

The exciting thing about this book is that maybe you will become a friend, too.

Table of Contents

Chapter One

*''You can't prevent the
birds of sorrow
from flying over your head,
but you can prevent them
from building a nest in
your hair.''*

Columns to cope by...

Chapter One

"Life is difficult," writes noted author, Dr. Scott Peck. "Once we truly know that life is difficult — once we truly understand and accept it — then life is no longer difficult." This realization started me on a life-long pursuit of education to help me understand how to help myself and others accept and cope with the "difficulties" of life. That journey has been an exciting one, if sometimes exhausting. In response to perceived need, my own and others, I went after training as a Hospice and a Community Caretaker Volunteer, then I jumped into a two year Family Minister Training Program. Somewhere in there I also earned, as a non-traditional student (meaning "old"), an undergraduate degree in communications and a Masters in Psychological Counseling. The education I've gleaned from these pursuits, and from just getting to the age to be considered non-traditional, I have insisted on sharing with my readers, and it is the following essays that the readers say have most helped them cope in times of need.

*　*　*

Send 'Birds of Sorrow' Flying

May 1983

I have just received what is destined to become my favorite proverb from a very unlikely source. You'll love it too. Here it is:

"You can't prevent the birds of sorrow from flying over your head, but you can prevent them from building a nest in your hair."

It's an old Chinese proverb. And living by it is probably why the Chinese got old.

My source was unlikely because it was given to me by a friend, Shirley, who is a world class worrier. You name it and she has already worried about it. She is a dear, dear friend. But she is a worry wart. I'm thinking of putting her up for the Guinness Book of Records.

She worries about anything bad that might possibly happen now or in the future to every one of her relatives and her friends and she has loads of both.

She sees bad omens everywhere. Especially if something good happens. She worries then that it won't last.

I'm always fussing at her about it. "Worrying gets you nowhere," I tell her. "Look at all the worrying we do about the weather and we haven't changed the path of one single cloud!"

Now I've got her worrying that she worries too much.

The thing is that a person can legitimately wallow in worry. A person can get into a veritable rage at the injustices in the world, can fume at the unfairness of life. A person can stew about getting wiped off the earth by a bomb or a tornado, both of which are possibilities. A person can stew about dying, which is a certainty. But all the worrying and the rage, in and of itself, will not accomplish much.

One should take action, if one can. But if one can't, one could just as well turn one's attention to the butterflies and the roses.

Dr. Joel Goodman runs a school teaching people to laugh (imagine, having to go to school to learn to laugh). He says that stress is not caused by an event but by our perception of an event.

Dr. Goodman says changing our perception with humor will keep us from going bonkers.

We are intelligent human beings. We are told we use only about 10 percent of our mental powers, that for all intents and purposes our ultimate mental capacity is infinite.

That means, at the very least, that we can turn our minds to other things. When we are wallowing, we can simply refuse to continue to wallow. Nobody said it was easy. I'm just telling you it's possible. And I've done my share of wallowing.

You can't prevent things happening that are not joyous, you can't prevent the birds of sorrow from flying over your head. But you can prevent them from building a nest in your hair.

It is true that in this life we can choose happiness. The inequities of life will not go away because they make us unhappy. There's always going to be somebody luckier, somebody richer, somebody better looking. There's always going to be something to worry about.

And there's always going to be butterflies and sunsets, and things to learn, and people to hug. There's vast quantities of good to be done. One just has to shoo off the birds of sorrow and get busy!

Fear Helps Bring Success

December 1981

An article on Erica Jung, the noted authoress, said that she believed that all the good things that have happened to her have come from a willingness to change, "to risk the unknown, to do the very things that I feared."

Every new venture, it seems, has an element of fear. **We fear failure, and yet, the truth of the matter is, failure is our best learning tool.** If I hadn't failed at everything that had anything to do with being a homemaker, I might never have tried to do anything else. In fact, I am sure of that. If I could have successfully mastered the art of sewing, growing things and attacking dirt and clutter, I would have been content.

But, as I've often fibbed, I am such a lousy housekeeper that our house was ransacked and we didn't know it for three weeks. The only thing I grow with any great degree of success is the mold on the leftover vegetables in the refrigerator. I am so good at sewing, that with my help Juli couldn't make a pot holder in 4-H. (Now she's costuming whole plays in Omaha, so you know with whom the problem laid.)

So my venturing out of the household to get a degree and do whatever else it is I do was a necessity. And boy was it scary. But I've found that I thrive on challenge, and **that fear might be uncomfortable, but it's seldom fatal.**

It is with this in mind that I share a brief bit of prose on "Risks" which I've borrowed from a pamphlet put out by the Nebraska Livestock Feeders Association. If you're not contemplating something scary but exciting, I hope it spurs you on.

"Risks"

"To laugh is — to risk appearing the fool.

To weep is — to risk appearing sentimental.

To reach out for another is — to risk involvement.

To expose feelings is — to risk exposing your true self.

To place your ideas, your dreams before a crowd is — to risk their loss.

To love is — to risk not being loved in return.

To live is — to risk dying.

To hope is — to risk despair.

To try is — to risk failure.

But risks must be taken, because the greatest hazard in life is to risk nothing. **The person who risks nothing, does nothing, has nothing and is nothing. He may avoid suffering and sorrow, but he simply cannot learn, feel, change, grow, love — live. Chained by certitudes, he is a slave, he has forfeited freedom.**

Only a person who risks is free."

You Really Look Awful!

May 1982

Have you ever had this happen? You're bouncing along the street feeling pretty good, and up comes this person who takes one look at you and says, "You look terrible, aren't you feeling well?"

And you felt fine — until that very moment. All of a sudden your spirits start to droop.

There are in this world otherwise kindly and well-meaning people, who seem to knock themselves out to bring you the bad news. Everybody knows somebody who insists on saying just exactly the truth on any subject (as he or she sees it) no matter how it hurts others. And the more unflattering the truth is, the happier they seem to be. They are telling us something "for your own good!"

When the truth of the matter is, it's for our own "bad," so to speak. At least, so say the experts quoted recently in an article in the New York Times.

"Silence" is preferable, say the experts, or at least a "gradual, more gentle approach to the truth."

Motivation is important here. If a friend walks up to you at a party and says quietly "your slip is showing," you're grateful. If she calls up the next morning and says, "Do you know your slip was showing all evening at the party?" you're not grateful, and you wonder about her motivation.

It would seem that sometimes the teller of truth does it for the sadistic pleasure of seeing you squirm, no matter how it's glossed over in the teller's mind.

There really are things that you should know "for your own good." But there are also some things that you never need to know. A wise and loving friend knows the difference.

Of course, we all slip up once in awhile.

Years ago, when I was in my "salad" days of public speaking; green, very tender and easily bruised, I was just heading out the door to make a local speech when a usually wise and loving friend called. She repeated a remark made by so-and-so in which he made some rather

5

ugly, derogatory comments about my speaking (he's never heard me) and ended by saying "I wouldn't go across the street to hear her!" Something like that. My friend concluded the tale by saying, "I thought you'd be amused." (My speech that night was not so hot!)

Well, now, I'm a realist, and I'm well aware that there are hundreds, perhaps even thousands, of people who feel the same way as so-and-so does. My whole family included. But at that particular moment it was a psychological blow. I was not amused. It hurt. **Later — I was amused, but that was much later.**

Truth which is unkind and won't help anything, is better left unsaid. This is true for any age, but particularly for children. Tell a child she's a klutz, and she will grow up to be one. I know from personal experience.

Dr. Willard Gaylin, a psychiatrist who knows all about these things, says "If you tell a young girl she's beautiful, even if she's not, she's likely to become a very attractive woman." The reverse is also true. "If you tell her that she's ugly, even the prettiest girl will believe it and act accordingly."

Dr. Karl E. Scheibe, a professor of psychology, suggests we sometimes need some "elaboration and embroidery of the truth" to meet each other's needs, and that all of our doubts and suspicions don't need to be voiced. "You cannot say everything that goes through your mind and also maintain a long-term relationship."

People need to be told they are loved and they are beautiful. And if you love someone — they are always beautiful.

That's the truth!

Trumpet Blasts Signal Election

November 1982

A passing stranger, observing the little white country schoolhouse, might not see it as a bastion of democracy. He might look at the uncut grass and the peeled paint, and get the idea it was an abandoned school, picturesque in its way, but of no use whatsoever.

He'd be dead wrong, because **on the first Tuesday in November, that little old schoolhouse is the most important place around.** It's the place we vote.

I don't know how you feel about voting, but I consider it a sacred trust. I think of the people who fought and died, who withstood pain and humiliation, who marched and petitioned and persevered, just so I might have the right to vote, and I march to the voting place as if a brass band were playing and an honor guard were accompany-

6

ing me. I vote as if my country depended upon it. I really believe it does.

I've taken part in too many elections where one vote made the difference to feel apathetic about my vote. I've watched what happens in countries where the people have no rights. Too many times I've heard, **"The only thing necessary for the triumph of evil is for good men to do nothing."**

Besides I enjoy complaining about things. If I don't vote, I have no right to complain. I long ago made a pact with myself: "If you don't go to the meeting, don't complain about the decisions made by the people who do." Which boils down to: "If you don't vote, don't gripe." It gets me to a lot of meetings and it gets me to the little white school.

Besides, voting is a social occasion in our Precinct 12. The people on the election board are all our friends and so we get a little visiting in. We only have 136 registered voters in our precinct, and all of them don't vote (though we usually do better than the national average), so the board members have time on their hands. They play Sheephead or Pitch and harass each other and passing voters, all in good fun.

Every 25 votes, the counting crew gets to go to work. When there's an interesting race, that's the exciting time. They count behind the piano. **They used to count in the basement, but found a family of snakes had moved in for the winter. Sort of took the fun out of it.**

Our voting stalls are not classy, but they're adequate. Wooden booths with moth-eaten beige curtains drooping about two-thirds of the way down the opening. Wooden shelves with pencils attached to them with string.

What they lack in elegance, these voting booths make up in prestige. People mark their ballots there, and decide upon the fate of our states and our nation. What could be more important?

It's an awesome responsibility.

The stuff that makes a country go happens in that little white schoolhouse. Democracy. The pencil on the ballot sheet. The strongest weapon known to mankind. And we wield it.

Do you hear the trumpets blare as you march to the polls? You should. They're there if you listen.

Radiant Vision Shared

November, 1982

I am indebted to Gene Day of Norfolk, Nebraska for sharing. In a letter received more recently, he included a couple of his favorite quotations.

Gene says he's carried the following quote in his billfold for many years. "It's pretty beat up...I guess we're getting pretty beat up together...but it seems to bring me back to square one." He attributes it to Richard Jefferies.

There comes a time when we all need to be brought back to square one.

Here's the quote:

"If we had never before looked upon the earth, but suddenly came to it man or woman grown, set down in the midst of a summer mead, would it not seem to us a radiant vision? The hues, the shapes, the song and life of birds, above all the sunlight, the breath of heaven, resting on it; the mind would be filled with its glory, unable to grasp it, hardly believing that such things could be mere matter and no more. Like a dream of some spiritland it would appear, scarce fit to be touched lest it should fall to pieces, too beautiful to be long watched lest it should fade away."

Thank you, Gene. I look out at my meadow this morning with renewed appreciation. I suspect a lot of people will see the vibrancy of their world in a new light because you shared your beat-up quote.

Marching To Your Own Beat Works Best

May 1983

There are individuals on this earth who seem to thrive on stress, and only go at one speed — fast!

And there are other individuals who are always saying to the above-mentioned fast-paced-persons that they should "slow down." They usually say that they should slow down after they've gotten them to agree to serve on a committee, or make a speech, or direct a choir, or build a house, or take care of their kids or whatever. **People who want other people to slow down never want them to slow down in an area which will affect what they are doing for them,** if you know what I mean.

These high-powered people work hard and play hard and frequently die young. But, if you stop to think about it, they've crammed a lot of living into their years. And we've all got to go sometime.

I am sort of one of those people, and sort of not. I only get things done under stress, and I'm continually taking on more than I should. But I can also do nothing with absolute aplomb, very happily. Not often, but often enough to refresh my soul.

However, I've been thinking about this for a long time, and I've decided that everyone has some kind of an inner instinct about the pace at which he or she works best.

I hear people say, "I'm a morning person," for instance, and know that they really race around in the morning, and hit the skids come evening.

And I also know "night people" who seem to light up after the sun goes down and perform tasks that require prodigious amounts of energy.

Although I echo Henry David Thoreau's sentiments: **"Why should we be in such desperate haste to succeed, and in such desperate enterprises: If a man does not keep pace with his companions, perhaps it is because he hears a different drummer. Let him step to the music, which he hears, however measured or far away."** I suggest to Henry that sometimes a person's drummer is doing a march double-time.

You can almost tell the beat of someone's "drummer" as they walk down a street. Some people are definitely stepping out to a march beat, and some are strolling along to a drummer dreamily tapping out a waltz.

And there are people who definitely respond to two drummers. I have a friend who says of her husband, "Oswald" (not his real name, thank heavens), "has only two gears, super high and super low." And it's true. The man literally runs while at work but on vacation he operates at a speed that would make a snail look hyperactive. It's amazing.

It would be nice if your occupation kept step with your drummer. Such as, ideally, the people who work on an afternoon paper, who have to go to work at unmercifully early hours in the morning, should be morning people. And the ones who work on a morning paper, who have to work half the night, should be night people. I would like to do a survey and see if this is true.

It is doubtless true, since we all have different drummers, that we will never set our pace to suit other people. And sometimes, I'm sure, we don't even suit ourselves. Nevertheless, we will step to the music which we hear, "however measured or far away."

Grief Cycle Runs Course
Leaving Strength Behind

November 1984

There's been a lot of talk lately about grief. Maybe not at your house, but at mine. A beloved niece talked to me about the calmness she felt at her mother's funeral. "We worked through the stages of grief while Mom was so sick," she said. "Now we can just be happy for her and glad her suffering is over."

And Judy Dye, the gal who mans the Farm Crisis Hot Line in Walthill said, "You've got to realize that some of our farmers are beyond stress, they are into the denial and anger stages of grief. They'll have to work through that before they can cope."

Whenever we lose something we love or value, we go through the grief cycle. It does, indeed, have to be "worked" through. It is interesting that we go through a mini-grief cycle when we miss a phone call, or break a treasured gift, or dent the car.

It goes like this, according to Dr. Elisabeth Kubler-Ross, who is the author of "On Death and Dying," and an authority on working with terminally ill patients: First there's the shock and denial. "This could not have happened to me! It can't be true."

Then the anger. "Why me?" And the depression. And finally, the acceptance, and the peace that comes with that.

In the matter of the phone call or the dented car, the whole process is over in minutes.

It is another thing with the loss of a loved one, or the loss of a job, or the loss of a farm. The process is long and painful, and sometimes people need a lot of help.

The shock might last for a while — an emotional numbness while you struggle to believe and disbelieve what's happened. When the pain comes, it is important not to run away from it. It is important to the healing process.

It's good that we know this because grief, and its stages, are a part of life. We work hard to make our life full and enjoyable. We build friendships, nourish family, acquire jobs and material comforts. And then we lose something, or somebody, and we have to deal with that loss.

Everyone has to deal with loss. It's a part of life. Understanding the nature of the grief process may make us better able to do that.

How we handle "little griefs," for instance when the Cornhuskers lose (Little?), will in some way give us an idea of what will happen when the major griefs hit.

This may seem depressing, but I don't mean it to be. I'm really talking about survival. Realizing that the grief process is normal, and **we** all go through it, is a step toward survival, because it is the nature of the healing process that you will survive. Nature is a powerful ally.

It takes time. The greater the loss, the more time. And it does not progress upwards in a straight line. It has dramatic leaps and depressing backslides, but if you're aware of this, you know it's underway.

Seek the support of others. It's not only okay to ask for help, it's darned smart. It's also okay to feel angry and depressed. It's not okay to be destructive or hate yourself. Your anger and depression will go away as your hurt heals. It's part of the process, remember.

Grief is an emotional wound which requires healing. Recognition of that, and looking at past situations wherein you've experienced grief and survived, will give you the confidence to survive again. **Weathering a crisis makes you stronger in the broken places.**

'Not Holy' Person Shares Prayer

December 1984

Although I'm a person of fairly strong religious convictions, I am not very holy. I've never liked to go to church, for instance.

I discovered why in a book I recently took part in. My early memories of church were entirely disciplinary. **I grew up thinking it was not a fun place.** I had to be quiet. Couldn't talk to my friends. Didn't really understand why I was there.

Intellectually, now, I've accepted the fact that I am a better person for going to church. And it is a source of emotional strength. But way back in my subconscious, something is telling me "if it snows a lot, you won't have to go to church." And part of me is glad.

I only tell you this because I want to share a favorite poem with you as a Christmas present. And I don't want you to think I'm trying to convert you. I don't care what faith you are. I just think for survival's sake, we all have to have some faith. And I hope you do.

Because, if you do, this poem will speak to you too, in the places in your heart and soul where you need it most. I want it to seep into your soul and give you the kind of comfort it gives to me.

I think, in these perilous times, when we are up to our ying-yang in stressful situations, we should share the things which give rest to our souls.

The author is unknown. I wish it were me.

Here tis.

11

Dear Child,
   God does not say to you today, "Be Strong" —
   He knows your strength is spent —
   He knows how long the road has been —
   How weary you've become, for
   He who walked this earth along —
   Each boggy lowland and each rugged hill, understands —
   And so He simply says, "Be still,
   Be still and know that I am God."
   The hour is late and you must rest awhile —
   Let life's reservoirs fill up, as slow rain
   fills an empty unturned cup.
   Hold up your cup, dear Child, for God to fill.
   He only asks that you be still.

   The Christmas season is a time for all of us to "be still" and let God refresh our souls. Without him, we will accomplish nothing. With Him, all things are possible. And we can and will survive with enthusiasm.
   And that's from someone who doesn't like to go to church.
   God bless you all. He does you know.

People Like Geodes, Shine Inside

August 1985

   Have you ever thought about how much geodes and people are alike?

   A geode is a rock that's not much on the outside, but when you open it up, it's full of crystal and other beautiful stones and it is a thing of beauty. Dictionary definition: "A rock, usually globular, having a cavity lined with crystal."

   I found one in Colorado. I would like to say I found it while wandering through the hills, but I found it while wandering through the shops. It was in a pile of geodes that was for sale. "You want to buy a rock?" Kip said increduiously. "What on earth for?"

   And I said, "To make a point."

   I picked the ugliest geode I could find and when the man cracked it open, I got so excited Kip was embarrassed. **The ugly geode was full of crystal and beautiful inside. "See," I said to Kip, "just like people." He didn't see.**

   The point is that we're all like geodes sometimes — ugly on the

12

outside, but it is our inner spirit that counts. That's where we develop the sparkling stuff. Yet we get so obsessed with how people look on the outside, we don't see the beauty.

Little kids who are not "beautiful" in the sense we define beauty at this point think less of themselves than their "beautiful" friends.

Teachers especially need to understand the geodes theory. People are looked down upon because they're not good looking or are too fat, too thin, too short, too tall, have funny-looking noses or whatever. We even judge ourselves by what we look like. Balderdash!

Sometimes, just thinking about it can change the way we feel. My favorite example is to think about our best friends. Chances are they aren't perfect. Who'd want a perfect best friend? We don't give a hoot if they are fat or thin or have funny noses. We love them because of their inner selves. Each of us needs to learn to be our own best friend.

We have a body just so our spirit has something to get around in. We are not our body. It's nice to keep it up because it's the only house we've got for our spirit. But it is not the essence of who we are.

I remember when the overwhelming reality of this hit me. It was when I was very young and went to the funeral of my favorite Uncle Bert. I was devastated and didn't even want to view his body. But I did. And I realized that though his body was there, Uncle Bert was gone. Does this make any sense? That body was not Uncle Bert.

And I remember another time, when I was taking a nap on the couch and son Bill, who was about 3 at the time, came up to me, lifted up an eyelid, and said "Mom, are you in there?"

Conversely, people who are great-looking may rely on their physical appearance and forget to develop internal motivation. **And when they get to be past 40, the body just gets to be something of a maintenance problem and they lose their sense of self-worth.**

So when we start to judge somebody by how they look, especially when that somebody is the person looking at us in the mirror, we should remember the geode, and look for the spirit sparkling inside.

Good Stress, Bad Stress, and Wild Beasts

1985

"When is the last time you ran from a wild beast?" asked the curly-haired lecturer. He was talking about stress.

There's good stress and bad stress. The good stress makes us function at peak level. The bad stress gives us ulcers, migraine headaches and heart attacks.

That's because the body's response to stress is to produce energy. The blood pressure rises, the adrenalin starts to flow. And in prehistoric times, when stress was caused by such things as wild beasts, we had a place for that energy to be used.

In this day and age we cannot often respond to stressful situations with action. We bottle the energy up. A bad situation.

And we become victims of "the fearsome foursome," which are anxiety, depression, inadequacy and guilt. There's a lot of that going around.

It helps, according to our lecturer, if we recognize the physical and emotional symptoms of stress and do something about them.

"Well, sure," you say, "but what?!"

I'm going to tell you.

Too much of the time we cause ourselves stress by worrying about things over which we have no control. We have to stop that. We have to "let go." It isn't easy. It helps to make a list.

On one side of the list we put the things over which we have no control. And an important thing we must take into consideration is that we have no control over any other person. **Someone else's problems, no matter how much we love them, are not our problems to solve. We can pray for them, and we can love them, but we cannot do for them what they will not do for themselves.**

Then we list the problems that we can do something about. Even the seemingly insurmountable ones, like financial catastrophes, or our own personal tragedies.

And we start to do something about them in a positive way. If someone is taking advantage of us and it's driving us nuts, we very politely put a stop to it. It will relieve tension immediately. We're the ones who're letting it happen. We're the only ones who can change the situation.

If you perceive a situation to be completely out of control, then stress management calls for you changing your perception. Get all the information possible, look at all the options, and make your deci-

14

sions based on the best of those options.

For some people that might mean quitting an impossible job, turning to a new career, taking bankruptcy either emotionally or in reality, and starting all over.

The important thing is that you DO something. Whether it's gathering the courage to go to a self-help group like A.A., or Al-Anon, or Recovery, or making the best of a terrible situation, or positively confronting someone who bugs you, the minute you do what you have to to change you, that's the minute you're going to start running your own life, and not let life run you.

We may not have to run from wild beasts, but we do have to confront a multitude of stressful situations which make running from wild beasts look easy. The more knowledge we have about dealing with bad stress, the more we'll be able to keep our modern wild beasts at bay.

'Luck' Requires Hard Work

1985

"You're a lucky person to be where you are!" said a friend of mine.

"Luck has nothing to do with it," I replied testily.

It's like somebody telling you you're lucky to have your teeth when you get to be 90 years old, and you've spent your lifetime flossing and brushing and seeing the dentist for checkups. Luck has nothing to do with a lot of things in a person's life. You make your luck.

It's a thought I've tried to pound into a lot of people's heads. What happens to you in your life is what you make happen. And, often as not, it takes a lot of hard work. A lot of studying, learning and giving up things which are not fun to give up.

It takes a willingness to try some things and fail. There's no crime in trying something and failing. Failure is simply a learning tool. The crime is to spend your whole life wanting to try something, but failing to try.

It's not always fun to do what you have to do to improve your life. It takes an enormous amount of courage, sometimes, for a person just to sign up for a class. Or take a chance on a new career. Or read a dull but educational book. If you can't find your way alone, it takes even more courage to look for counseling. But it's all part of making your own luck.

Even if you're pretty sure who you are and where you're going with your life, it takes a lot of dedication to get up every morning and face the unpleasant things one sometimes must in order to cause the pleasant things to happen. Like working at a tedious job, or doing an unpleasant but necessary task. Or flossing your teeth. I've always hated to floss my teeth, but the alternative is unthinkable. I have trouble finding my glasses now. Lord help me if I also had to look for my teeth.

Luck doesn't have a lot to do with the care you give your teeth, just as it doesn't have a lot to do with what a person becomes in life. Work does. And work is not always fun.

"Variety may be the spice of life, but it is monotony that brings home the groceries."

There's nothing that says work can't be satisfactory. But often, it's the end of the job that brings the satisfaction. Or the end of the day. And the thought that you've accomplished something worthwhile, if that accomplishment consists only of earning the money to put bread on the table. What am I saying "only?" That's one of the most important accomplishments we accomplish.

We got into trouble some years back when there was a rumor going around that everything was supposed to be joyously fulfilling. And a whole generation wandered around attempting to find this state of euphoria. Finding themselves, they said.

Nobody finds themselves by wandering around looking elsewhere. People find themselves by looking inside, and then making the best of what's there. We get discouraged when we start comparing ourselves to others. Or start trying to build who we are according to other's specifications.

We are what we are. And we do the best we can. We don't have to achieve like our neighbors or our sisters or our brothers. **We only have to achieve in the areas where we can, in ways which are possible to us. And God knows we have to work at that. But at least that's possible. Trying to be like somebody else is not.**

All of this is not a lecture for you, although you're certainly welcome to it if anything's of use. I'm glad to be of service. Actually, however, it's for me.

This week I'm seriously starting on writing my book. It's going to be a whale of a lot of work. I know it's the next step for me. And I want in the worst way to have written a book. So, I suppose I have to write it. I've dedicated myself to the project.

If — I mean — when I get done, there won't be any luck involved. And it's not going to be fun. But, oh the satisfaction of having done it. I can hardly wait.

Some Things Writers Have To Get Out Of Their Systems

February 1986

Just as everybody seems to remember exactly what they were doing the day Kennedy was shot, I suspect we will remember where we were when the Space Shuttle exploded. I'm sure that you, like me, have listened and read about it until you're overwhelmed with the details.

And yet, I have to write about it myself. Ferdie Peitz taught this to me. After my mom died, I thought it would be too painful and too personal to write about her, but I couldn't write about anything else. And Ferdie came up to me in the Chief Bar at a Friday night fish fry, put his arm around me, and remarked on the fact he hadn't seen my column for awhile. He said, **"You're going to have to write about your mother, you know."**

I was at my Mackintosh writing about getting lost, when Kip came in and said, "The shuttle exploded."

"Oh, my God!" I said, "It's the one with the teacher on it."

It dawned on me later that the horror was brought home even more by that fact. One of "us" was aboard. A civilian. An ordinary person plucked out of her ordinariness by fate, to become a martyr to technology and find a place in history books forever. But at the price of her life.

I got to a TV set and watched, ignoring the tears that couldn't seem to quit running down my face. I declared the TV people heartless and inhumane when they showed the picture of Christa McAullife's parents watching the shot, and of the children, and all other intensely personal and painful pictures.

I got up and turned the set off angrily, and then I went into the kitchen and turned that set on. **I could NOT watch.**

I kept hoping for a miracle, like a great bunch of parachutes descending, or the spaceship suddenly appearing out of the giant cloud of smoke and zooming off into space, just like it was supposed to do.

Some of you will remember, on May 5, 1961, watching Alan Shepherd blast off. I was so scared. I knew the thing was going to blow up. I watched and I prayed. Boy, how I prayed. If the Lord didn't have some control up there, where did he?

But I didn't even bother to watch some of the last space shuttles blast off. It had gotten to be ho-hum business. I feel guilty about that. It blew up and I wasn't even watching. Or praying.

As the incredible horror of what happened sunk in, the pain in my heart began to feel familiar. It seemed a part of all the sadness we endure in life. **Those of us who have lived — well — a number of years, have a lot of scenes stored up in our heads.**

I again saw, mentally, the riderless horse at the Kennedy funeral, and the little boy saluting his father. And I remembered, good Democrat that I was in my grade school years, how terrified I was when President Roosevelt died. Crying, I called my dad at the bank and said, "All we've got is that dumb Truman, and all he can do is play the piano."

And Dad said, "Don't you worry, Joan, Truman is a very capable man, he'll make a great president." (Prophetic words.)

We've all had loved ones who have died, less spectacularly, but no less painfully for us. We planned on having them around for a lot of years. We understand the pain of personal loss.

As survivors in this sad old world, we should learn never to let things get "ho-hum." We need to hug our loved ones, relish the sunsets, smell the violets, listen to the birds sing. **The unforgettable sight of the shuttle making its own sun in our sky should remind us, and remind us, and remind us.**

Losers Deserve Congratulations, Too

May 1986

The following wise words have been variously attributed to Teddy Roosevelt and John Kennedy.

"The credit belongs to the man actually in the arena whose face is marred by dust and sweat and blood... who knows the great enthusiasm,... the great devotion to duty... and spends himself in a worthy cause. Who at best if he wins knows the thrill of high achievement, and if he fails, at least he fails while daring greatly... His place shall never be with those cold and timid souls who know neither victory nor defeat."

Speaking as one of the cold and timid souls, I'd like to extend my heartfelt congratulations to all the losers in Nebraska's primary. Everybody congratulates the winners, but the losers also deserve a word of thanks, because they "fail while daring greatly." **Most of us prefer the role of complaining from the side lines.**

Nebraska's primary is behind us, with the confusing abundance of good candidates running for governor. Other states have their primaries yet to come, and are still bearing the brunt of the claims and counterclaims.

So it's probably a good time to pause and contemplate those who have the courage to file. Many recognize they are pitting themselves against enormous odds, to say nothing of opening up their life to the unmerciful public scrutiny. I think anyone who's even vaguely in the public eye is approached about running for office. I have been. But I always have a million reasons not to do it. The truth of the matter is, I'm chicken.

I'm afraid of two things. It is not in my nature to do anything halfway, so if I ran for an office, I'd go all out. **So first — I'm afraid I'd lose.** I know from experience, losing is painful. I ran for cheerleader once and lost by one vote. And it was my vote. I voted for my best friend who was running against me. I learned an important lesson there. I learned in this life one has to vote for oneself. It's stood me in good stead. Nonetheless, in the far reaches of my mind there's a little notation to myself that says **"losing is painful."**

But there's another side to this running for an office which might be even worse, and that's the second problem. **Suppose a person wins.** You have to have a skin as thick as an elephant's. The minute you file for an office, all the other candidates for the office, and everybody in the other political party, has a vested interest in discrediting you. And all the silly things you've done and said in your lifetime come back to haunt you.

Forces over which you have no control come into play. One has little enough control anyway, but once one is in a political office, every word and every act is scrutinized. Not only of the candidate, but — and I suspect this is the hardest part — of the candidates family.

Following Harry Truman's advice, most of us, contemplating the heat, do not go willingly into the kitchen. So congratulations to those who have the courage. **Winner or loser, we owe you a debt of gratitude.**

Ultimately, Everyone Is A 'Single'

1986

I cannot find the author of the words I'm going to share with you today. But I've been trying to express something like this for years so I am grateful to that unknown. I think you'll love it.

I wish I'd had it some weeks ago when I spoke at a "Singles" convocation. And my kids said to me, **"How can you do that, Mom, you've been married 38 years."** I couldn't exactly explain.

But I had no qualms about it because we are all in a sense "singles." True, some of us are attached to other singles. Spouses or best friends or beloved relatives. But nothing is forever and survival is the recognition that we have the ability to carry on by ourselves.

The past few years I have survived with some degree of enthusiasm despite the fact that dear friends have died, friends with whom I'd planned to grow old. I never imagined for a minute that I would have to live in a world without them. And if anybody had suggested it, I would have simply said, "Well, that's nonsense, I just couldn't survive." But I did.

We've all had to say goodbye to people because of death or divorce or some other reason. And we've survived. Although there are times of gut-grinding pain when we wondered if we would. The knowledge that we can, and indeed, we must, sometimes comes slowly and painfully. But when it comes we are much stronger in the broken places.

That's when we learn we are all, in a very real sense, single. And though we sometimes have company along life's passages, we must be prepared to traverse them alone. A friend who spent most of her years as a dependent wife has — after the death of her husband — learned that she can do things like fly into O'Hare in Chicago, and drive to Kansas City by herself. She is exuberant, and her enthusiasm is contagious. "All by myself!" she says grinning. "I did it myself."

It's not so easy. After his wife died, Ferdie Pietz, Hartington's beloved philosopher/auctioneer said, **"It's hell to have to go in single-hitch when you've been in double-hitch for so long."**

But enough of this philosophizing. Here 'tis:

Comes the Dawn

After awhile you learn the subtle difference
Between holding a hand and chaining a soul,
And you learn that love doesn't mean leaning,
And company doesn't mean security,
And you begin to understand that kisses aren't contracts
And presents aren't promises.
And you begin to accept your defeats
With your head held high and eyes open
With the grace of an adult, not the grief of a child.
You learn to build your roads
On today because tomorrow's ground
Is too uncertain for plans and futures
Have a way of falling down in mid-flight.
After awhile you learn that even sunshine
Burns if you get too much.
So you plant your own garden, and decorate
Your own soul, instead of waiting

For someone to bring you flowers.
And you learn you really can endure,
That you really are strong.
And you really do have worth
And you learn and learn and you learn
With every goodbye, you learn.

Sleep Deprived Reader Gets Advice

1986

"Unraveling Insomnia: No More Sleepless Nights," proclaimed the front of the June issue of Psychology Today. Sounded good.

Some months ago, a kindly but apparently sleep-deprived reader asked me to write about insomnia. I started gathering material. Occasionally I have a night when I cannot get to sleep. A little voice in my head will not allow it. The more I fight to sleep, the wider awake I am.

I learned an effective technique at a seminar given by a biofeedback expert. You outsmart the little voice.

One way is to designate an uncomfortable chair in your house as a "worry chair." If you can't sleep, get up and sit in that chair and worry for ten minutes. Decide what your problems are and what you can do about them. Perhaps confront the worst possible scenario and decide how you would handle it. Soon the little voice feels uncomfortable, thinks longingly of the warm bed and lets you go to sleep in peace. You may have to do it a couple of times, but it works.

Considerable research has been done in this field, and the good news is, "there is real hope for poor sleepers." Because of the complexity of the underlying causes of insomnia, researchers now call it "disorders of initiating and maintaining sleep," or DIMS. Thirty million Americans are estimated to have DIMS.

The least serious is what I diagnose myself as having, and it is called transient insomnia. **Virtually everyone suffers occasionally and the sleeplessness comes from worrying about a fight with the boss, an upcoming test or some other schedule interruption or stress.**

More serious is "short-term insomnia," which can last days or even weeks and is fueled by such factors as on-going psychological stress of bereavement, divorce or relocation. The most serious type is chronic insomnia, which may last for months or even years. No case is the same and in more serious cases the key to helping insomniacs is careful diagnosis.

Sleeping pills are not the answer on a long-term basis. One suggestion from the article to "treat" insomnia, was to "grab patients by the feet and shake all the pills out of their pockets."

Sleep researcher Peter Hauri says one problem is fear of insomnia, which becomes its own self-fulfilling prophecy and he makes the following suggestions:

— Most crucial is to never oversleep because of a poor night's sleep. Get up at the same time every morning.

— Try to set a regular bedtime, but delay it if necessary so you go to bed only when you are tired. If you awake in the night, relax in bed for awhile and let sleep return. Try reading or listening to music. If this doesn't work and you grow tense and frustrated, get out of bed and do some quiet activity until you're sleepy once again. Repeat this as often as necessary.

— Cut down on alcohol, smoking, chocolate, tea and caffeinated soft drinks, avoid them in the afternoon, or eliminate them entirely.

— Schedule a time in the early evening to write down worries or concerns and what you will do about them the next day.

— Experiment with your bedroom's noise level and temperature.

— Avoid heavy meals too close to bedtime or snacks during the night. But a midnight snack of hot milk and crackers helps some people sleep.

— Stay fit with regular exercise, but not too close to bedtime. Keep physically active if possible the day after a bad night's sleep and avoid napping unless you're sure they will help you sleep at night.

— Try each of the above suggestions for at least a week before discarding it. If it becomes necessary, get professional help in coping with life stresses or learning biofeedback or other types of relaxation training. Find out if medical conditions or prescription drugs, including sleeping pills, could be keeping you awake.

If necessary, consult a sleep-disorder clinic. For a list of centers available, write "The Association of Sleep Disorders Centers, National Office, 604 2nd Street S.W., Rochester, Minnesota 55902.

'Grief Work' Needs Time, Friendships

1987

Deanna Edwards, a noted music minister for people who are dealing with pain and grief, said at a recent workshop that we must realize that a person has to heal from being psychologically broken, just as we have to heal from having a broken arm. It not only takes time, it takes "grief work."

We've had a lot of grief work to do around here lately.

Deanna says we can take the pain and we can make something beautiful out of it. We can take our suffering into our hands and transform it into the stuff from which a fragile miracle of regrowth will spring.

But it's a painful process and takes time. **We need to cry. Even Jesus wept.** Men and women, boys and girls, should welcome tears as a healing gift. Tears are our God-given human right. We need to cry alone, and we need to cry together as family and friends. "Crying is a wonderful experience and a great way to say I love you," she said. Deanna gave a workshop in Randolph at the behest of her friend, the Rev. Rick Arkfeld. Father Rick has cancer and his outlook on life is an inspiration to all who know him.

There's another side to this weeping business. A young friend who'd lost her mother said, "I feel terrible because I can't seem to cry." **Tears don't come on cue. They spill over when they need to.** Daughter Juli was driving down the road and saw an elderly man beside the road with a hat on "just like Grandpa's." She said, "I just started crying and couldn't stop."

Something will trigger a memory, and grief will overwhelm you. You won't have much control over this. You may be in the middle of a public place. Let the tears flow. It's your right. But don't expect anything of yourself. People handle grief in different ways. For some people, crying comes later — down the road.

It is important that we allow our grief to happen, that we work through our pain. Hidden grief does not go away. We must expect to go in and out of the stages of grief, first the denial, the depression and the anger, before we can come to the gentle gift of acceptance and getting on with our lives. There is no shortcut. And, as many people who have walked this road know, we become stronger in the broken places.

But we need to be there for each other. Mostly, we need to listen. Before we can help others, we have to face our own feelings and fears about death. We are afraid of the unknown. And we need to have worked through our own losses. I know about this because I spent

23

a lot of time denying some of the losses in my life. They came too close together and I couldn't handle them. And I put in even more time being really angry at the Lord.

I kept super busy. I seemed to be possessed. For me, this might have been a necessary part of the process. But I didn't recognize what I was doing to myself until I sat down with a therapy group and it surfaced, as plain as day. I was avoiding. It was my way of denying the grief I couldn't possibly cope with. I had to allow myself to feel the pain, cry a mountain of tears, recognize the suffering and work through it.

I will restate this for emphasis. The important thing is just to listen, to be there. Hugging is good. Advising is not. Do not tell them how they should feel or say, "I know what you're going through." Nobody fully understands the depth of another person's grief. Just be there with your love and let people talk their grief out while they are learning to survive. Deanna emphasized listening with leisure. She said a wonderful thing, **"Don't just do something, stand there!" "Listen with your heart,"** she said, **"and you'll hear love."**

Follow-up is important. Deanna suggested that when you take something to the house — which we all do — **take it in your best dish and don't put your name on it. Say, "I'll be back in a couple of weeks and pick this up."** What a terrific idea!

Chances are if you're not grieving yourself, you know someone who is. Hope these thoughts are helpful.

Chapter Two

*"A merry heart
doeth good
like medicine..."*
Proverbs 17/22

He Who Laughs, Lasts!

Chapter Two

Humor is an elusive element. It has a ''you had to be there'' quality. I agree with the wise person who said that analyzing humor is like dissecting a frog, you can do it, but when you get done you have a dead frog. So analyze it I won't, but stress its importance I will. Humor is a necessary element in our lives. The ability to laugh at oneself and with others is a significant indicator of one's mental health. So, if nothing else, I'm hoping the following columns will indicate to you that this writer is mentally healthy. Perhaps not. Whatever your judgment be on that, I hope you find a chuckle as you recognize your own foibles. You have them, you know. Of course you do.

* * *

He Who Laughs, Lasts

March 1986

Have you heard about the Protestant couple from the Deep South who traveled to Rome? They had nothing to do with Catholics, but they were interested and willing to learn, so they went to a Mass the Pope was saying at the Cathedral. The husband said to the wife, ''We'll just do everything they do so we won't be conspicuous.'' Watching the others carefully, first they knelt and then they sat, and finally, as the Pope entered, they stood up. Then the Pope made the sign of the cross and the wife said to the husband, ''What should we do now?''

The husband said, ''I don't think we have to do anything. I think he's going to make a free throw.''

That story pokes good-humored fun at many things I hold dear (Catholics, Protestants, the sign of the cross and free throws), but I laughed heartily when I heard it. There are those who say my ability to laugh at that story is an indication that my mental health is good.

Some years ago, a group of eminent psychologists met in Wales

26

and proclaimed, "More and more people are becoming sick because they cannot laugh at themselves." Taking oneself too seriously, they warned, could be endangering our health. Health experts say that a good laugh can be as important to your health as jogging, racquetball, aerobics, and all those roots and herbs we read about.

Psychiatrist Joel Goodman started "The Humor Project" at Sarasota Springs, New York, to teach people to laugh. He has trained some 60,000 crabby folks to laugh their way to better health. **Stress is not caused by an event, he says, but by our perception of an event, and if we change our perception with humor, we puncture the balloon of our stress.**

According to Dr. William F. Fry, Jr., associate clinical professor of psychology at Stanford University Medical School, laughing raises skin temperature and heart rate; flexes the diaphragm, chest and abdominal muscles; exercises the shoulders, neck and face; and releases adrenalin-like hormones called catecholamines. These stimulate the brain, increase alertness and ready the body for action.

Also, says he, "When you stop laughing, your blood pressure dips below normal for a short period of time, giving the body a rest."

Interest in humor therapy is spreading, and dozens of conferences are scheduled in the United States this year. Humor techniques are used to fight diseases, relieve back pain, and release the tension which causes one to develop ulcers, colitis, or high blood pressure.

You don't learn humor by studying it. I agree with Mark Twain who admonished, **"Studying humor is like dissecting a frog. You might learn a lot about it, but you wind up with a dead frog."**

You learn humor by experiencing it, by reading funny books and watching funny movies and listening to funny people, by giving yourselves opportunities to laugh.

Hearken to what it says in the book of Proverbs 17:22, "A merry heart doeth good like medicine, but a broken spirit drieth up the bones."

Who wants dried up bones?

Dead Cat Humor

October 1972

A friend of ours, Shirley Bogue, who writes a column in her husband Bob's paper, the Oakland "Independant and Republican," told a cat tale recently which she claims rival some of mine. And although some of my readers have threatened me with personal violence if I tell one more cat story, I feel it my duty to share this one with you.

(The devil is making me do this!)

Seems a young matron was entertaining the bridge girls at a luncheon. She prepared a molded tuna-fish salad and just as the guests were due, she stepped into the kitchen for last minute details. Imagine her horror when she discovered the family cat was up on the table chewing away at the tuna salad.

Well, quick-like she kicked the cat out the door and carefully cut away the part of the salad that the cat had touched. She covered the whole thing with a cream cheese frosting to disguise the cat damage, then she served the tuna salad to the guests. It was duly appreciated and rated with usual superlatives.

It wasn't until she returned to the kitchen for more coffee that the bombshell fell. Opening the back door for some fresh air, her gaze fell upon a heap on the doorstep and she froze with horror. **For there lay her cat, stretched out and very much dead.**

She went back to her luncheon guests with much red-faced embarrassment and confessed what must have happened to the salad and what HAD happened to the cat. Collectively the horrified bridge club gals decided that the smart thing to do was rush to the hospital for some quick stomach pumping.

It was not at all surprising that by the time the caravan arrived at the hospital, a couple of the gals were actively ill and all were feeling definitely queasy. The consequent stomach-pumping session at the hospital was one for the books, complete with sobbing theatrics. Just picture, if you will, eight rather hysterical matrons vieing for position in the stomach-pumping line!

The payoff came a bit later when all the frenzy had died down, the gals had gone to their respective homes and the hostess had returned to the scene of the story.

It was then that a neighbor knocked at the front door.

Said she, "I knew you had a luncheon in progress, so I felt I shouldn't interrupt. Your cat was killed by a car, so I picked her off the street and laid her on your back steps."

(I haven't asked, but I suspect that Shirley's source for this story was just as reliable as mine for my cat in a paper bag story.)

The Machines Are Out To Get Me

November 1978

"If you're looking for the toast, it's in the wastebasket," said Kip, the friendly farmer, as I was busily dishing up his breakfast. "The toaster shot it in there."

The toaster has just recently taken to firing its toast, instead of merely letting it pop up.

It's a little unhandy, retrieving your toast from a wastebasket, but I can't say as it surprises me. I consider it only the latest salvo in the war my many machines are conducting to drive me loony.

If it wasn't the toaster, it would be something else. Just about the time you think your house is in shape, completely equipped with all the modern equipment known to mankind. Just about the time you've gone in hock for a dishwasher, or a disposal, or even — glory be! — a trash compactor, that's when something else breaks down.

I've read that it's planned obsolescence, meaning that manufacturers build equipment so that it will wear out, or otherwise how would you get anybody to buy anything new.

I think that's reasonable of the manufacturers. And I even expect things to wear out. My main objection is to how and where they choose to do so.

For instance, my clothes dryer just couldn't quit. No way! It had to make a scene and have a fire. And my automatic washing machine — instead of just refusing to run, it flipped its hoses and flooded the laundry room and the basement under it.

And the way the fry pan gave notice it was getting ready to retire was also melodramatic. It began giving out high voltage shocks to anybody who happened to touch it at the same time they touched the metal rim of the counter.

But I don't have to tell you these things. You probably have horror stories of your own.

The meanest machine, from what I hear, is the garbage disposal. We don't have one. Our sewage system couldn't handle it, for one reason. For another, the friendly farmer is too tight. "If you want a garbage disposal," he said cleverly, "I will bring in one of the pigs and pen him under the sink."

I decided I didn't want one. Though I still envied the people who had them and didn't have to deal with drippy sacks.

But my friends have had problems with their disposals. My friend, Shirley, had 24 guests for dinner. Served several courses and used every dish in the house. Her garbage disposal not only quit, it backed up in both of her sinks. Have you ever had a house full of fancy company and tried to be sweet and hospitable when your garbage disposal was disposing backwards? My friend smiled, but she kept getting redder in the face and her neck kind of expanded. All in all, it wasn't a pleasant sight.

But machines are like that, and we just have to face up to the fact. Not only do they break down, they do it at the most inopportune moment possible. For instance, when does a deep freeze break down? When it's empty? Of course not. When you've just butchered a beef. Or filled it with ice cream and frozen food which you bought on sale.

And your air conditioner wouldn't think of quitting unless it was 110 degrees in the shade. I suspect, however, we wouldn't want to go back to the olden days. **Even toast in the wastebasket is preferable to no toast at all.** If we think about using a washboard instead of a machine, a broom instead of a vacuum sweeper, a horse instead of a car, we probably would quickly retreat like the elderly lady on Saturday Night Live, saying "never mind."

Neats 0 — Messies 1

May 1980

Show me a neat person and I will show you a reformer. A person has a legal right to be disorderly if a person should happen to want to, but a neat person wants everybody to be neat. Individual rights are violated by neat people, who invariably disagreeably push their fanatic neatness upon their family and their friends, frustrated by the failure of those fine folks who do not find the fullness of life in being fastidious.

Neatness is not always a virtue, but try to tell that to neat people. Unfortunately, neat people marry messy people, so trying to tell that to neat people is what messy people do a lot of the time.

I know I've expounded on this very subject before. What brings it up again is my office. To say it is not neat is the understatement of the year. There is no way that I could exaggerate the mess in this office. But I am happy here.

However, the friendly feeder, my husband Kip, is building us a new office. This plan has been in the works for many a year. Up until now, my office is a converted bedroom and his a converted closet. Soon, it will be a real office, jutting out from our house at a friendly angle, for BOTH of us. Therein lies the problem.

Kip is insisting, loudly and to everyone who will listen, that I will move into the new office and become a new woman. I will be neat!

And he says it that way, with an exclamation point.

One does not spend 51 years perfecting her sloppiness and become suddenly neat because of a new location. Even if one wanted to — which one doesn't.

However, to get the bedroom back will be a real plus. So I can see some compromise will be necessary. Neat people, however, are inherently unable to compromise. Neatness means "a place for everything and everything in its place." Those words send shivers of terror into us sloppies.

Neat people are frustrated from birth, you see, because their goals are impossible. Life isn't neat, nor is the world. But they continue to strive for total neatness, making everybody around them miserable.

And consider this fact; a sloppy person is seldom bored. Even the two hours a day we spend looking for things are not dull. **When a neat person goes to find something he knows with dreary, dull certainty just where it will be.**

For a disorderly person it is an adventure. Poking through layers of stuff, the disorderly person finds treasures he's forgotten or overlooked. Unopened letters are not unusual, and old letters become adventures into the past. It is not unusual for a disorderly person to chuckle his way through the debris, forgetting ultimately even what he's searching for, because of the treasures he stumbles on to.

A sloppy person never tries to inflict his disorderliness upon a neat person. You never hear a "messy" saying "why don't you mess up your desk" to a neat person. On the other hand, neat people are constantly trying to clean up a disorderly person's act. They want you to file things. Even referring (Lord help us) to something called cross-references.

Can a neat person and a sloppy person find happiness in the same office? Can the neat person find the sloppy person? Can the sloppy person find anything? Tune in next month...

Spraying Mold Gold?

October 1981

"Joanie!" bellowed Kip at the top of his non-smoking lungs, "where in the heck is the butter?"

"Right in the refrigerator," I responded in my sweet placating tones.

"There are ten butter dishes in this refrigerator full of moldy vegetables," he continued crabbily, "but no butter!"

And he was right! Although all of them didn't have moldy

vegetables in them. Some had moldy gravy, moldy rice, moldy whatever we'd had in the last month — that my conscience wouldn't let me throw away.

I have read that the C.I.A. and F.B.I., and other investigative agencies of that ilk sometimes sift through a person's garbage to find out what the person is like. They analyze the liquor bottles, the torn-up letters, the publications and any other refuse that's there and develop a pretty good composite picture of a person. You can see how they could.

I maintain they could find out almost as much by analyzing the contents of a person's refrigerator.

They would figure out in a hurry that a person with ten butter dishes full of moldy leftovers and no butter could not be criminal. Her conscience wouldn't allow it.

Guilt will not let this person throw one thing away. She thinks she will some day make vegetable soup. Or some time she will come across a gourmet recipe to disguise these leftovers. Believe me, if she were a gourmet cook, she wouldn't have all these leftovers in the first place.

Fizzled out half cans of diet pop would also add to this picture, as would a half bottle of wine with a cap that screws on and a Christmas decoration.

Also ancient and wrinkled fruit, curled up bits of leftover meat, a soggy and aged box of soda (to insure refrigerator freshness, of course), a leftover hunk of pizza (is there **anything** so unappetizing!), an ancient and brown corsage and other bits of flotsam and jetsam cast off from the dinner tables of life.

But we were not in nearly as much trouble at our house until we began to pile up such a supply of empty butter dishes. Little butter dishes, big butter dishes, all with handy lids. A person who is a born saver — a keeper of refuse of any kind — cannot throw even the most unappetizing tidbit of leftover away under these circumstances.

One even has a sense of virtue as one piles it in the handy empty dish, slaps on the lid, and then places it carefully in the refrigerator never to be thought of again.

It is delaying the inevitable, of course. But one can feel almost the same sense of virtue when one throws out the moldy little bit of stuff, and washes the butter dish for the next round of this farce.

Since I have trouble growing almost anything but the mold on the leftovers in the refrigerator, I have thought seriously of using these containers full of charming green fuzzy stuff for centerpieces. Perhaps if one sprayed them with gold and added a sprig of evergreen?

NO? Well — it was just an idea born out of desperation. In the meantime, I better get myself to town for some more butter. Another container. Oh boy!

Ruling One's Passions

March 1982

There are things in life one has to do if one wants to accomplish other things. Things one hates.

For instance, if you want to keep your teeth until you're done with them, you have to take care of them. That means brushing them and flossing them.

I hate to floss.

Something about getting one hand inside of my mouth to get at the little critters gets me all perturbed. But the threat of plaque moving in and taking over my mouth overcomes the displeasure of flossing.

So I do.

Then there's the desire to be thin. Or at least to keep one's girth within reasonable boundaries. To do that you have to diet.

I really hate to diet!

Passing up all the foods I dearly like is very hard for me. **There's a fat lady inside of me that keeps fighting to get out.** Little globs of her stay on me even when I am at my thinnest. Feeding my face is a favorite pastime. I like to eat when I'm depressed, when I'm bored, when I'm happy, when I'm celebrating, when I'm trying to forget. But — again — the threat of fat coming in and taking over my life, the vision of splitting seams and unzipped zippers, overcomes the displeasure of dieting.

So I do.

Nothing worthwhile is achieved without some sacrifice. Milton, the famed English poet, wrote: **"He who reigns within himself and rules his passions, desires and fears is more than a king."**

I hate Milton.

Now I'm kidding. I don't even know Milton. Probably because he was born in 1608. (And Marge, even I'm not that old!) (Marge is the friend who always gives me a bad time about being old. She's six months younger than I am!)

But about the other things I am not kidding. The examples could go on and on. This morning my house is a mess. I like a clean house. To get one I'm going to have to tear myself away from this typewriter and clean the danged thing. I hate to clean.

Yards and gardens take an enormous amount of work, not to say money, if they are to look nice. Even friends need care and consideration if we want to do right by them.

There is no greater feeling of achievement, however, than the moments in life when you have these things under control. Nobody's perfect, so they do not last for long. But when the scale says you're thin, and the dentist says that you have no cavities, or you achieve some other goal in life for which you've worked hard and long, a feeling of — well — accomplishment takes over, and you know what Milton is trying to say.

We can wallow in our miseries blaming them on everybody else, or we can take charge. Everyone wallows occasionally. It seems to be a prelude to the "taking charge" phase.

I hate to take charge. But I guess the truth of the matter is, **I hate to wallow even more.**

End of protest!

Trying Out Jokes On Cattlefeeders

November 1983

A mighty groan rose from my kitchen table and with eyes downcast, I returned to my office. It isn't easy.

When I give my little talks hither and yon about the country, I like to illustrate my points with humor. Sometimes I use personal experiences, sometimes anecdotes, sometimes quotes and occasionally an out-and-out joke. The kind you preface with, "Did you hear the one about . . ."

The challenge, when working up a new talk, is to find just the right touch of humor. I know when I hear it, or read it, a chill goes up my spine.

However, I run across a lot of borderline material, and when I do, I try it out on the cattle-feeding types which seem to congregate about my kitchen table drinking coffee.

I plop myself amid them and inflict my jokes upon them. They are a tough audience. I shall share two of their rejects at the close of this column.

It's hard to come up with the perfect humorous bit because although a rose is a rose is a rose, a joke is not a joke is not a joke, if you know what I mean.

Jokes that some people find riotously funny, offend others. People laugh at different things. Ethnic jokes are out. Shaggy dog jokes (which I love) have a small audience. Jokes with even the gentlest sexual connotation are dangerous. Sexual revolution notwithstanding, the very word still offends some people. You can purchase a book of 10,000 jokes and not one will work for you.

A friend of mine, who is in the business of hiring speakers for conventions, goes to some place down south and listens to dozens of speakers, one right after another. She says that there will be one "new" joke and they'll all have it. What an awful thing to have to do. (Listen or speak.)

Because I'm such a good audience, and always looking for a good story, my family and friends attempt to bring them to me. Eldon Hartman, our Iowa Beef buyer, brings in about one a month. So far I haven't been able to use any, but I appreciate the effort.

Now, prepare yourselves for the rejects, and don't say I didn't warn you.

A nice little lady told me this one. She said it was making the rounds at the nursing home. Seems mother and father and baby carrot were picnicking at the park when baby ran out in the road and got run over. He was rushed to the hospital, and the doctor came out of intensive care and said, "I've got some good news and some bad news."

And the anxious parents said, "Tell us, please!"

And the doctor said, "The good news is that baby carrot will recover. But the bad news is, he will always be a vegetable."

And this from a beloved nephew. A painter was painting a church steeple and as he got towards the top his paint was running out, so rather than go all the way down for more paint he thinned it, not once but twice. And when he started to thin it a third time, a great voice rumbled out of heaven and said very firmly, "Repaint! Thin no more."

Do I note a mild grin out there? Not a single tee-hee did I get from the mighty cattlefeeders. Only groans.

Well, like I told you, it isn't easy.

Confession of a Chronic Shopper: "I Needed It!"

September 1984

One of the joys of being in a business which requires travel, such as writing and public speaking, is that once in awhile I get a chance to shop.

Kip would say, "Once in awhile!" and grab for his Rolaids. The very thought of me entering a shop upsets his tummy.

I don't know why. I am very thrifty. I look for bargains. **I love sales. The very sign "sale" sets my heart beating at a rapid rate.**

There was a time, I readily admit, when he might have had some cause to worry. I would hit a store with a "20% off the regular sale price, one day only" sign and I'd consider it my duty to load up on "stuff."

I didn't care if the size was right (it would fit someone), the color was right (I could wear a scarf) or if it went with anything. Often, I didn't even know what it was, except that it was cheap.

Wisdom has come with maturity, however. Wisdom, and thirty-some years of hearing Kip holler, "If you don't need it, it isn't a bargain."

So now I shop judiciously. Even so, I seem to find things I "need" in strange places.

Kip was totally relaxed, for instance, when I went to Center to do a feature story on Ethel Clark, who had directed her choir for fifty years. (Center is one of my favorite places).

Until, that is, he looked in the back seat of the car upon my return. "What are those things?" he asked.

"Rag rugs," I replied. "I bought them at the church in Center."

"You even found something to buy at a church?" he said in disbelief.

I needed them.

And then, he wasn't too worried when I took off for Omaha a week or so ago to make a speech. I was just going and coming in a hurry, without much chance to shop.

Except that my friend, Helen Dwyer, went along, and I dropped her off at her son Tim's house. Tim and his wife, Tootie, had just had a garage sale. As I drove down the road after letting Helen off, I remembered seeing in the corner of the garage some glass trays with cups, the kind I always have to borrow when I'm serving club, or having a graduation party, or some such thing.

I could hardly wait to get back to pick up Helen. That would be a bargain; if you ever saw one.

And I needed them.

When I got home, again Kip looked in the back seat of the car. Sixteen plates and cups wrapped in newspaper and stuffed in a big box look ominous.

"What in Heaven's name have you got in that box?" he asked crabbily.

I explained what a wonderful bargain I had and how much I needed them. **I talked fast, as I always do when I suspect I don't have a perfect case to present.**

"How often do you have the club when you borrow plates like these?" he asked. I was afraid he would think of that.

"Every other year," I replied.

"And how many kids do we have left to graduate?" he asked.

"None," I answered.

Well, nobody's perfect.

Do you want to borrow some plates?

Conquering Clutter?!

September 1984

As the kindly lecturer spoke, I slumped down in my seat and reddened with guilt. How did he know all this? Had he been in my house?

"Is your life being disrupted by clutter?" he asked. "Do you waste precious hours out of the day looking for something? Do you spend a lot of time moving clutter from one place to another? Do you have hundreds of used twisties hoarded in a drawer? Do you have the jewelry boxes from every present ever given you? And the wrapping? And the ribbon?"

Then came the indictment. "If you answer yes to any of these, you are a junkie!"

For me the disease might be terminal.

"A book you might want to read is 'Clutter's Last Stand,'" he said. "It could help."

I bought the book. It cost $8.95. It helps. In fact, it is changing my life. I realize this is no way for a charter member of Messies Unanonymous to talk, but I am de-junking my life.

It is not easy. **When throwing away an empty olive jar takes an enormous amount of will power, you know you're in trouble.**

So it's with personal pain and emotional upheaval that I am carrying great green garbage bags full of stuff out of this house.

We keep things for many reasons. I was raised by my banker father to believe that the depression was always around the next corner. "Fix it up, wear it out, make do or do without," was a motto imprinted on my mind. That and a constant concern (while cleaning my plate) for the starving children of Armenia.

Therefore, I keep everything — broken electrical appliances Kip might (laughter here) fix, bushels of lone socks, single earrings, used disposable razors, pilled-up blankets with frayed bindings, faded curtains, puzzles and games with pieces missing, leftover ends of wallpaper rolls, dresses and pants I haven't been able to zip in years, outdated packets of garden seeds, pens that won't write, expired coupons for products I don't buy, and on and on.

If you recognize yourself in any of this, don't despair. There's hope. Take one closet at a time so you don't get emotional bends, and follow the advice of the book's author, Don Aslett, a professional cleaning expert.

Start with three large heavy-duty bags and one box. Label the first one "Junk," the second one "Charity," the third one "Sort," and "Emotional Withdrawal" for the box.

In the "Junk" bag put everything that's broken, outdated, without a mate, out of style, ugly, useless, dead or moldy. It will fill up fast. Then dump it.

In the "Charity" bag, put everything that's good but you don't want, won't use, or just don't like. Then take it to your local charity outlet and give it away.

In the "Sort" bag, put all the loose, misplaced or homeless stuff that is still useful and needed but should be in a more convenient place. Sort what you can, relocate it and keep what you will use. Leave the rest in the bag, and sort again in one month. Some of it will go.

In the "Emotional Withdrawal" box, put the inactive, unused and outdated sentimental stuff. Keep it for six months. With this detachment period, you'll be amazed what you can chuck out.

I've gone through four closets and have a feeling of lightness and virtue. I really wanted to get rid of all that junk, I was just chicken.

But it isn't easy. **Take heart from Ecclesiastes (3:6). There is "a time to get, and a time to lose: a time to keep, and a time to cast away..."**

Trivialities Try Us

December 1984

"Greece!" Kip bellowed, "Why would you pick Greece? Greece is a terrible choice. Used to be you always wanted to go to Ireland. Now you're saying you always wanted to go to Greece. I should have never let you go to Ireland!"

"*Let* me go to Ireland!" I bellowed back, my latent feminist sensibilities rising to the surface. "*Let* me!!" And we were off and running.

You won't believe the ridiculous premise for that heated discussion.

It all boils down to letting yourself get in an uproar over trivialities. **Dr. Abraham Lowe, the founder of the wonderful self-help group called Recovery, says that 95 percent of the things that get us down are trivialities**, and if we handled them one at a time, with a sense of humor, we would never have the stress problems we inflict upon ourselves.

I think the "sense of humor" part is something I added to Dr. Lowe's wise pronouncement, but nonetheless, the argument Kip and I got into is an example of getting in an uproar over trivialities.

I mean what could be more trivial than the trip you choose on one of those sweepstakes offers. Who's going to win it anyway? One has to choose something if one sends in sweepstakes offers, and if one is hurried, one might even choose Greece. I send in a multitude of those dumb things. I choose fancy cars that would never do for a farmer, I choose the option that would get us the most money at this very moment and I choose vacations that sound the most glamorous, or educational, or whatever. . .*like Greece*.

What I usually do that's smart, *however,* is keep my mouth shut. I never discuss the sweepstakes options I pick with the crabby cattle-feeder. I just choose them with a great sense of glee, as if I thought I might win, and then forget the whole thing. Fifty-six years of never winning anything tends to do that to a person.

It never occurred to me that Kip would bother to have an opinion on them. He thinks I'm crazy to take the time to send them in. Why would he care what options I choose?

But times are tough. I wouldn't say we're in trouble, but I should have known Kip was taking sweepstakes offers more seriously when he took the Reader's Digest Sweepstakes tickets into the bank to see if he could use them as collateral. To give you an idea of how tough things are, the banker was interested. A 33 billion-to-one chance is better than none, right?

It came up when we were discussing vacations with friends, and I laughingly told them how I'd gotten three of the giant sweepstakes offers in the mail that very morning. It was fresh in my memory. Like a dummy, I mentioned I had a choice of winning one of six vacation spots. I said, "I chose Greece."

And Kip said, calmly enough, "Greece, why would you choose Greece?"

And I said, "Because I've always wanted to go to Greece." That's when the match hit the gasoline! See what I mean? Let us all make a New Year's resolution. **Beware of trivialities. They strike when you least expect them.**

Aversion To Pain Halts
Ear Piercing Thoughts

May 1985

It's embarrassing, but I have to admit it. My ears are not pierced.

I know, I know, it's shocking. Not everyone could own up to such a thing with the courage I display, but that's just the way it is.

I don't know why, **but people with holes in their ears go about with a sense of missionary zeal trying to convert people with virgin ears.** They seem to think happiness comes with pierced ears. They act as if it's a sign of maturity. Some people even pierce the ears of helpless, little bitty girls for Lord knows what reason. Little girls don't need to be mature. What's the use of being a little girl if you can't be free of the burden of jewelry?

You can see that I am not only of the non-pierced persuasion, I am militant. My ears aren't pierced despite the fact that I have strewn earrings all over the country, one by one. I have a box full of earrings bereft of a mate, waiting for a one-eared person to come along.

My ears aren't pierced in spite of the fact it's a disappointment to salespeople. When I look for earrings of a certain shade, they show me a mass of earrings for pierced ears. When I tell them my problem, they look at me with disbelief, if not disdain, and say, "You mean, you don't have pierced ears?" They say it softly, as if they were discussing a dread disease. Customers turn and stare as if I were terminally dense. I slink away.

I also claim that my ears aren't pierced because I am leaving that for something exciting to do when I get older.

I have three good friends who decided at age 75 to get their ears pierced. It was a big event. There are not too many things you can do at 75 that you've never done before. I liked that idea.

I also claim my ears aren't pierced because I don't want to give up the nice looking earrings, antiques and all, which I have for non-pierced ears. Friends tell me that's nonsense. In the first place, one can wear clip earrings whether one's ears have holes or not. Who's to know? And one can get one's earrings fixed to work with pierced ears.

The reasonable plea of the salespeople, who seem to feel sorry for me, is that I should try getting my ears pierced. *If I don't like pierced ears, they say, I can always let the holes grow back together.*

What a dumb idea? Why would I do something like that?

You see, it comes down to this: the real reason I don't get my ears pierced is because I'm chicken. Why would any sane person undergo the traumatic process of having a hole made in each ear (and sometimes two and three) if it were not to avoid a dread disease? Why would one allow themselves to be poked if it didn't serve a medical purpose? Don't you know that putting holes in a person hurts? People tell me it's a simple process, but I've seen friends (excuse this grossness) with oozing ears. With my luck, my ears would fall off.

So don't talk to me about piercing my ears, and don't patronize me because I don't have pierced ears. I'm happy this way.

Maybe when I'm eighty and my ears thin out...

The Reluctant Grasshopper Gardener

1985

Whenever I hear the story about the grasshopper who fiddled all summer while the ant industriously worked, I always relate to the grasshopper.

I think it has to do with gardens. The vegetable kind.

When we were newly wed, and I became a farm wife, I used to think I had to plant acres of land in a garden. **And I loved the planting part.**

I soon found, however, that was all I loved. Weeding was enormous work, and canning was even worse. Vegetables always get ripe on the hottest days of the summer, when you have a wedding to go to.

I was spared a lot of that, because many a summer my garden was ruined (to my outward dismay, and inward delight) by wandering cattle or hogs.

I finally got it down to just a few tomato plants. And my canning, for several years, has consisted of making chili sauce and freezing corn.

I made 40 quarts of dill pickles one year, and they were all soggy, so I've never had to make them again. We always have a supply. Nobody *ever* eats them.

This year, however, was different. My nephew Jim landscaped the hill beside our house, just outside of our office, and he put on the top of the hill, right out the windows over Kip's desk, a tiny plot so I could have a garden.

"Cute," I thought, "and fun." And I planted a few vegetables. Somehow, the tomato plants looked tiny, and the seeds even tinier. So I put in 16 tomato plants, a row of carrots, a row of green beans, a row of cucumbers (nobody ever told me they were supposed to be mounds), a few strawberry plants and some petunias.

For awhile, everything was under control. But the tiny plot had rich soil in it, from Kip's feed yards. And you will remember the rain we had this spring.

So the plants just took off. And since they didn't have any place else to grow, they grew on each other, straight up in the air. The garden looks like a baby jungle.

Only good thing about it is there wasn't any room for the weeds.

The bad thing was that we were picking cucumbers out of the tomatoes, green beans out of the cucumbers, the carrots were lost in the underbrush, and I don't know what happened to the strawberries.

And it has produced.

Kip came in this morning with a huge cardboard box full of tomatoes and cucumbers and he said, with just a touch of sarcasm in his voice, "I thought you picked these yesterday!"

"I did, I swear I did."

"So why do some of these cucumbers look like small watermelons?" he asked.

"I can't imagine where you found those," I said.

And he said, "You might try lifting up the vines."

Are you kidding? I've already canned more pickles than we'll ever eat. Kip doesn't even like pickles. The kids are all gone.

I make lousy pickles anyway. What's a nice grasshopper like me doing in a situation like this?

The last Kip saw of me I was out at the cattle yards opening the gate, and urging the cattle toward my garden.

Wasted Worries and Holey Underwear

1985

People get hung up on silly things. Like I have a friend who will never go on a trip wearing holey underwear. She says if she's in an accident and goes to her eternal reward, she does not want the local undertaker, who is a mutual friend, to find out she occasionally wears holey underwear. I told her (she's kind of ornery) that **if she had an accident and went to her eternal reward, she would have a lot more to worry about than her holey underwear** — she'd have to worry about her eternal reward. But it doesn't faze her. She keeps fancy underwear on hand just for trips and our local undertaker.

Personally, I've always thought that when it came my time in life to make the last trip, it would be in a tornado. At least I used to feel that way. For many years I was petrified of tornadoes. I had this vision of being lifted up like Dorothy in the Wizard of Oz and then smashed straight into a tree with only my feet sticking out. I think it came from (first) seeing the Wizard of Oz too many times and (second) hearing the "grown-ups" talk about a tornado (when I was young) which somehow had such force that it blew a long stick of straw straight through a tree trunk. If it could do that to a straw, what couldn't it do to a short lady?

Consequently, until several years ago, I would go into a panic at a tornado watch, and if there was a tornado warning I had everybody in the corner of the basement — whether there was a cloud in the sky in our area or not.

And, to take nothing away from my friend's above-mentioned idiosyncrasy, if the friendly cattlefeeder could finally convince me to leave my frantic sky watching and get some sleep, I would be sure to go to bed in my best jammies. If the rescuers were going to find me in the morning with my legs sticking out of a tree, those legs would be well clad.

Then, a strange phenomenon occurred. At first it seemed rather terrible, but it turned out to be a blessing in disguise. It was the spring several years ago when we had a tornado warning every night for nearly 60 nights straight.

Well, nobody — even the most paranoid person — can keep up a state of panic for 60 nights straight. It got to be ridiculous. So, one night I looked at the clouds and the only emotion I felt was disgust. The reign of tornado terror in my heart was over. What remained was only healthy respect for the weather, and a lot less wear and tear on my good pajamas.

We waste a lot of time in our lives worrying about things that don't

ever happen, and if they did happen, we couldn't do anything about them anyway.

For instance, I have another friend who has predicted a drought for all the years we've been on the farm. Twenty years this went on, and we'd get pretty good rains. Then, when the drought finally came, she said, "See, I told you so." But we'd had to worry about it twenty years before it came.

The friendly cattlefeeder is a case in point. The beautiful rains we've gotten this spring have just left him suspicious. He's sure something bad is going to happen, it's going around, and if it looks as if it's coming right at us, he's almost certain it's full of hail.

I think a farmer gets this way because he doesn't want to be disappointed, and he is so often. So, if they think the worst then they won't be in for any letdown. It's kind of a crabby way to go through life. But I think it's a cover-up. Basically, farmers have to be optimists or they wouldn't be farmers. Who could plow all that money in the ground every spring if they didn't believe it would pay off in the fall?

And once in a while that optimism peeks out in spite of them. Like this spring, for the first time in three years, we put out a rain gauge. And first thing you know it had two inches of rain in it. Incredible, I thought, at least this will have to make the friendly cattlefeeder grin.

"Well," he said, "we've got the corn planted and it rained. Things couldn't be much better." A tornado watch was on the air and thunder rumbled in the background.

But he caught himself up short, looked a little startled, and said, "But it's too wet to cut hay and the cattle market isn't too hot."

Well, what's a person to do? I just put on my good pajamas and went to bed.

Sister-In-Law Refuses To "Have A Nice Day"

1985

I have a beloved sister-in-law, Rhea, who gets into a royal tizzy when people — especially passing strangers — say, "Have a nice day!" She thinks they are insincere, trite, and she would like to whomp them.

Because she makes such a thing out of it, we've given her anything we can find with "Have a nice day!" written on it.

This all came to mind the other day when I was working on a speech for an ecumenical occasion, looking for just the right biblical quotation. One of my favorites popped up. "This is the day the Lord has made. Let us be glad and rejoice in it."

I had a sudden insight, one of those "Aha!" experiences. I said to myself, "Self," I said, "This is the Lord's way of saying 'have a nice day.'" Think about it. I'm sure you'll agree.

I wondered how my sister-in-law would feel if a cheerful store clerk said, "This is the day the Lord has made. Let us be glad and rejoice in it." I must ask her.

Personally, I've never minded being told to "Have a nice day." It's better than a lot of things people might say. And it reminds me of an important lesson. I'm one of those who need a lot of reminding. The decision to have a nice day or not to have a nice day is up to me. Or you — if it's your day we're talking about.

Some people have the wonderful knack of making every day a "rejoicing" occasion. I have friends like that. Relatives, even. And I know people who live with serious handicaps, who look at every minute of life as a gift, and appreciate, appreciate, appreciate. **They have a kind of "walk into the wall and it will fall" faith, and live life courageously and with joy.**

Then there are the poor souls who seem to have everything, but sit around on their duffs and howl like hound dogs because they aren't having a nice day, don't expect to ever have a nice day, and don't want anyone around them to make the mistake of even thinking about trying to have a nice day.

I fall somewhere in between. Sometimes I appreciate and sometimes I howl. There are days when rejoicing gets to be a problem. Some days we get up to face tasks that are not pleasant. Like the days I have to clean . . . anything.

Some days we have to deal with people who are not favorites. Like tax men or dentists. Some days tax men and dentists have to deal with us.

Some days we just wake up feeling plumb grumpy, and we don't really know why. We have an itch somewhere (physical or psychological) we just can't scratch.

According to eminent psychologists who know about such things, it will help if we make ourselves smile, even if we don't want to. Especially if we don't want to. Just by smiling we start a process which will make us feel good all under. We've talked about this before, but I'm afraid you haven't tried it yet. It really works.

When we get up in the morning we look in the mirror and grin. And the person in the mirror grins back. A great way to start the day. Sure you'll feel silly. That's the idea.

Then say to the person in the mirror — sincerely — "Have a nice day."

And you'll be glad and rejoice in it.

Meal With Bugs Always Remembered As Defeat

April 1986

Human beings have to work at enjoying their successes. The memory of the defeats linger longer, and hurt more, than the memory of successes last, or feel good. If you know what I mean. For instance, I consider myself a good cook. Not a gourmet cook, you understand, but a cook who has a plethora of great recipes.

However, do I remember the meals when guests have stuffed themselves to the gills and gone away singing my praises? No! I remember the time when a bridge-playing guest tried to cut into one of my picture perfect meringues and shot it across the living room. And I remember the time I served an eminent priest cereal with bugs in it. His name was (and still is) Father John Flynn — he heads the Omaha Archdiocese Department of Education.

It's good to have an overactive sense of humor at times like that, because it allows one to laugh and point out the humor to other people. The guest who shot the meringue across the living room laughed as soon as she saw that I was laughing. It took a little longer for the gal to laugh who had the meringue (with strawberries) land in her lap.

As for Father John, well even I didn't laugh right away at that one. He was a friend of ours who was in our neighborhood giving a talk. His decision to stay with us was an unusual one, because he is a dear man but stuffy. And he likes things neat. With six kids and no inclination to be that way myself, our house was not his favorite place to be.

However, I'd worked at it before his eminence's arrival and his room was immaculate. The bathroom fixtures gleamed, the curtains were freshly washed. The towels new. He was, I could tell, impressed.

It was at breakfast time that we got into trouble. As many farm-wives do, or used to do anyway, I prepared bacon, eggs and homemade rolls for breakfast. I sent the kids off with a hearty, not to say heavy meal. That was long before I became a born-again roughage enthusiast. I said, "Father, how do you like your eggs?"

And he said, "Eggs?" as if I was asking him how he liked his arsenic. "Oh, I never eat eggs. I will just have some cereal, thank you, with skim milk."

I had plenty of cereal in my cupboard. No one ate cereal at our house. So I poured him a hearty bowl full, and put the milk (two plus) on the table. We had a lot to visit about, and Father was busy talking so it took me awhile before I noticed that there were little critters doing the backstroke on the top of Father's cereal.

I honestly didn't know what to do. He'd eaten half of it. I started talking about the view out our kitchen window. I brought up skiing, Father's favorite pastime, guaranteed to make him forget what he was eating. I suffered.

Breakfast over, Father folded his (cloth!) napkin carefully, briskly wiped off his mouth, and said "Thank you for the breakfast, Joanie, the bugs were delicious." And he left. And he's never been back.

Barn Swallow Battle Won But War Lost

June 1986

For the last few years Kip has, with no success, tried to apply that wise old saying, "You can't keep the birds of sorrow from flying over your heads, but you can keep them from making a nest in your hair," to the barn swallows that nest every year above the door which opens out onto our patio.

His version is like this: "You can't keep the barn swallows from flying around your house, but you can keep them from nesting under your eaves." In the last ten years I suspect the score has been barn swallows - 10, Kip - 0.

This year he was determined. He went after the barn swallows like a countrified Rambo with all the arsenal of weapons he could muster. Barn swallows are beautiful creatures if you watch them in flight. But they built their nest with mud, and they aren't neat. And what's worse, they potty train their babies to doo-doo over the side of their nest. So wherever they decide to make their home, it gets to be such a mess that you would think the deer and the buffalo also roamed there.

The reason Kip's attempts to keep them off the eaves have failed heretofore is that they were more persistent than he. He would remove their nests once, or twice, and think he'd discouraged them. The minute he turned his back they'd be back, and in seconds (or so it seemed anyway) they'd have a bunch of kids.

Now, who can destroy a home with a bunch of kids in it?

This year it was going to be different. Kip queried everyone about deterring barn swallows, and he did everything they said to do.

Except shoot them. He's threatened to do that, but I have a problem with thinking about him shooting things. Not that I don't think a person's entitled, you understand. And he used to be a crack shot. But he's not shot that gun for years. He'd be mad, you know, and I have visions of blasted windows and pock-marked siding dancing in my head.

So this year, besides removing the nest the minute it was in progress, he used other tactics. Although he thinks both wind socks and the Irish are sometimes frivolous, he hung up a bright green Irish wind sock. It did not even phase the swallows. They flew in and out of it. It did, however, cheer me up.

Then he hung up three sets of wind chimes. When the wind blows it sounds like an orchestra of bells tuning up. **For the swallows it was "music to build nests by."**

Someone recommended mothballs, and Kip put them everywhere. Ah-ha and eureka! The barn swallows, after swooping around for a day or so, gave up on the patio area. So did the human beings. What a smell!

Kip was jubilant. Until he sat at his desk and realized they were now swooping about the eaves above his office window.

Emphasize With Exaggeration

1986

I started to write this column as follows:

"Occasionally messy and disorganized people come out on top. As a charter member of Messy's Un-anonymous, I only thought about putting my winter clothes away when we had a brief and intense bit of summer a week or so ago. I didn't do it. My neat friends did.

My closets, which are always a mess, are even more so, because I've brought my summer clothes out of hiding piece by piece and simply stuffed them in among the winter clothes.

Nonetheless, my messiness has paid off. At a recent meeting wherein the landscape outside was again covered with snow, I comfortably cavorted in one of my winter suits while my more organized friends shivered in seersucker."

At this point I stopped writing and became introspective. All because of a letter from Phyllis Jensen and her "Practical English" class at Madison High School. She wrote, "We read your article, 'Meal

With Bugs Remembered as Defeat' in the April, 1986 issue of the Norfolk Daily News. Our class was discussing the term 'exaggeration.' **We were curious to know whether the story of the bugs is true or exaggerated. We would also like to know if most of your other stories are true."**

My reply came under the heading of the "Yes, Virginia, there is a Santa Claus" school of column writing. Every word of the story about the priest eating the bugs was true. Would I make a thing like that up?

But, as I wrote to the Madison students, exaggeration is a columnist's tool. We use it to grab your attention, to make a point, or teach a specific lesson, often in the fond hope of being amusing. It's a ploy which we know is recognized by readers so that together we chuckle over it.

Because my subjects, my family and my friends, are real, I care how they feel, so to exaggerate unkindly is out. Besides, it could get me sued.

Erma Bombeck, who is a superb columnist, uses exaggeration as a good artist uses caricature. She takes a nugget of truth and elaborates. If people sue, she doesn't care. She has money.

What I'm saying is that even though there might be some kindly exaggeration in the telling, my stories are basically true. Truth is not only stranger than fiction, it's often funnier. And readers recognize the ring of truth. **Face it, weird things happen to me.** Always have. Ask Kip. Of course, it helps that I'm open to them and was born nosy.

Now, about the beginning paragraphs. A good example. Every word is true, except that my friends were not wearing seersucker. But "shivering in cotton" does nothing for me. "Shivering in seersucker" is alliteration and pleasing to my ear. "Alliteration," according to my trusty dictionary, is "the occurrence, in a phrase or a line, of two or more words having the same initial or sound clusters, as in 'a fair field full of folk.'" **Have you ever seen "a fair field of folk?"**

You see, even the dictionary uses exaggeration to emphasize.

The Trauma Of Attempting To Bust A Gut

1987

In this day and age, I think we are too concerned with trying to stay young. Next thing you know, they'll be selling us support bikinis. The thing is, like it or not, you're only young once. It's just as well. Being young at my age would probably kill me.

Staying young at heart is another thing. Some of my oldest friends are my youngest, if you know what I mean.

Doing what you can to stay healthy and in relatively good shape is smart. That's part of staying young at heart.

However, I'm not sure the latest move we've made toward the end is the wisest one we've ever made. **Kip sent for a Gut Buster. Don't snicker.** According to our friendly UPS man, so did a lot of you.

A couple of years ago, we didn't have any guts to bust. But that's when Kip gave up smoking, and I just gave up. Kip's chest began to develop, but only after it had slipped a few notches. And I, well, I just developed.

Of course, I'll take worrying about a potbelly over worrying about cancer of the lungs any day. But, there gets to be a point when that rationalization is no longer justified.

It was after our eating orgy in the Dominican Republic and the equally fattening holiday season that we reached that point. We decided to take a determined stand against the encroaching fat. We developed a diet and exercise plan. We have had moderately good results. (Knock on fat.)

The Gut Buster's purchase was an afterthought. To those of you who haven't the slightest idea what I'm talking about, the Gut Buster is a powerful spring with stirrups for your feet at one end, and a handle bar contraption at the other. The idea is to exercise with this thing, and bust your gut. An inelegant description but, for those of us with guts to bust, effective advertising. Although I'd bet you 100 to one odds, the man and woman in the advertisement never had a gut to bust in the first place.

But Kip responded to the advertising, having a somewhat ludicrous vision of the two of us exercising together, eventually looking like the couple on television. The fact that for us to look like that would take major surgery, plastic and otherwise, did nothing to quell his enthusiasm.

The Gut Buster arrived, and Kip's first move was to get a bunch of copies of the shapely woman on the front of the direction sheet and send it to his friends saying soon he would look like that. That amused him and was probably worth the $19.00.

His enthusiasm was momentarily squelched by the fact he found what looked to be an exact replica of the Gut Buster advertised in a magazine, two for $10.

"Probably not the quality of ours," he decided.

The first night we tried the fool thing, it made Kip sick to his stomach (perhaps psychosomatic, as it was the very stomach he's trying to get rid of) and it gave me a pain in my lower back. I, of course, overdid it.

We started slower, with a little less enthusiasm, but more sense, and have used it ever since on a more or less regular basis. The jury is still out on the results. Combined with our other efforts at exercise, and an attempt to regulate our diets, we've lost five pounds apiece.

Kip says if we keep on at this rate, he's afraid in two or three years we'll completely disappear.

I'll keep you informed, of course. If you note a difference in our physical profiles, especially Kip's, I expect you to comment in a congratulatory fashion. If you read we're in the hospital for abdominal repair, or lower back surgery, I hope you'll have the decency not to bring up the Gut Buster.

Chapter Three

*"Children are an inestimable
blessing and a bother."*
Mark Twain

*"A friend is one to whom one may
pour out the contents of one's heart,
chaff and grain together, knowing that the
gentlest of hands will take and sift it,
keep what is worth keeping and with the
breath of kindness, blow the rest away."*
Arabian Proverb

Family and Friends

Chapter Three

This chapter was the hardest one for me to prepare. In the first place, much of my writing has been centered around family and friends, so I had too many columns from which to choose. So I have simply chosen too many. This chapter goes on and on. I kept putting in one more essay about Grandpa Burney, or almost Perfect Grandchild Kate, or this friend, or that kid, until I'm a little — but not much — embarrassed. In the second place, by the time a writer gets to be my age (which is 58, even as I write) there have been a lot of good-byes. The readers have generously encouraged me to include many of those essays, sending them as "keepers," and writing such things as "I've kept every column about Kate" and "Your farewell column to your mother helped me with my grief for my own mom" and "Your column about your son's winning battle with alcoholism gave us strength to face our own son's problems." Consequently, dear reader, you have all aspects of our life represented here, the happy, the sad, the preposterous, the poignant. You have, in other words, the patches of living that make up the crazy quilt of life.

* * *

Aunt Lenyce Marsh, 74, Takes Over As Editor

July 1969

As you probably noted from the rogues' gallery on the front page, this newspaper is experiencing a change in administration. Lenyce Marsh, better known to me as Auntie Lenyce, reluctantly agreed to assume the editor's seat and oversee the rest of us for the next few weeks. No easy job — I could fill the whole paper with stories about Auntie Lenyce, but because it just would not do for an Editor to sue her own paper (the first week, anyway), I will confine myself to my favorites.

Lenyce has had a great deal of newspaper experience, and is really adept at ferreting out the news. Her cheerful voice saying, "Say, didn't you have a party last week?" and thereby shaking your mental tree for fruit for her newspaper has become familiar to us all.

Besides this, she knits, quilts beautifully, makes rugs, bakes the best pies in the country, plays a good game of golf, wins her share of bridge prizes, and is almost as nutty as I am.

And her never-to-be forgotten appearance at the Cedar County Fair was one of the highlights of my directing careers. Lenyce, Lola Samuelson and Margaret Stockwell, in short skirts and a mass of ribbons, with perky parasols perched on their shoulders, minced enthusiastically about the stage singing "Three Little Girls from School" from the opera Madam Butterfly. They brought the standing room only crowd to their feet in a rousing ovation.

Her prize winning appearance as Eve (need I say more) at the Country Club Ladies' Fun Day, still sends a shiver of appreciation running down my spine. This same Lenyce, at an outrageously youthful 74, can trot circles around me at the golf course, and in almost any other field of endeavor she so chooses.

So, you see, I think we can assure you that we will put out a paper that will attract your attention, hold your interest, and give you a laugh or two. (Probably some we haven't scheduled.)

We Spent A Week At The Fair Last Saturday

September 1969

We spent a week at the State Fair last Saturday. At least, it seemed that way. We were joined by 37,500 other presumably sane folk, all of whom were proceeding rapidly in the opposite direction of what we were. We set out on this adventure at six in the morning and arrived home at two-thirty the next morning. The cow-milkers in the bunch had gotten up before four to get their chores done. The reason for this Odyssey was (what else?) our kids. **Fifteen members of our Pleasant Dale Beef Club, many of whom had never even sung in the bathtub before, worked hard all summer, won the County Fair contest, and won the chance to go to the State Fair.** The State Fair is a long way from the bathtub, and it was quite an experience.

54

And what could be more fun, thinks their leaders (Dean Marsh and Jim Potts), than planning a whole day at the state fair. As it turned out, Dante's Inferno might have been comparable. Most of the parents went along: Jim and Leona Potts, Dean and Laura Lou Marsh, Donavon and Jeanette Lammers, and Bonnie Hoesing and I (The Odd Couple). Then we conned some of our neighbors and friends into coming along to fill up the bus. The Clarence, Richard and Robert Husses, the George Bargstadts, the Leo Boeckers, Sally Bart and Mrs. Burt McFarland rounded out the lively group. With that crew, how could you go wrong?

It wasn't hard. We had a wild day, and I laughed so hard my jaws ached when I got home. **Only someone who has been at the state fair on a hot, steamy, muggy, dusty, crowded day can know true misery.** The only thing that was hotter than the fairgrounds itself were the exhibits and the barns, and we hit them all. I insisted everybody sign up for everything, and so we expect anytime to win a three-point hitch, bushel of barley, Bible, four tickets to the Nebraska football games, etc., etc. We gathered all the free loot we could, and this included free yardsticks, which proved almost lethal in that crowd. I saw everything but the chicken barn, and of course, everybody tried to convince me on the way home that the chicken barn was the only thing really worth seeing.

A real high point was when an unsuspecting exhibitor got talked into giving us a pen (writing) for each of our children. **When Leona Potts mentioned casually that she had fourteen, and Bonnie Hoesing came up with eleven, Jeanette Lammers and I came up with seven and six respectively, you should have seen his face.** Fortunately, there was a Protestant in the group, and I thought the poor man would kiss Laura Lou Marsh, who just had three.

As the day wore progressively on, we wore progressively out. Our ankles were swollen up to our knees, and we ended up sitting in front of the grandstand on the curb like a bunch of hot, lumpy rag dolls. That's where the men-folk found us to lead us willingly into the Country Western extravaganza. It was a place to sit.

At this point, it started to rain. It rained buckets and sheets and cats and dogs. They shot off the fireworks during the program so they wouldn't get ruined. It was a little weird having a rocket shot to the moon (the fireworks display) to the beat of country western music. We literally swam back to the bus.

John, our No. 3 son (a real farmer), stood out in the downpour with upstretched arms, shouting exultantly, "Rain, rain!" The rest of us, scattering like a bunch of drowned rats, easily suppressed our enthusiasm for the needed moisture, and arrived at the bus.

Our idea of sleeping all the way home was soon shattered by Leona Potts, who took over my job as song leader, and indefatigably led the group, many of whom were less than enthusiastic. Leona has gained much strength this summer, you see, from picking pickles in Potts pickle patch. (For perfection in pickles try Potts' pickle patch.) (Try saying that after twenty-three hours of no sleep.)

Whenever I'd start to doze, they would come up with a good harmony song, and the old alto blood would boil and off I'd go. (Who can resist 'Sentimental Journey'!)

Oh yes, our kids won a blue ribbon, Sally Bart won three teddy bears, Jeanette Lammers won at bingo, we came home with 40 pens, three red caps, a lot of good laughs, and numerous tired and happy kids. You can hardly beat that!

Summer of Bad Breaks

September 1969

No matter how you look at it, this summer seems to have been a series of mishaps, misadventures, mistakes and just plain misses. I missed the Laurel Calf Sale and Barbecue for the first time in umpteen years, because one of the calves so honored had the gall to step on my daughter's foot.

We missed a trip to the Black Hills because another of the critters broke my son's jaw, Kip missed a fishing trip because he had to go to some cattle sales — (and not because I browbeat him into staying home for our 22nd anniversary, as is so loudly being stated by his fishing cronies) and he missed the anniversary party I browbeat him into staying home for because he had to sell cows.

As a matter of fact, the person whom I've seen the most this summer (in a purely professional capacity of course), is Dr. Vlach. **He has hinted in his subtle (?) manner that he is preparing a photograph album for us as a Christmas gift — with all of our families' X-rays.** He's also threatened to set up a permanent appointment for me so I can bring in whatever emergency I have that week. It would certainly come in handy, but seems a touch pessimistic.

The Ordeal Of The Family Portrait

November 1969

One fine Saturday, late last summer, we went through the excruciating agony of having a family picture taken. Nobody in the family was too interested, but I put on my crabby face and insisted.

I had an appointment for four in the afternoon, plenty of time for leisurely preparing clothes, etc., or so I thought. I went merrily off to the beauty parlor, only to get a call from harassed husband to inform me of the fact that he HAD to go to a cattle sale in Bloomfield that afternoon, that he had trucks coming in with cattle that morning, and that he'd changed the appointment to 11:30 and I had better get a move on.

Well! There we were, Rob's hair was too short, he'd just come back from camp; Bill was too skinny, he'd just had wires removed from a formerly broken jaw; I could do nothing about that. But the little boys would have to go without the needed hair trims, Juli without the right color ribbon, Mother without any makeup (ugh!) and nothing, but nothing, that matched anything was readily available.

In total disarray, we roared in upon poor Bud Hesse and his lovely crew. Kip announced that we had fifteen minutes — no more! Imagine — fifteen minutes for a picture that has to last for eternity. (I'll never go through THAT again!) There we sat, stood and/or wiggled. Snap, snap, went Bud. Growl, Growl, said Kip. Smile, Smile implores Mother, and it was over.

An unusual photo, all the Burneys still and quiet. Kip's white socks sticking out of his black boots would have to be colored with Bud's magic marker. The remarkable thing was the smile on Kip's face. That was worth recording for posterity. He had the most angelic look of complete self-control. Can it be that the Art Center has a magic camera?

While picking out my proofs (procrastinating as usual, I just got around to that!), I noted a marvelous picture of the John Fleming, Jr., family. I gazed with admiration and awe at the impressive array of 12 color coordinated children, surrounding calm and collected looking John and Theresa. One wonders — how did THEY ever do it.

Creek Captures Kids

June 1971

A gentle little creek meanders through our farm. That is, as a rule it meanders. After a hard rain, it crashes, thunders and roars, taking out bridges and dikes in its wake. However, its dual personality is hard to imagine on an ordinary day when all it is doing is meandering.

Another type of devastation is sometimes wrought by the gentle little creek, though. City people are unaware of it. Just how unaware became evident to us Sunday when my poor unsuspecting sister, Anne, and her husband, Bill Millea, arrived for a relaxed visit.

With them were their five children dressed in cute little color coordinated outfits as bright and shiny clean as new pennies. Swimming suits for a late afternoon swim in our local pool were the only change of clothing that was thought necessary. They reckoned without the creek.

Before they went for a swim, the Millea kids decided to accompany the Burney kids on a tour of the farm, including the fishing hole, creek, etc.

About an hour after they left, my sister and I decided to take the bitty kids down for a wade in the creek and check on the older ones. Little did we suspect the devastation that awaited us. We were driving across a bridge with Annie admiring the scenery. All of a sudden she let out a shriek. **Coming down the middle of the creek was an apparition which can only be described as a walking mud pie.** Annie was not fooled. "Tim Millea!" she bellowed. We jumped out of the car and quickly perceived five other sitting mud pies, soaking in the water up to their color coordinated necks, long hair floating in the water, smiles rapidly disappearing from their sandy pusses as they perceived the outrage of the pair of ornery mothers standing on the bank.

The walking mud pie explained with no little logic, "But Mom, I came to this deep water and tripped and fell in," and, with his 9-year-old Irish mug a picture of outraged innocence, "I just couldn't help it!"

Actually, the odds were always against us. Ninety degree weather plus creek plus kids — we never had a chance. And after we ran the sandy clothes through the washer a couple of times and scraped some of the sand and mud off so that we could recognize the kids underneath, the humor of the situation began to sink in.

Also, one of mine swears that I gave permission. He said that Annie and I were talking and he asked if they could play in the creek with their good clothes on and I said yes and Annie heard me.

In all probability, that might have happened. When Annie and I get to talking, I would probably give the kids permission to set an atom bomb off in the living room when their daddies were sleeping.

And considering the reaction of their daddies as the gritty, grimy little goons walked forlornly in the house after their unscheduled swim — it might have been a smarter move.

Grandma June Rossiter Turned 80

July 1971

Whomsoever the sage is that runs around saying "Everything is relative," had to be around the Burney household this last week.

My mom, considering the alternative, decided to turn 80, and we kids(?) deciding that this was an event of outstanding proportions, put on a celebration for her.

Therefore, Rossiters and people closely and vaguely related to Rossiters, gathered from far and near to sing Happy Birthday to Grandma. Led by Mike Rossiter, who remarked (cheerfully looking over the bubbling mass of humanity which his grandmother was in some way responsible for) that **to some this must look like an ecological disaster.**

And there are those who consider a family reunion at least a disaster, agreeing with one of my brothers-in-law, who always says (among other things) that "relatives are like fish, after three days, they all stink." I don't feel this way...about relatives...or fish...with the possible exception of my brother-in-law, for among other things, a family reunion is a great place to observe human nature.

For instance **the interrelation of organisms and their environments (ecology) in our family have produced a real variety of folk.** From a 6' 5" grandson to a 4' 7" granddaughter, in Mom's case.

We represent all varieties of views politically, also. Accordingly, we have all ranges of haircuts, from a butch cut to the John the Baptist variety.

Our longest haired relative, Jed Livingstone, took kidding about his haircut or lack of it with great aplomb, such as when he was riding our horse across the yard slowly and son, John, told him that he has uncontrollable urge to lay palms before him.

Mom's total count of grandchildren is at 42 and holding, and the countdown on the great-grandchildren is at the moment 23 with no end in sight.

This is pretty small potatoes compared to some of the families in this area, who number their offspring in the 100s.

As in all these things, the planning beforehand was thorough and well thought out.

So what if we forgot to put out the guest book which we had so carefully bought, and if Mom will be using lovely napkins that say Happy Birthday June E. Rossiter...80...for the next 80 years because they spent the day of the birthday on somebody's shelf.

It's the thought that counts.

Isn't it...MOM?

Old Car Turns 00,000.0 Miles

April 1972

I hope you're up to the following exciting announcement. Old Car has just turned over 00,000.0 miles.

Breathtaking!

This great event took place last Sunday with the car loaded with excited eye witnesses. Appropriately, the turn over from 99,999.9 to 00,000.0 took place as the car was driving by the city dump. **A hushed silence accompanied the event, followed by subdued cheering appropriate to the occasion.**

All has not been beer and skittles for Old Car as it made its way to last week's historic event. And as it drew closer and closer to the momentous occasion, it became apparent that there was some controversy about who the driver would be when the event actually took place.

Kip felt that since he was the owner and older that he should have the honor, but No. 3 son John felt that he'd been with the Old Car during some of its more traumatic moments and put enough miles on it that he should be able to turn it over.

The discussion was raging Saturday afternoon when Editor Rudy Froeschle happened by. Our excitement about the impending event was not readily understood by Editor Rudy, but he soon got caught up in our enthusiasm. He even noted that he could hardly wait to tell his friends from Minneapolis about it, saying **"And they were worried about me moving to a community where exciting things didn't happen!"**

Finally, the negotiations about Old Car's driver were settled. Kip was to be first pilot, and John co-pilot.

The car was sitting in the garage with its speedometer, or whatever that is, registering 99,997.0. The entire family and a few friends crowded into Old Car and it headed down the road. It was an awe-inspiring sight.

I didn't accompany the revelers because I am not a hypocrite. I've publicly chastised Old Car for its cranky attitudes and, just between you and me, I never thought to see this day. In spite of myself, however, I wished Old Car and its occupants well.

The excitement proved too much for Old Car, though, and subsequently, it lost its water. However, its personal physician said that after a short rest and a water hose transplant it would be as good as could be expected.

So, Old Car has been rewarded with a thorough checkup and a short rest. The family has settled down after all the excitement, back to our hum-drum everyday existence. Not for long, however! We have to rest up for the next exciting events on our calendar.

You see, two of our mother cats are expecting!

I better tell Rudy about that!

Laidback Bill Almost Misses Graduation

May 1972

The commencement speaker at Creighton University's graduation used the following quotation: "Life is more like wrestling than dancing." Marcus Aurelius was the fellow that made it, and he really said a mouthful.

The commencement itself was a case in point. We packed up our tribe and journeyed down to watch our second eldest son Bill graduate, as he put it, Magna Cum Lucky. Bill is, to say the least, relaxed about life. He enjoys it. And we enjoy him. Most of the time.

This day we were bursting with pride as we watched the graduates file into the auditorium in a dignified procession. Try as hard as we could, however, we couldn't spot Bill. We'd gotten to the auditorium 45 minutes early just to get a good vantage point, and we watched eagerly for that familiar figure. To no avail. Kip muttered into my ear "He overslept." I vigorously denied it. The kids stood up on chairs and craned their necks. No Bill. Then the cry went up. "Here he comes!" I looked with renewed interest at the final graduates filing ceremoniously in the door, but I quickly had my attention redirected to the side aisle nearest us. There, loping in unconcernedly with his gown trailing out behind and a grin on his face, was Bill. He'd overslept.

Go, Kidney, Go!

October 1973

A very dear friend of ours, plucky little Darlene Miller, had a kidney transplant last week in the Clarkson Hospital in Omaha. We were terribly concerned about her, but she had said that it would do no good to come down because she would be in isolation and all we could do was look at her door.

Well, I don't know what you do when you get very concerned about something that you can't do a blamed thing about, but I go into

61

frenetic activity. So I started to paint. I painted the living room, then the dining room alcove, then two halls, and then our bedroom. Then I gave up. I realized I was just going to have to go down and look at Darlene's door.

So, I crawled in the pickup with Darlene's sister-in-law, Marge Miller, and we headed for Omaha. If we couldn't see Darlene, we could sit with her husband Don and look at the door.

And just looking at the door turned out to be an incredible experience. You see, **her progress is charted minutely on the door with an ever growing list of sheets.** They are scotch-taped firmly together, and when one gets too long, another is started on the top. Darlene was on her first sheet when we got there, and on her second when we left. But the kidney transplant patients in the room beside hers, who'd been there one week, two weeks, or three weeks, had reams of these neatly charted pages, one on top of the other.

Besides all the technical information on the charts, there are personal comments at the end of each line. When that personal comment said "turning easily" or "resting easily," we were pleased. And when it became apparent by the charts, which Don deciphered for us, that the kidney was functioning beautifully, we were elated.

But we weren't the only ones who were elated. The whole fifth floor of Clarkson Hospital seemed to resound with the news. This floor houses all the kidney patients, with those receiving the transplants and their donors being the very special ones. Some of the transplants came from cadavers, but many come from close relatives. Darlene received hers from her brother, Leo Arens, Jr. Better known to all of us as Curly.

There is a tremendous esprit de corps on this floor. A fellowship, if you will, between all these kidney patients and their relatives, and the nurses, and the doctors. The relatives have spent many hours in the waiting room together. Waiting out the patients on the artificial machines, waiting out the long hours of the operations, comforting one another when a patient seems to be rejecting. They've laughed together and cried together, and they are tremendously supportive of one another. It is quite an experience just to sit and watch.

But Darlene was our chief concern and all night and all the next morning we haunted that room and those charts. Don could go in if he completely gowned up. But we, of course, couldn't. We would stand in the door and peek at her, really unbelieving of this miracle that was taking place, but so thankful for it. Finally, we were rewarded, because she was taken out of complete isolation so we could holler words of encouragement from the door. **We made signs on paper towels saying, "Go, Kidney Go!" and stood and beamed at her.**

We were cautioned against over optimism, of course, but we couldn't get over the fact that our little friend, for the first time in many, many years seemed to have a working kidney.

So we stood at the door, waving and making fools of ourselves and watching the broad grin on Don's face. And we read the chart one last time. The nurse had written, **"patient cheerful."**

Now, we could go home.

Belt-Tightening Month
Bad For Ketchup Users

January 1976

Figuratively and literally, January is a belt-tightening month for many of us.

This is the time of year when a farmer figures out one of two things He didn't make money and has to cut down to survive. Or, he did make money and has to cut down to be able to pay the income taxes.

Both conclusions bode ill for the farmer's wife. It is the time when we get the "times are hard" and "need to be frugal" lectures. At our house, this is bad news for the ketchup users.

For whenever we are in one of our frugal periods, the friendly farmer gets the maddest at how much ketchup we use.

It causes blowups at the dinner table. "Look how much ketchup you've left on your plate" he's inclined to bellow. And all heck breaks loose. **"Do you think we are made of money?"** is usually the next question. The kids, having been through several "frugal" periods in their lifetime, are pretty sure we're not.

But the belt-tightening not only includes the spending of money, you see. It also includes the actual tightening of belts.

Not on purpose, you understand, but as a result of all the holiday festivities and the eating, and more eating that occurred during that time.

So, all in all, it makes January a pretty miserable month. **One sits around in one's too-tight jeans, afraid one will use too much ketchup.**

Farmers aren't the only ones who have tense periods like this, however.

I remember times at home when the tension was so thick you could cut it with a knife and gigantic explosion might occur at the supper table when something happened as simple as a water glass falling over.

These occasions happened spasmodically throughout the year and

63

when we became aware that we had one upon us, we learned to tread lightly.

It was when the bank examiners showed up. My dad was a banker, you see, and bank examiners (state and federal, as I remember) tend to show up when one is least expecting them.

Bank examiners make bankers tense even though they have nothing to worry about. But if their best customer happens to be slightly over-extended — which I think might have occurred occasionally during the depression years, well, it made for an interesting few days.

It occurred to me to wonder if other families in other businesses go through such cyclical stress periods.

I don't think that newspapers, or plumbing and electric shops, or grocery stores, have examiners. And I doubt that they wait until January to figure everything up to find out where they stand for the year.

Weekly newspapers have a mini-stress period every Tuesday night, however, which is when the paper gets wrapped up. It is best to avoid annoying an editor at that time, I've learned. Although the same person can be agreeable and lovely on Wednesday, after the paper is out.

In schools, I suspect the stress period is toward the end of the term. Exam time. Trying to get everything finished up.

For coaches it is constant.

For us it is January. Which is why I must leave you now to spoon the excess ketchup from our supper hamburgers back into the bottle. After all, do you think we are made of money?

Burney Reunion Baseball Synonymous

May 1976

It wasn't what you would call your run-of-the-mill baseball game. It had all the earmarks of one — (hollering, yelling and a couple of Mexican players) — but you would have immediately recognized its distinctiveness if you had seen the roster. That is, if there had been a roster.

The youngest player was seven and the oldest 84. It would have been difficult for a bystander to decide which of those two had the most enthusiasm, because they both moved with great spryness and put out a lot of chatter.

Except that when his softball got caught in the tree, it wasn't the oldest one that cried.

Burneys from all over the state and points West had gathered for a family reunion. The baseball game was and is traditional, there's never been a Burney gathering without one. Everybody plays except for a few chicken women and the competition is fierce.

Four generations of Burneys were playing ball. Chad Willard Burney was the 7-year-old son of Lincoln lawyer Travis Willard Burney. He (Travis) is the son of Willard Wales Burney (Hartington farm manager and appraiser at whose home we were reunioning) who himself is son of Dwight Willard Burney the first, our 84-year-old.

In between were all kinds of brothers and cousins and aunts and uncles, including the honoree, Grandpa Burney's 88-year-old brother Quay, who'd driven in from California with his son Gerry.

It was great fun to watch the various sizes (and shapes!) of Burney and Burney-related people as they played ball. **There was so much cheating going on that there was some doubt as to who was the winner.**

There were enough players that a runner might get held up, physically, while getting to a base and there might even have been a little tripping. There were no umpires, of course, so the rules were rather loosely applied and some of them were interpreted in Spanish, making it all very interesting.

In fact, it looked so interesting that I was about to go out and join the game, when they took an ice cream break. I always have the best of intentions of getting into the games but try to procrastinate just long enough to miss most of them.

The wisdom of my master plan was born out as the middle-aged types who were playing came in moaning and groaning about their various infirmities.

All, that is, except for the 7-year-old and the 84-year-old. Both little Chad and Grandpa Burney could have gone a couple more innings.

Good thing for Grandpa he didn't though, because Grandma Grayce was watching out the window and I heard her mutter, **"The next time he tells me he doesn't have the strength to wash the windows..."**

Messy Office And Fish Named Dog Make For Bad Week

June 1976

I knew last week was going to be a bad week when the kids showed up with a hyper fish whom (which?) they named Dog.

I knew the fish was coming, because I'd wandered through the carnival which was gracing the streets of Hartington last week, and I saw a fish concession. Seemed that if you could toss a ping pong ball into a tiny fish bowl you could have the fish therein. (That's the reason the fish is hyper. How'd you like having ping pong balls thrown into your living quarters all day long?)

Anyway, I knew when I saw the fish concession that one of my boys was bound to bring home a fish. **One year we got 38 beer mugs, and we aren't particularly fond of beer.** We've been overwhelmed with ash trays and funny little plastic creatures, to say nothing of a few dogs, teddy bears and ugly snakes. And a couple of frogs.

So my day started with this fish, Dog, who was racing around his fish bowl like a nincompoop. Then Kip brought up my office. "It is ridiculous," he said. And it is. I've been so busy running around doing whatever it is I do, that I've let everything pile up in here, and not only are all the desks and tables covered, so is the floor. And I don't know where anything is. Usually I have organized chaos. This is just a mess.

So, I started to clean it up, and I discovered a stamped addressed envelope which was supposed to go to Maverick Media in Syracuse. It was my column. The one that was to be in the paper last Wednesday. This was Friday. I'd lost it on my desk.

Francis Moul, the man who runs Maverick Media, is a very fine fellow. We've been associated in the journalism business for many years, and even ate a shrimp pizza together in the wee hours of the morning once. You have to really like someone to eat a shrimp pizza with him — any time — but especially in the wee hours of the morning.

He's also very understanding, and knows my peculiarities. That's the reason he wasn't surprised when he got an envelope some weeks ago and it contained nothing. No column. Nothing. Just an envelope. Maxine, his lovely wife called, and asked what I might have had in mind for that envelope. The column was folded neatly under some of the inordinate amount of stuff which decorates this desk.

I was appalled and swore that it would never happen again. It didn't. This time I lost the envelope, too.

And Grandpa Burney's 85

January 1977

It was probably your typical family reunion, if any family can be called "typical," with the kids and grandkids and great-grandkids, but for us it was special because it was in honor of Grandpa Burney's 85th birthday.

And Grandpa Burney, just back from a very short (very short!) personal appearance in California leading Lawrence Welk's orchestra, looked more hale and hearty than any of us.

He assured us that if we could get to be his age and have as good a life as he was having, and be in as good a shape as he was — well — it was just pretty nice.

And we all agreed.

There was a little grumbling in the group, because this celebration was taking place on Super Bowl Sunday. It was especially irksome to the rabid sports fans in the Burney family because thirteen years ago Grandpa married Grayce Hahn of Polk, Nebraska on New Year's Day, which just happened to be the day Nebraska played in the Cotton Bowl. So, everybody was giving Grandpa a bad time about that. (Personally, not being a rabid sports fan, I thought it did them good to miss two games in thirteen years. It builds character.)

Referring to their thirteen years of marriage, Grandpa said that we should all give Grayce credit for keeping him out of our hair, and there was a round of applause for Grayce.

We had a cake made in the shape of the state house in honor of the years Grandpa spent there, and Grandpa opened presents which included two lovely pair of gloves from sons, Doctor Dwight and Wid. He said they'd go nicely with the pair of gloves he got from son, Don for Christmas. It's always been a problem knowing what to get for Grandpa because he has no faults one can contribute to, and so he probably has more good looking shirts and pajamas than anyone in the country.

No, he has more gloves.

Uncle Doc brought slides, and we all were exposed to much younger versions of ourselves in living color on a wide screen, so we relived for a moment brief snatches of the "olden days."

One picture was of Kip in his uniform standing with me before we were married. Kip looked dashing and debonair and I looked coy and shy. Boy, those were the olden days.

Another family picture was taken later (after we were married) (of course) in which I was quite pregnant. The thought passed through my mind that in those early years it would have been difficult to catch a picture of me when I wasn't pregnant.

In spite of missing the Super Bowl game, which was lousy anyway, we all had a good time, retelling favorite family stories and reliving favorite memories.

Kip remembered when he discovered a red wagon in the basement before Christmas and confided in "Junior" (Dr. D.W. Burney II) and Junior said, "You stand here and talk like there's two of us and I'll go down and check." (I think they were 18 and 20 at the time.)

All of us should sit down and write down all of the family history and memories we can, and save them for posterity. I've got an edge on all of you because I'm doing that every week, as we go along. But — of course — there are personal memories which nobody (even old blabbermouth herself) would want to share with anybody but family. Anyway, it would mean a lot to our kids. We should think about it.

P.S. I forgot to explain about Grandpa doing his "a-one-and-a-two" bit in front of Lawrence Welk's orchestra. It was during an entertainment session Lawrence was putting on for this tour troupe Grandma Grayce was leading, and they were called out of the audience because of Grandpa's being a "former governor." Grayce danced with Lawrence while Grandpa directed. As far as I know, he isn't considering going into it professionally, but he said it was fun.

Death Does Not Extinguish The Light

February 1977

Every time I sat down to write a column last week, the words wouldn't come. I whipped out some articles and did some interviews and took some pictures, happy to be busy. But a personal column I could not tackle.

My friend Ferdie Pietz took me aside just last night and told me why. He said, "You know, you're going to have to write about Mother." And I suppose I am.

All during the last five years that Mother was bedridden with a stroke, Ferdie would come up to me and say, "How is Mother?"

And I would say, "Well, she seems content, she's not in pain, she likes television, and she enjoys company." Something like that.

As I think about that now, it is incredible. How could a vivacious, active, beautiful lady like my mother be "content" to be bedridden, saying only "yes" and "no," and watching her family come and go, the seasons change, the holidays go by. But she was, or made us think so, always smiling at us, patiently waiting for her care.

Oh, occasionally she could be a little grumpy. If I hadn't been there for a couple of days, I'd have to have a pretty good explanation before I got that smile. And she laughed out loud at all my stories. She was my very best audience.

And always when our visit was over, I would kiss her on the mouth and on the forehead and say, "I love you," and I think she knew that, too. Her eyes told me she did. And sometimes she would say "yes."

I would sit on one side of her bed and hold her hand, and her very dearest friend and companion, Clare Schmidt, would sit at her "post" on the other side of Mother's bed and we would talk and laugh. Clare must have spent most of the last five years in that chair, doing fancy work and mending, keeping Mother company.

Mother especially enjoyed visits from her grandkids. My boys would go in and she would hold their hands and beam, and say "yes" most emphatically.

My daughter Juli and she had a game going. She wouldn't say "yes" to Juli at all until Juli would say "Well, I guess I'll go now, Grandma," and then Grandma would get a big grin and say "Yes!" and Juli would make a big thing of that.

Sister June would bring her mail, and brother Vince stopped almost every night and watched TV with her.

But now she's gone. Last week she just gave up and slept away. God knows she must have been tired of it. She who traipsed the world with aplomb until she was 81 years old, must have been tired of being confined to a bedroom participating in the edges of everyone's life.

We talked a lot the last week, when we knew she was leaving us — about how good things were going to be for her. She looked at us with unseeing eyes and held our hands so tight. Selfishly, not until the last couple of days was I able to pray that the Lord would take her home. As long as that smile was there, our mother was with us.

So now, Ferdie, I have written about "Mother." And even as the sound of the "Alleluias" we sang at the funeral fade in my memory, the memories of the bedridden lady fade too.

And memories of the mother who walked regally into my kitchen every Sunday, who polished my silver, sewed on my buttons, and advised me (in no uncertain terms) how to run my life, take precedence. That's the way she would want it.

We buried her in the red suit she always wore when she traveled, with her NCCW (National Council of Catholic Women) Mrs. Arthur Mullen Award medal and the gold Rosary that was a gift from Daddy. On her casket was a spray of yellow football mums. Every anniversary Dad had sent her two dozen of them, and after he died, sister Mary sent them still.

Everybody said she looked wonderful, certainly not like she was 86 years old. That always strikes me as a little ironic, but nonetheless I hope I look wonderful when the time comes.

We shall miss her. But our strength comes from knowing "Death is not extinguishing the light; it is putting out the lamp because the dawn has come."

Appreciating The Ordinary Day —
After Agonizing Accident

June 1977

A week ago Saturday was just an ordinary day. People in and out, phones ringing, lots of talking, laughing, arguing, sun shining. Just an ordinary day. And I didn't appreciate it for the beautiful thing it was.

Because by Sunday morning, things were mighty different. Saturday night we'd gone out to dinner, and when we got home I checked on the kids. Only daughter and #4 son were safe in bed, and so, I presumed so was the #5 son, who was staying with a friend. Ever since I've had a kid old enough to toddle out the door for an evening, I've stayed up to welcome them in. Then I trundle off to my bed and sleep soundly.

This night, at exactly 4:06, the phone rang. I guess every parent has a terrible dread of that phone ringing in the middle of the night. In the innermost recesses of our minds it is a fearsome thought.

But, as a rule, we get phone calls any time of the night from Kip's truckers. Clarifying orders, checking on where they are supposed to go, that kind of thing. So, we don't think too much of it. And Kip usually answered the phone.

It was his terse "Yes," "Yes," "Yes" answers that made my heart stop. He came back into the room grabbing his clothes and informing me that our youngest had been in an accident. His friend was all right. But he was unconscious in the emergency ward, and we should come right away. "They wouldn't tell me any more," Kip said with fear clutching at his voice.

Juli said we went out of the door at 4:08.

That ride to Yankton was one of excruciating agony. We've had too many of these accidents in our country. When the parents reach the hospital, it has never been good. Sometimes it's been terrible. You don't say much. You don't have to, you pray a lot. It didn't make any sense. The boys had never been out that late. It just couldn't be. But it was. And when we got to the hospital, things weren't much better. Professionals informed us cooly that our son, who was badly cut up and bruised and looked just awful, was awake and was only slightly disoriented, so they were hoping no head injuries. But they couldn't rule out broken leg, broken nose and possible internal bleeding would indicate other problems. Our son's friend was beside himself worrying about our boy, and our boy's only concern was his friend. "Tell him not to worry," he kept saying. And then, "Mom it can't be this late."

Turned out the accident took place about one o'clock. The boys had gone over to Yankton to get something to eat, but they'd both worked all day and were tired.

On the way home they both went to sleep. Unfortunately, one of them was driving. They went in a ditch and would have successfully pulled out, except for a wash-out by a culvert, which propelled them into the culvert and catapulted them end over end down a twenty to twenty-five foot embankment.

Miraculously, the driver, who had his seat belt on, was not hurt and with difficulty got himself out of the upturned car. But our son was no place to be found. He'd been thrown some 60 feet from where the car landed. **It must have been a nightmare.** Cars wouldn't stop. And when one finally did, they couldn't find our son, either. They tried to flag down someone with a C.B., but two more cars and two more trucks went by without stopping. Finally, we were told, a camper pulling a boat stopped. They had a C.B. and a floodlight, and finally they found our son, unconscious, and apparently seriously hurt. It took another 45 minutes or so before the ambulance came. "Seemed like forever" they said.

Hence, our phone call at 4:06 (blasted digital clocks!). It wasn't until three o'clock the next day that we learned the X-rays showed no broken bones, only badly sprained ones. And other tests showed no internal injuries. And all the facial cuts were superficial. And everything would heal. Lot of aches and pains. But otherwise okay.

There are no adequate words from those of us who were involved to properly thank the people who helped our boys. I can understand people being afraid to stop in the middle of the night, but thank God for the people who weren't. And thanks to the professionals who work all hours just doing their job. And to the good Lord.

Because it is going to be a long time before I have just an ordinary day, people in and out, phones ringing, lots of talking, laughing, and arguing, and sun shining. Just an ordinary day. When I don't appreciate it for the beautiful thing it is, and thank God. A fellow just doesn't know what he's got until he darned near loses it.

It's All Water Down
The Old Irrigation Ditch

September 1977

It was the morning of the thirteenth of September and I was sitting on the couch going over some papers when our bookkeeper, Bill Bernhard, came in and congratulated me. You see, it was our (Kip's and mine) thirtieth anniversary.

It dawned on me that we'd been married longer than Bill had been alive: Seemed funny, somehow. It seems as if we've been married forever, and — on the other hand — the time has gone so fast.

Memories crowd in — mostly good — like when we set out on our honeymoon and Kip spent the first hundred miles giving me a lecture on finances. (I've laughed about that a lot!) I guess he decided he wouldn't take any chances on my being a spendthrift, since he was marrying the banker's daughter. Little did he know that the banker, whose daughter he was marrying, came through the depression and was probably the — hmmm — thriftiest man in town.

But we didn't have much to start out on, and somehow it didn't seem to matter. Kip was going to ag college, Ft. Collins on the G.I. bill. I was going to go to college, too, but after a decent interval (a couple of months) I was suddenly seized with this strange malady, and spent every morning violently ill.

Funny thing, the same thing was happening to the three young couples we ran around with. That's the way things were done (or not done) in those days, you know. Jack and Therese Thielen, who got married within three days of us, had their first son, Kenny, within ten days of the birth of our first son, Rob.

The Thielens and we lived in apartments in a converted chicken coop by an irrigation ditch. I can remember sitting at the edge of that stream eating watermelon after we'd sold our books to get food at the end of the semester. That sounds more melodramatic than it was. Kip, ever thrifty, had us putting away a large portion of our incoming salary against the day we could start farming. So we were budgeted to the nth degree.

Anyway, I'd written my mother that we were living on a cottage by a creek. Romanticist that I was. I didn't tell her that sometimes the "creek" didn't run (when the irrigation water was turned off) and it might smell a little and have a few (!) mosquitoes.

Then a week before Rob was born, I blew up a gas stove in my face, leaving me with no eyebrows or eyelashes and my hairline set back a couple of inches. Also, a brown mask all over my face.

We'd decided that we could have this baby by ourselves and didn't need our mothers to come since Kip was on vacation from school.

Everything went well, we had our baby and good thing Rob was a boy, because Kip took me to the hospital, and then left and came back to the waiting room with a baseball and a glove for his son, and he wasn't even born yet.

But after Rob was born I developed something that I think we call milk fever in cows, and our mothers got together and decided one of them better come. It was my mom that came. Kip picked her up and brought her home to the chicken coop and the ditch and a daughter who looked like she'd been burned at the stake and scalped, and **she just put her arms around me and cried.**

But after she discovered we were really happy and despite the looks of things, relatively healthy, she being not one to sit still, immediately suggested a trip and Rob was touring the mountains before he was a week old.

Lordy, Lord. A lot of water has gone down the old irrigation ditch since then. That was a long time ago. Strange that it should seem like yesterday.

Graduating #6
A Last Look At The Long Line...

June 1978

The feeling was strange, almost indescribable. It really wasn't sad, though tears were inevitable. It's just that everything was happening for the last time. And last times are almost as hard to take as first ones.

The school bus stopped by our house for the last time. The familiar red graduation gown came home to be pressed, for the last time. I watched, for the last time, one of my own march slowly up the aisle of the Holy Trinity gym with his classmates.

Handsome young people proud and assured, and — somehow — never more vulnerable. A giant lump forms in my chest, and memories of other proud young people crowd in. Six to be exact.

Mothers do all kinds of things for graduations. They clean and bake and prepare for festivities. They smile a lot and laugh a lot and sit around looking proud. And cry a few secret tears. Just enough to keep their heart lubricated, and keep the big lump in the chest from bursting.

Now the sixth graduation picture can go up beside the other five, balancing out the six baby pictures on the other wall.

I can remember when I hung the first picture and the young man in the picture headed out to Creighton University. I could hardly stand to let him go and, on the other hand, I could hardly wait to get rid of him.

Mothers have mixed feelings, you see. By the time kids get to be 18 or 19, they need to get away. And you need them to go. They've been flapping their wings in your face for some time now, and it's time they tried them.

By the time that sixth one flies away, you know from experience that the flight isn't permanent. They will be back with their problems, their triumphs, their boy and girl friends, and their dirty clothes.

But as they march in that graduation line, they look so young. This is the moment they've been waiting for and working for, and now they wonder why they were in such a hurry.

You can see it in the six pictures that hang on our wall. So self-assured, yet so vulnerable. Different hairstyles denoting the different years. The first a crew cut, the second a little longer, the third with hair gently flowing over his glasses, the fourth with hair to the waist (of course, she was the girl) (still is) and so forth.

In any case, Chuck, the sixth and last one walking in that line was almost more than I could take. I snapped pictures and splatted tears all over.

Until I looked around and saw a friend, Joan Vlach, sitting behind me who was graduating her first. First of six. And I thought about all the graduations, proms, sports events, father-son banquets, parent-teacher conferences, report cards, first driver's licenses, first dates, first car dents, etc., etc., she had to go through.

And I started to grin. Better she than me, I thought. We'd raised six pretty decent kids, and enjoyed every minute of it. Well — almost every minute. But I wouldn't want to do it over again.

And I watched those gallant young people march slowly out of that gym into the world without a tear in my eye. This might just be the class that really would go out and save the world. I certainly prayed so.

Meanwhile, Kip and I . . . well, by golly, **we'd survived!**

Don't Put Off That Reunion!
A 1978 Reunion With Duchesne Classmates

September 1978

Mary Higgens Brennan looked at us all and said: "If I expected this reunion to rate 57%, I'd have to say now it rated 157%." Which is the way we all felt.

It's hard to explain why we've remained so close over all these intervening years. After all, our only exposure to each other was one year at the Duchesne boarding school attending college in Omaha.

But we were all primarily small town girls, and we were more or less trapped in the boarding school because that's the way they were

74

in those days. We signed in and signed out, had to be in by six on weekdays, had strict hours on weekends, and never appeared ANY PLACE in slacks.

I think it was probably a little like surviving the war together.

We laughed together over memories of studying in the closet after "lights out," of sunbathing on the roof of Duchesne College, much to the consternation of the good Mothers of the Sacred Heart, and of hurrying to the Masses that required caps and gowns with our pajamas on under the gowns.

All sounds very tame in this day and age, but then we were rascals, I tell you.

There were five of us able to get together. Mary was the one who initiated this. We'd tried for years to plan a reunion but could not come up with a mutually agreeable time. There's never enough time, you know.

And suddenly it dawned on Mary that time was a fleetin' and we weren't getting any younger. And, laying that on the line, she made the initial phone calls. Amazingly, with just a couple of days' notice, we arrived at a date, and the movement started toward Omaha.

It was an emotional high from the first wild hugs of greeting to the tearful hugs of farewell. **Many of us hadn't seen each other for 25 years or more, and still the get-together was as natural as if we'd been studying in the closets together just yesterday.** There was a lot of catching up to do, and about the time we'd covered ourselves and our families, it was time to go home.

Monte Sibley Darner had come from Huron, Mickey McGlaughlin Morehouse from Lincoln, Mary from Wisconsin, and Rosemary Foster Mullen from Omaha. Well, actually, Rosemary was there all the time which was handy for her — and us too — since she drove us around and allowed us to descend on her lovely home.

We seemed to laugh a lot. We also told each other we hadn't changed a bit. Of course, the reason for that might have become apparent when we sat down at the table to eat and all pulled out our glasses to read the menus. "You frauds!" Rosemary cried, and we laughed some more.

I'm sure it would be necessary now, if we were to see a lot of each other, for us to establish our friendships on the basis of the people we have become. **But for one delightful session we were still five girls in a dorm, and we had a whale of a time.**

The lesson here is, there is enough time...you just have to take it. And my word to you, if you have a reunion you've been putting off, is get with it. Time's a fleetin'!

Dealing With The Empty Nest Syndrome

December 1978

Like a lot of people, I am very good at hellos and terrible at good-byes. This is the season wherein we seem to be saying a lot of both.

As people get — well, ahem — older, and their children start to scatter to the four corners of the earth, hellos get further and further apart, making goodbyes even more devastating. Are you following me?

What I mean is, you wouldn't want those great big kids who've suddenly become adults around all the time. Heaven knows, nobody could stand it! **But it is such a deliciously wonderful feeling to have them all back together for a short time, that it's hard to give them up.**

All six of ours, plus one wife who is now also ours, were home for Thanksgiving. Probably the last time for awhile because one heads to California, and another — eventually — to France for a year's study on his way to a doctorate. They won't even be in the same direction.

So I tended to hug a little tightly and get a little teary as each one took off. Mothers have every right to do that, you know.

Since most of the kids are natural-born hams, our reunions are somewhat tumultuous, with spontaneous song and dance teams springing up from the supper table, and ordinary conversations liberally sprinkled with bits of dialogue from everything from 'Fiddler on the Roof' to 'Romeo and Juliet.'

I remember one meal during which everyone talked in rhyme, which got very bad indeed.

In any case, it's very quiet when all these characters take off. One tends to fall back on the couch and take a little nap.

This fall, when my youngest headed out to the college of his choice, I was somewhat worried about the "empty-nest syndrome" which I've read so much about. So much so that I took on every assignment my editors wanted to give me, and almost every speech I could work into my schedule.

Consequently, I was so busy I couldn't even think about being depressed. However, I forgot one thing — Kip, my friendly cattle-feeder husband. Although he's gone five days a week to cattle sales — allowing me a great deal of freedom, you see — he does occasionally show up at home. And he's kind of gotten in the habit of having me there when he gets there. Seems the least a person can do.

Now he might not stay there even if I am home, you understand. He may go off to bowl, or play cards, or play golf, or whatever it is men do in their leisure time. But it's important to him to think I spend at least some of my time at home. I mean . . . he'd like to run into me occasionally.

So toward the end of fall, he asked me how I was doing with my "empty-nest syndrome" and I replied happily that I thought I had it licked. The secret was just to keep too busy to think about it. **And he said: "But you know what? You're never home. Now I've got the empty-nest syndrome."**

Well, a person can't think of everything! However, I'm scheduling more carefully now that my first panic is over. But I still don't like the goodbyes. A person just has to offer them up, and look forward to all the hellos to come.

Uncle Wid's Office Party

January 1981

I wouldn't say my brother-in-law, Willard, was tight, but I don't know too many people who have their office Christmas party at the John Deere pancake days.

With the savoir faire of a man leading his guests into an elegant restaurant, he gathers his office personnel and other "invited" guests about him like a covey of quail and leads them into the giant shop area where John Deere personnel and their wives are busily putting out several million pancakes.

He took great pride this year in the fact that the Dairy Princess was at his Christmas party and that all the other people were there. **"A lot of people come to my Christmas party," he said proudly, survey-ing the multitude of people wolfing down the pancakes, "and it doesn't cost them a cent."**

He completely ignores the fact that his Christmas party doesn't cost him a cent either.

The Burneys are a thrifty lot, and they come by this trait naturally. Dad Burney has been known to drive miles to get to a gas station that had a price war (when they used to do that) and the whole family was sure (since he only bought a few gallons at a time in case the next station would have cheaper gas) that the top of his tank was rusty.

Kip will spend money on something big — like a cruise — and then absolutely refuse to spend any money on clothes to take along. Not for me, you understand, he long ago lost control of that, but for himself.

All he ever wears are boots and white socks. He claims he wears the white socks in self-defense because it's the only way he can guarantee that he has a matching pair. I think that's unkind, but I do have two bushels of unmatched socks that give some credance to his claim.

I gave up on talking him into purchasing a dark suit ("I already have a suit," he said) but I remained adamant about his purchasing a pair of tennis shoes, or jogging shoes, or something to wear on the deck besides his boots. He says, "I can wear my slippers." He loves his slippers! Jack Konz orders him a new pair every four years or so, just like the old ones.

I wouldn't have to sit next to him, of course — a man in white work socks and his slippers on the deck is bound to cause a stir — but I would still feel somehow responsible.

My friends and relatives have a great deal of influence on their husbands' clothes. My influence is minimal, if any. I have to trick him into a clothing store, and then make a scene, and he makes a scene about prices, etc., and I usually manage to out-scene him.

Thus it was with the tennis shoes. With the help of an obliging clerk, I shamed him into a purchase. But he has fussed about it ever since.

Now — a lot of people would be fussing about the cost of the cruise. Not Kip — it's a cattle feeding cruise and will include touring six Florida ranches and daily seminars, in which he is to have a part. That all sounds very sensible to him. **But the price of the tennis shoes!!! That may send him into cardiac arrest.**

Dr. Dwight Burney Jr., the third brother, has equally interesting idiosyncrasies when it comes to spending money. He just never carries any. They tell about him sticking a $50 bill under a mattress at the lake to have for emergencies, and driving home with that same $50 still safely under the mattress. And no money to buy the kids the promised "meal out."

Their father would be proud of them.

90-Year-Old Grandpa Burney's High School Reunion

June 1981

Grandpa Burney, my much beloved father-in-law, has an adventure ahead of him this month. He's heading for Turtin, South Dakota for a big, all-school reunion.

Grandpa taught there when he was 20 years old. It's also where he wooed his first wife, pretty and petite Edna Wales, the mother of his four sons. He has wonderful memories of Turtin.

He can't wait to get back there and see the "kids" he taught. Grandpa will be 90 years old on his next birthday. He taught in high school, so you can about figure how old those "kids" are going to be.

In fact, Grayce, his present wife, has tried to prepare him for the fact that some of those "kids" might not even be around. Grandpa is undaunted. Somebody will be around. No matter who's there, he plans to enjoy it. That's the way Grandpa is. That's why he's lived to be 90 years old.

Grandpa Burney has in great abundance that magic quality that makes people young. Enthusiasm.

Besides, he knows one of our favorite cousins, Kenny Wales, will be there. He is a banker from Minneapolis. Kenny went to school in Turtin, and he also has this unbounded enthusiasm for life that characterizes Grandpa. It's going to be some reunion.

Grandpa, however, is worried about remembering names. "I don't remember as well as I used to," he said, while trying to think of someone the last time they visited. A funny thing, none of us could remember the name either. In fact, we spent all one evening trying to think of this one name. You know how something like that can bug you.

Kenny won't have that problem. We've always been amazed at his phenomenal memory of names. He lived with Kip's folks for a year while his mother was sick, and Kip says he can walk down the streets of Hartington today and still know those people.

Kenny's memory only failed him once. He tells this story on himself. He once met a man on the streets of New York whom he thought he should know. He decided the man was a banker from Minnesota, and stopped him to visit while he waited for his marvelous memory to come back. The man visited with him very cordially, Kenny said, and finally Kenny's memory came through. The "friend" he'd stopped on the street was Garry Moore, the famed TV personality.

Grandpa's enthusiasm for life does not include spending money. Quite the opposite. Just this last year he broke down and purchased a riding lawn mower for his large yard in Polk, where he and Grayce live. We've been trying to talk him into it for years, but he views this kind of "frivolity" as nothing short of decadence. A man who can push a mower should not ride. **But we tried to tell him that at 89, he's entitled.**

He finally succumbed, but reluctantly. In fact, he takes visitors out to show them the lawn mower with just a hint of embarrassment.

Now we're trying to talk him into a new car. Seems as if a former governor of Nebraska could drive up to the reunion in something besides a 9-year-old Chrysler. "You can't trust those old cars," I tell him, "and think of all the safety features on the new ones." He just grins. **Don't tell Grandpa you can't trust something old.** He knows better!

Kip — The Agony Of Smoking Years

October 1981

I walked into a book store at the mall this past week and the kindly clerk, seeing my name on my charge card said, "I liked it when you gave it to your husband about smoking!"

And I said, "I'm about to give it to him again."

But first I want to say how much we've appreciated the letters of encouragement we've received regarding Kip's noble attempt to quit smoking. Letters from people who've tried and know how painful it is.

Secondly, I want to tell all of you from whom Kip's been mooching cigarettes that I'm aware that he hasn't quit smoking as much as he's quit buying. I suggest you avoid him. I don't suppose you'll be able to.

One of his arch-targets — mooching-wise — is his brother Wid. Wid is what I call a militant smoker. He defies anyone to make him quit, saying "it takes real courage to smoke in this day and age." It takes "real" something, but I'm not sure courage is the word.

At any rate, Kip is something of a militant moocher. I've observed him from behind pillars and potted palms, and he hovers about a known smoker like a buzzard ready to pounce, then moves in smiling broadly for the kill. I've told him that I'm not his mother, and I'm not going to check up on him, but that's a lie. I mean — I'm not his mother, obviously, but I check up on him all the time.

Anyway, back to Wid. Wid was complaining because since Kip has "quit" smoking, his (Wid's) cigarette cost has grown appreciably. Kip says blandly, and with a certain air of martyrdom, ignoring his own culpability there, "If you can't afford to smoke, you should quit."

Tom Tideman, our local insurance man, is "quitting" smoking too. Kathy, his wife, gives him all the help she can. **When he mooches one, she mooches four — sticks two of them in her ears, two in her nostrils, and follows him around.** It tends to draw attention to the two of them, and has cut down considerably on Tom's smoking in public places.

We realize, of course, that it's not up to us, it's up to them. Maturity is assuming the responsibility for your own actions. And the fact is, you have to. No one else can.

Everybody who knows anything about it tells Kip he has to quit cold turkey. His father, who's lived to be nearly 90 years old by not smoking, is adamant about it.

I think that's probably right. But if you just can't seem to do that, I think cutting down from a pack and a half to two or three cigarettes a day is a reasonable alternative. And then maybe — who knows — one day that wonderful inner conviction that "I can lick this abominable weed!" might appear full-bloom in one's subconscious. And the yucky cigarette will be out of our lives forever.

Until that time — thanks again for your encouragement, and I'm sorry about the mooching. The only way I can think of keeping Kip from mooching cigarettes off of you smokers is for you to quit smoking too. That will show him! How about it?

Saint Willard, He Wasn't

December 1981

Our son Tom said, "Mom, what I remember best about Wid was when I was a little kid and I had chicken pox and he brought me two six packs of orange pop, with a letter that told me how orange pop had a secret chemical that cured chicken pox. I still have the letter."

That little nugget of a story is the essence of what the life of Willard Burney was all about. He died suddenly this past week, in the early morning, seemingly in the midst of his life. His wife Virginia said almost immediately, "This is the way he would have wanted it. He couldn't stand getting old."

But he was the only one who would have wanted it. His concern about Tom's chicken pox is just one example of the way he moved through so many of our lives with wit and wisdom and loving care. The whole community is still reeling from the blow of his death. The family has letter after letter saying "I can't imagine a world without Wid."

Saint Willard he wasn't. When the minister came into the kitchen the day before the funeral and asked all of us there to recollect our favorite stories about Wid, it was quite awhile before he heard any he could use in his funeral homily. But when he told the stories he finally gathered — everybody in the church laughed. I can't help but think, if Wid's soul was hovering over us as they say souls do, he would have liked that. He liked to make people laugh.

He was an excellent speaker and a writer. His wit punctured holes in many a pompous situation, not to say person. He was a practical joker, and bedeviled his closest friends with pranks and anonymous letters. His favorite target was his beloved group of Hartington liberals, he being an ultra conservative and one of the first backers of Ronald Reagan. Just the week before he died, he'd sent ultra conservative material, anonymously of course, to these poor "misguided" men.

The minister said he celebrated life. That he did. He loved his family and friends, and he brought such a warmth to his business relationships that those people became his friends. He refreshed his soul with people. With the fellows at the morning coffee, his lifelong bridge club friends, and especially with the beauty of Hideaway Acres, the development he helped get started at the lake, and his multitude of friends up there.

And with every foray he made into the world, he brought back more stories to regale Virginia and the rest of us with. Many a morning coffee at our house was enlivened by Wid's retelling of the little "slices of life" he loved so much to share.

He was easily led astray, he happily admitted. He'd call Virginia and say that "the boys" were making him bowl, or golf, or play cards. Then he'd bring to whatever game it was a spirit of competitiveness and fun that kept everything more than lively.

But for all his orneriness, his love of teasing, he was a gentle soul. He was a man who cared deeply and felt deeply. He hid it sometimes with gruffness and humor, but we all knew it was there. He was a man who gave to all of us to such an extent that finally his big heart gave out, and just had no more to give.

Heaven will not be the same place with Wid up there. His kids and his brothers wondered if the Lord really realized what He was in for. By now he will have reorganized everything — he will have hugged his mother and gotten her laughing, he will have had some wild joke with Marge Seim, and he will be settled down for a gin rummy game with Dick Wintz and Benny Johnson.

But our world will never be the same, either.

Writer Needs Confusion

March 1982

There are advantages and disadvantages to writing at home. **The advantages are you're home to stir the stew, be available if your husband needs you, or if emergencies arise.**

The disadvantages are that you're home to stir the stew, be available if your husband needs you, or if emergencies arise.

Therein lies the problem. If you want to have long uninterrupted hours for writing, forget it!

Problems arise in several areas. For instance, as all writers will tell you, once you get to writing, the house could fall down around your shoulders and you wouldn't notice it.

So, chances are the acride smell of scorching stew would be one of the first emergencies to arise.

Also, our office overlooks the whole farm. So farm emergencies are readily apparent. Cattle in the cornfield, for instance, or hogs in the garden. The latter can be particularly disruptive to my train of thought.

Then there are family emergencies. A button needs to be sewn on "right now!" or a call from a college kid makes an immediate transfer of funds necessary or kids and kids' friends arrive to "surprise!" us.

Then there are business emergencies. The urgent phone call that means I have to find Kip. Lord knows where. Or the times you're needed as a "go-fer" to get a part, fill the car with gas, or get a check to the bank.

Then there's that need for personal contact with your friends that can happily eat up a whole day in a hurry.

So I write in snitches and snatches of time, sometimes in the wee hours of the morning. And read and research on the same spasmodic kind of schedule.

There was a time when I had the notion that I might really accomplish something if I just had some solitude. Kip got the bright idea that I could go along with him when he took one of his two-day trips to cattle sales and I would have all those days in the motel room with not a soul to interrupt me.

It was probably the worst two days I've ever spent. It was terrible. Just me and the danged typewriter. Nobody to interrupt, nothing to bother.

I was bored out of my skull. I was lonesome. I couldn't write.

I began to hear things. It was hot summer weather, and I imagined I heard a bird caught in the air conditioner. I have a thing about birds, so I raised a fuss.

I could just hear the motel owner. "Some crazy lady thinks there's a bird in her air conditioner. I think she's got bats in her belfry!"

I got the bird things settled. (Turned out it was a bird, but she wasn't caught, she was nesting. Noisy thing!) I still couldn't write. Kip was four hours later than he thought he would be from the sale.

He'd said, "I'll meet you at seven for supper if I can" and he showed up at 12. I was mad as I could be. He was truly amazed. "You never get mad at me when you're home," he said. "You know I never show up until the sale is over."

When I'm home I have things to do. Scorch the stew, chase the hogs, sew buttons. Interesting things like that. Up there I just had to write.

One lesson learned, the hard way!

Big Brothers Mend Broken Dreams

August 1982

My sister, Anne, and I are the "little girls" in a family of seven. We came along as afterthoughts, sort of, two little black-haired girls who were alternately spoiled and teased by our five older siblings.

The oldest two were boys, and we were the luckiest little girls in the world to have two "big brothers." They carried us around on their shoulders, fixed our things when they broke, teased us and made it so we weren't afraid of thunder and lightning. We worshiped them.

They were long gone from home when we were growing up, Lawrence the dreamer and Vincent the do-er, and people often thought they were our uncles rather than our brothers. But we still tended to lean on them. Call on them to solve knotty problems. **Or just to mend broken dreams, like they fixed our toys when we were little.**

So you will understand what a terrible ache it left in our hearts to say goodbye this past week to our big brother, Lawrence. We've said so many goodbyes this year, it seemed incredible that we would have to say another one. And a person has this silly notion that big brothers are indestructible. Lawrence wandered in and out of our lives with much love and good cheer. Indeed, he wandered through all life that way, appreciating all the goodness the Lord had to offer. He and Florence made each of our kids feel special. And with their appreciation for education, they were the most influential in encouraging anything and everything that I've done.

I knew from the time I was a little girl that Lawrence was a "brain."

He was so smart in some areas it was amazing. He could wander by his own sister on the street, however, and be so wrapped up in his thoughts he wouldn't say hello. A tug on his sleeve would be responded to with a bemused grin.

He was a superb photographer. He captured the world he loved and the people he loved that way. He helped me pick out my first camera, announcing "any fool can operate this!" I soon proved him wrong. Even that trusty Minolta couldn't take pictures when this fool forgot to put film in it. But he'd done the best he could to help me. He'd tried.

He tried with all of us, always thinking we might be better than we were, always having a little more faith in us than any of us deserved.

And he had lived, at 70, many more years than prior generations of high-powered Rossiter men. The credit goes to Florence who (depending on the weather) saw to it that he walked daily in the Yankton Mall or along their beloved Lewis and Clark Lake, who fed him tofu and other healthy things, who made his home a gracious and beautiful place.

He died because the Lord was ready for him. Even his "little sister" has to accept that and be happy for him. But he will not wander, humming away, into my kitchen and muse about the beauties and peculiarities of life. Not any more.

Cacti Friends Are Best Of All

1982

Last week I was watering my plants and noticed one was terminally ill. My cacti were flourishing. My philodendrons were cheerfully winding their way around the room, even a touchy baby tears seemed to be surviving. But this one particular plant had put up with all the benign neglect and spasmodic watering it cared to. It was definitely going, going, gone.

Reminded me of my friends, strange as that might seem. And my proven theory that friends are a lot like plants.

Friends are people who know all about you and like you anyway. They are more valuable than silver and gold. More to be cherished than diamonds and pearls. And probably just as rare.

At least, the cactus friends are. Those are the friends who are always there when you need them no matter what. But they require no care, so to speak. You may not see them for a year or longer, and their friendship remains the same. Cactus friends are quite often old army buddies, or old classmates. If you are lucky, your spouse is a cactus friend. Often favorite relatives are.

Although a cactus friend also could be somebody you meet tomorrow. Someone you are as comfortable with as if you'd known them forever. Cactus friends are never jealous, never demanding. They are just there. And they understand.

Now, philodendron friends require a little more care. They have to have a phone call now and then to keep their friendship alive. An occasional luncheon. Whatever. But they are still very valuable friends. One must be careful not to lose a philodendron friend because they confuse him or her with a cactus friend. This is a sensitive issue.

Then there are the baby tears type. They require moderate reassurance much as the baby tears needs its regular cup of water. But they can be worthwhile too. Great friends if you give them the proper care, and don't mind the coddling. And very hardy in the case of a little benign neglect. Allow you to make up for it with a little extra care.

Then there's the kind of friend that my dying plant represents. I call them the African violet type of friend. They require constant reassurance, constant care, as it were, but are as suspicious of too much as they are of too little. They are, to be truthful, sometimes a pain in the patootie. But, if you really like them, they too can be worthwhile.

Busy people have little time for African violet types. They are usually lost by the wayside. They're just not worth the effort.

Friends are usually better kept when we remind ourselves that people are more important than things, easily lost when we begin to put things ahead of people.

Sometimes we have to remind ourselves of this. And we have to take time to give our friends a little lovin', even the loyal cacti ones. Maybe send them this column and say "this is for you!"

There's an Arabian proverb that says it all: **"A friend is one to whom one may pour out all the contents of one's heart, chaff and grain together, knowing that the gentlest of hands will take and sift it, keep what is worth keeping and with a breath of kindness, blow the rest away."**

Compromise Is The Name
Of The Marriage Game

September 1982

"To what do you attribute the success of your looooong marriage," said a young friend, half kiddingly.

"Compromise!" I said uncompromisingly. "No doubt about it." Then I tried to tell her about it and she dozed off, so I'm going to tell you.

We started compromising even before we were married. Kip joined the Catholic Church and I joined the Republican party causing us both some misery.

That should have told us something right there, because it was only the beginning. We found out as our marriage progressed that outside of having handsome babies at regular intervals we had almost nothing else in common. I like my music, writing and communication work, Kip likes his cattle, cattle and cattle.

I could not understand how anybody could be so crazy about cattle. He'd go to a cattle sale and I'd think he should be home in time for supper. Sometimes, he almost didn't make it home for breakfast. And would I make a scene!

And I'd drag him to musicals and ballets, which he'd be miserable in and probably sleep through. He always said if his pants were that tight, he could jump that high too. No appreciation for the arts.

Then — when I went to the cattle sales with him and found out they really did last that long, I was bored to death.

So we figured out a new approach to togetherness, which is "apartness." Our marriage has lasted, indeed it has thrived, because we learned fairly early that if we were going to stay in double hitch for the long haul, we were going to have to give each other enough rein. In all friendships, especially marriage, sometimes if you hang on too tight you lose someone, but if you let them go, you keep them forever.

So we compromise about everything. It's not easy! Kip is a neat and I am a messy. He's orderly and knows right where to go and what comes next. I am totally disorganized, and lost more often than not. He likes beef and potatoes, I go for salads and crepes. He likes to be involved in any kind of sports, and if he's not playing them, he's watching them on television. I am a total klutz, and like to watch the Boston Pops on ETV. He loves any kind of game, especially cards and will play solitaire by the hour. Card games give me pains in the stomach. He's a mathematical genius, I can't even add the bridge score. I like picnics and camping out, he likes the Holiday Inn. It goes on and on. **So — sometimes we do things his way, sometimes mine,**

and sometimes we go our separate ways, happily.

I've learned to play bridge and golf and enjoy both most of the time. He stays awake during all musicals and even some plays. We have a high divider in our office so my messy desk doesn't drive him nuts. You see how it goes.

I think I have brought to his life a lot of foolishness and mostly joyful emotion. He's brought to mine some order, a solid goodness under his gruff exterior, and an uncompromising respect for honesty. ("Being honest is just like being pregnant, there's no such thing as being part way.")

By sharing our interests, we've enriched each other's lives and by going our own way we've become more interesting people to live with and retained our sanity. If there's a message here, it's just hang in there! We did and we're glad. In fact, we're going for another 35.

Sexy Bankers —
Pardon Me While I Chortle

November 1982

I couldn't believe my eyes. The headline on the Ann Landers column was "Are Bankers Sexier?" The poor demented lady who wrote the letter "in all sincerity" said, necessarily, "This is not a gag."

The letter came from, of all places, Nebraska.

For those of you who don't know, my dad was a banker, my brother is a banker, my nephews are bankers, my cousin is a banker, some of our very best friends are bankers.

There's hardly a thing I don't know about bankers. There's hardly a thing I haven't called them.

But sexy?

Pardon me while I chortle.

But the lady asks to be taken seriously, and I shall do that. Let's look into this matter in a little more detail.

She asks several questions. Are bankers sexier (her description, not mine) because they are rich, because money is an aphrodisiac, because they are classy and influential? What makes them so desirable?

And Ann Landers replies, "Maybe it's the way they dress — or their suave manner. Then again it could be the thought of all that money in the vaults." Ann says — "Whatever, it is a turn on."

If this was a surprise to me, a self-proclaimed expert on bankers, you can't imagine what a surprise it was to the bankers I know. Or to the friends of the bankers I know.

We all looked at our local bankers in a new light. Unfortunately, the new light didn't help. In fact, the less light the better.

Oh — they may look classy at work, but follow them home and see them in their grubbies, and that aura of power will disappear. It's funny what happens to the bodies when the three piece suits come off. They tend to droop.

And about all that money? Raised in a family of bankers, I can honestly say "What money?" If you think bankers are close with their customers — well — I can only sigh at the memories of being in a banker's family — a banker who had survived the depression.

Probably in preparation for the next depression, bankers are rather close with their money. Like tight. If you think of money as an aphrodisiac (which means something that arouses you sexually, if I did have to look it up myself) I can tell you, you'd better get turned on by the clinking of coins. The big stuff stays in the vault. Unless said banker has an important hobby. Most bankers rationalize that a new gun takes priority over the kitchen stove, for instance. That's not too sexy.

I'm only kidding, of course. Our bankers are as suave and sophisticated as any of us can stand. And they are also desirable, at least so their wives tell me.

I did my own private little poll, though, to see if the general public regarded them as sexy. The answers:

"This is a joke, right?"

"You've got to be kidding!"

"Certainly not when 'your note or notes are due!'"

"I know, you're doing a funny article."

Somehow this put things back in perspective.

State of Burney Household, Thanksgiving 1982

December 1982

One huge turkey, a couple of mounds of dressing and mashed potatoes, three pumpkin pies and two cakes past Thanksgiving, and we waddle merrily into the Christmas season.

No matter where I look, it's food, food, food!

If our Thanksgiving celebration was any indication as the start of the Christmas season, the season's bound to be a good one. Two-thirds of our family sat around our table, with the day being rounded out by phone calls from the rest. Rob called from California and Bill from Colorado.

In a strange kind of role reversal, Rob told us about California's tornadoes, and we told him about our earthquake.

Rob rubs shoulders with the stars out there on his way to being one. Fame and fortune are always just around the corner when we visit, and I'd be the last one to say they weren't. He keeps his body together dispatching cabs at odd hours while his soul pursues the acting career in prime time. I think that would make him a natural for "Taxi" but then, I'm always looking at TV shows and saying "Rob could play that part!" Some director is sure to figure it out sooner or later.

Bill reported on his move to Golden, Colorado, from whence he will manage a new Mexican restaurant in Denver. The economy in Idaho Springs, his former abode, hit the skids with the closing of the mines, so that the unemployment rate is around 37 percent.

The ham runs deep in this family, as one of Bill's experiences this fall was starring in a local melodrama.

Even John, in pursuit of his Doctorate of History, took time off to emote in a play or two.

And, of course, Juli is teaching in the theater department at Wayne State.

Kip blames it all on me, of course. Even though I've traced the Burney's lineage back to England and Scotland where they were dancing masters and actors.

He's not the only one who associates me with being a ham. On a recent speaking foray into Southern Nebraska, a kindly gentleman informed me that Hartington was becoming famous (infamous?) because of the notoriety of Jim Neu and his Neu Cheese commercials and my columns, TV segments and speeches. And I thanked him. A little too soon. Because he went on to explain, "A bunch of us were talking about how appropriate that was."

"Appropriate?" I asked.

"Well, he said with a grin, "you just think about it. **What could be more appropriate for a town. Joan Burney and Jim Neu. Ham and cheese!"**

Well, I don't know how Hartington feels about that, but I do know that there are a lot more hams here than just me. We have the hams everybody knows, and then we have the closet hams. And whenever we're hamming it up, sure enough, we usually have some of Jim Neu's cheese around to eat.

I start out writing about turkey, and end up writing about ham.

Just like I told you. This season we can't seem to get away from it. Food, food, food.

And if a person has to be called something, I guess it's preferable to be called a ham...than a turkey.

Rob's On TV

January 1983

Thanks to our readers for the lovely Christmas greetings. Especially to the dear soul who wrote, "Did you ever see your son on television?"

Because I did, and I'm dying to tell you about it. I will reconstruct the scene. We're at my brother Vince's house. He is standing by the controls of his videotape machine with an engineer's hat on that lights up in red and green Christmas lights. He's quite a sight.

And he has a long-suffering look on his face. Vince is a banker and they quite often have long-suffering looks on their faces, but this one has a different cause than money, or lack of it.

I am saying, "Let's look at it one more time," and he is backing up his videotape player for the 14th time to look at the 30-second segment of the NBC Christmas special in which Rob wandered in front of the camera.

And sure enough, there he is again. Robert. Big as life. He and this girl pass in front of two of NBC's stars who are supposedly singing at this big party.

No doubt about it. We've stopped the machine a multitude of times and admired the wonderful way he walked, the casual way he glances into the camera, the crispness of his mustache, etc.

"That's his new jacket," I say proudly as it blurs past us on the TV.

"It's very lovely," says my poor beleaguered relatives, stifling their yawns.

Vince has the whole program memorized, of course. He's had to play it for the various relatives who've passed through his house at different times. He must be ruing the day he ever invested in that videotape machine.

When Rob called on the Sunday following Christmas, having tried for two days to get through, I told him how good he looked and how much we'd enjoyed seeing him during the holiday season.

He said, "But Mom, I was only on for 30 seconds or so."

And I said, "You'd be surprised how long a mother can draw out 30 seconds."

Besides, we found his back several times, and his profile, etc. And we played them back and forth too.

So yes, I saw my son on TV. Boy did I see him. It was great fun.

I don't know about Vincent. As we left his house, after our long session of repeating the tape, he handed it to me. "Why don't you take this tape home with you?" he said, with some degree of enthusiasm.

"But I don't have a machine," I commented.

I thought I heard him mutter, "You're lucky," under his breath, but I'm not sure.

If you have a machine and want to see Rob, just give me a call. I'll be glad to drop in with my tape.

Shakespeare's 'Zest of Raunchiness' Provide Burney's Unusual Togetherness

February 1983

I came in from choir practice Monday night to find Kip ensconced in his favorite recliner peering at our TV set with what I suppose he assumed was a scholarly expression.

"I am getting culture," he announced.

"Sure you are," I replied with a degree of skepticism. Now, Kip is no dummy. He didn't graduate from anyplace that he wasn't top in his class, and he graduated from quite a few places. But "getting culture" has not always been the first thing on his agenda.

"Getting to a sale," yes, or "getting a nap," or "getting to a fertilizer meeting." (A group of businessmen in Hartington meet regularly on Thursdays and Saturdays to golf or bowl, depending upon the season. Kip has always said he's going to a "fertilizer meeting." Once, he actually did.)

And besides, this is the man who refuses to go to ballets with me because he doesn't care for the male ballerinas. **He says, disdainfully, "I could jump that high, too, if my pants were that tight."**

This is the man who went sound asleep in the middle of the award winning "Chariots of Fire," muttering, "Why don't they speak English?"

This is the man who chooses to watch sports, any sports — from the Super Bowl to girls' basketball — over any program, especially Masterpiece Theater.

And he tells me he's getting culture? I should live so long.

But he was. With just a trace of snobbishness he said, "I'm

92

watching 'The Merry Wives of Windsor.' It's by Shakespeare you know."

I knew. But I really only learned to love Shakespeare myself after I returned to college to get my belated degree. I was not crazy about the bard in high school and still bear a certain antipathy toward the "quality of mercy" speech which we were forced to learn.

Shakespeare has marvelous quotations for a writer to use, just about anything on which you need a quote. And when competent actors speak his words "trippingly on the tongue," it is an uncommonly pleasant experience.

Thus, I sat down with Kip and thoroughly enjoyed the rest of the evening, reveling in this unexpected togetherness. **Usually we'd be together apart,** with me reading and him watching sports, or in different sections of the house watching different programs. We're very comfortable with this. We've adjusted. But this was nice.

It was an excellent presentation. Even the director agreed with Kip that the language was sometimes "curious," saying in an interview "when you read the play, it almost seems as if it was written in a foreign tongue. Once the actors are on stage, there is a zest and raunchiness to the language that makes it sound extremely funny."

Also, Ben Kingsley, the actor presently being acclaimed for his role in "Ghandi," played one of the leads.

Whether it was the excellent acting or the "zest and raunchiness," Kip sat through the whole thing and seemed to enjoy it.

Visions of togetherness at future plays, operas and perhaps even ballets begin to dance in my head. Soon to be shattered.

"Well," he said as 'The Merry Wives,' concluded, "that's my culture for this year!"

It was nice while it lasted.

Antique Collection Finances Face Lift

February 1983

Collections can get to be an obsession. If you are a collector, you know what I mean. If you're not, you probably know someone who is, so you still know what I mean.

It's nice when you have a friend who collects something, because you always know what to buy them. It's even better when they collect things like match covers or beer cans, because your gift can cost very little, like nothing, and still be unusual enough to be appreciated.

I have a sister-in-law who collects little squat things. She doesn't care what they are — vases, pitchers, figurines, tea-kettles or whatever — **she just likes them short and chubby. I catch her eyeing me with interest, and have the feeling I might end up bronzed on her mantle.**

Then there's my friend, Marie, who collects butterflies. Butterflies flit all over her house in almost every form a butterfly can take, and they travel out of her house perched on her clothing and in her hair. I guess we can be glad it's the butterfly collection she chooses to carry around on her body, because she also collects bells and tigers. That could get noisy and cumbersome.

The beer can collection is really quite attractive. It lines the walls of a recreation room in a colorful display. I didn't know there were so many different kinds of beer. The cans are all empty, of course, and come from every country imaginable. If they could only talk, I bet they could tell us some interesting stories.

The matchbook collection makes an interesting and colorful showing too, displayed in huge brandy snifters.

The nice thing about the beer can collection and the matchbook collection is that they catalog themselves.

My beloved aunt and uncle collected antiques, mostly salts, blue plates and silverware. They spent their whole retired lives carefully cataloging them, displaying them, and lecturing on them to anyone who came within earshot. They had a wonderful time gathering these things, carefully shopping for each item. They were jubilant with the finding of some rare, long-desired item.

I learned more about antiques than I ever wanted to know. I cherish the knowledge now, along with a lovely pair of blue salts and a coin silver tablespoon they gave me. They'd be pleased.

My mother, on the other hand, was not so much a collector as an accumulator. She was an enormously intelligent and talented woman with a joie de vivre that wouldn't quit, sort of a combination Eleanor Roosevelt and Auntie Mame. But she was totally dominated by my Irish father, who was frightfully tight. When he died, she traveled the world joyfully gathering quantities of lovely things to stuff onto her shelves. And when she died, we had a great multitude of items to appraise and parcel out to her five daughters, ranging from salts to goblets to silver services.

Mother was never attached to any of these "things," she just bought them because, by golly, she could. And no one would get a bigger kick out of what my sister did with her share than my mom. My sister put an ad in the paper saying **"Must sell mother's antiques to fix up antique mother,"** and she sold them, and had a face lift.

Which goes to show you, one shouldn't get too attached to "things." Things break, wear out, or get sold to finance somebody's face lift.

Icebox Mother Deals With Refrigerator Son

March 1983

Surely you remember icehouses?

There are times in our lives when our advancing age becomes all too readily apparent.

Like the other day when I was driving by the beautiful Bow Creek on the south side of Hartington and I said to my son, "This is where the icehouse once stood."

And he looked at me a little strangely and said, "Icehouse?"

And I knew he was thinking igloo.

It dawned on me I was dealing with a refrigerator generation.

So I explained to my son that icehouses were not made of ice, they were for storing ice. For iceboxes.

Another strange look.

Actually, I hasten to assure you, the only place I remember an icebox was at Hidden Paradise in Long Pine where we had a rustic summer cottage which we frequented when I was a kid. I'm talking rustic! Mom cooked for multitudes on a two burner kerosene stove, the bathroom facilities were outdoors and around the bend, and the iceman stopped regularly to sell us ice for our icebox.

A glow of nostalgia comes over me as I recall our days in Hidden Paradise. I remember it as heavenly. No place is it recorded what my mom thought.

Meanwhile, back at the site of the used-to-be icehouse, I was still trying to explain to my son.

There was this huge building on this very spot. I remember it well because we used to pass it always as kids when we went for "hikes" in the country, giggling and picnicking along this very creek.

And my friend, Ferdie Pietz, tells me that in the early days it was the biggest business around. In the winter time it employed some 50 people, whose job was to chop the ice out of the creek and store it in the icehouse. The creek would freeze, be harvested (so to speak), replenish itself and refreeze.

I don't know what they did during a mild winter. However, to listen to the old-timers, there wasn't such a thing as a mild winter.

In Hartington, where we had a refrigerator, we used to get ice from the icehouse to make homemade ice cream. Big hunks of ice which we would put in a gunny sack to pound into little chunks to use in the outer bucket of the ice cream maker.

We'd be hard put to find a gunny sack in this day and age. "Gunny" is a coarse material made of jute or hemp. I don't know where we got them, I suppose with seed or feed or some such thing. But they were always around when we wanted to pound ice.

Well, that's enough fascinating historical data for one column. I'm beginning to feel like an old settler.

I think I'll wrap myself in my shawl, prop myself up in my rocking chair and smoke my corncob pipe.

Just don't ask me, "What's an icehouse?" okay?

Home Town Centennial Great Experience

June 1983

"The tumult and the shouting dies;
The captains and the kings depart...
Lord God of Hosts be with us yet,
Lest we forget, lest we forget."—Kipling's Recessional

...As quoted by Gee O'Hara in a rich Irish voice at the V.F.W. on the occasion of the reunion of the multitudes of friendly folks from afar and local folks, equally as friendly, during the Hartington Centennial.

Another quote, as carefully preserved on a napkin as the one above: **"I'd rather be a shooting star for five seconds, than a lamp post for eternity."**

And this week, as the shouting and the tumult does indeed die, it seems we will never forget. We have been for this brief moment of our history, a shooting star. **If we perhaps return now to being a lamp post, we return with a sense of history.** A sense of reaching a point which we'd never reached before and to which we will never be able to return.

One's hometown celebrates its 100th birthday only once and those of us who live here had been building up to these moments for many months, some with wild enthusiasm, some with a sense of resignation, and some with great reluctance.

But for all of us, I truly believe, whatever the quality or the quantity of our participation, including the friendly folks from afar (many of whom read this column), some moments have been almost magical. Meetings with old friends, moments with our families, sights and scenes and people and memories to be stored and savored in future years, when even the problems will become funny anecdotes to share around some distant hearth.

For me it was a joy just to walk down the street. You were bound to run into people you once knew, faces which would first bring a hazy recognition, and then a full-blown one, followed by the most satisfactory kind of hugging.

In my mind's eye, and in my heart of hearts, I knew this whole celebration was being hovered over by those who are no longer with us.

How appropriate that Memorial Day was celebrated in the midst of our centennial.

But enough of that, the celebration was a tremendous joy. While it was quite a balancing act for many of us to keep track of family and friends, old and new, it was also a great pleasure.

We have carved ourselves, by the sweat of our brows, a piece of history: "Lest we forget, lest we forget."

'Roots and Wings' Best Gifts

1983

I got a poignant letter from a reader this past week discussing problems with grown kids — and that reader's own problems dealing with the guilt that sometimes falls heavy on the parents of kids who've had trouble.

I am familiar with that kind of guilt. It's the kind that all of us have to deal with occasionally. "If I'd just taken more time," or "If I'd just realized how short a time they'd be with me." It serves no purpose.

Funny thing, when kids are little you think that time's going on forever. I can remember feeling that I would never get to the place where I wouldn't have to deal with diapers.

And then I can remember when I wondered if I'd ever get to the place when I didn't have to worry about teenagers.

Almost before you have time to look around, those years are past. That beautiful song "Sunrise, Sunset" from Fiddler on the Roof, says it best. "I don't remember getting older, when did they?"

A very wise lady said to me when my kids were little, "Enjoy them now, because believe me, the problem you have with these little children are little problems. When you get older, the big problems come."

And the older they get, the bigger they get, and the less we can do about them.

But that's the way it should be. Somewhere in the back of my mind a quote springs up, something like"The best thing we can give our children are roots and wings."

There comes a time when you have to let them try their own wings.

But it is hard to let them go. And sometimes they don't want to go. The tough job, for us who are parents, perhaps our very toughest job, is letting them fly — and perhaps even shoving them out of the nest. **Maturity is assuming the responsibility for our own actions, and allowing our children the right and duty to assume the responsibility for theirs.**

But that is tough. And the whole question sent me to my files where I remembered a letter from a lovely lady which came to me years ago. She discussed a tough period in her life dealing with the problems of a grown son. And she shared with me a prayer given to her by her Baptist godmother, which she said made a new person out of her. I can see it's time to repeat that prayer for all of us.

Father:

I've been crying over my child's "spilt milk," which is useless.

He's reached the age where the decisions are his own.

His is the milk, and his is the mess...and his is the responsibility to clean it up.

My motherly blubbering will only serve to confuse the issue.

He is always my son, Lord...but his decisions are no longer my responsibility. It is essential...for his sake...that I let him alone. I believe in him, in his ability to stand alone. Why do I deny that belief with my motherly blubbering?

Besides, I have promises of my own to keep, and things to do before I sleep.

Watch over my son, Lord.

Amen

"Getting In The Clear" — An Impossible Dream For A Cattle Feeder's Wife

June 1983

My dad was a banker who survived the depression. All of his life he was prepared for the next one and tried to convince his customers to do the same.

On the wall of the bank he had painted "Read the Handwriting on the Wall." And then, just in case you didn't see the "handwriting" on the wall as clearly as he did, he added "This is the Year to Get in the Clear."

It was quite a cultural shock, therefore, for me to marry a cattle feeder. Cattle feeders also have axioms by which they live. Kip's grandfather, a remarkable man who retired at the age of 40, instilled in his children, and his children's children, the firm belief that **"You can't make money with your own money."**

His reasoning, as I understand it, was that one is too conservative with one's own money. He had several choice examples of men who "got in the clear" and gradually went broke because they were protecting their own money.

You can readily see that those two diametrically opposite philosophies might make a few problems for two people who happened to be married to one another.

While Kip goes through life merrily working with borrowed capital, I am always peering into the future with the thought that we must "get in the clear."

Considering the state of the farming economy, the state of the cattle feeding business and high interest rates, that future goal seems remote indeed.

However, I have two solutions which seem feasible. **One may be a little drastic. We have to die.** Our insurance will take care of it. I'm saving that as a last resort.

The other solution is more to my liking. I must win one of those sweepstakes which are constantly flooding into the house.

Our future seemed a bit brighter just yesterday, when we got three Publisher's Clearing House envelopes.

It is not an easy task for me to enter all of these contests. In the first place, you have to scrounge through a multitude of enclosures to find the little paste-on things to qualify for winning free prizes or double prizes or whatever. As you do it, you are accosted by all this high-powered advertising. You just might succumb and order something.

Then you have to make choices. This can take hours. Do you want two fabulous new homes? Or $250,000 cash? Or $40,000 a year for life?

And you have to hurry. Because if you get your entry in before such and such a date, your prize will double. Of course it will!

I do all these things and Kip laughs at me. He claims I have more money tied up in postage stamps than the interest on our loan.

And it is entirely possible that winning that money would not solve a thing. You've all heard about the cattle feeder who won $1 million and allowed as he would just "keep feeding cattle until it was all gone!"

There can be no doubt that at this house, any sum of money coming in would simply be viewed as more collateral — additional borrowing power.

But one has to have one's dreams, hazy though they may be, and mine is to "get in the clear."

Grandpa Burney Says Enjoy Today

October 1983

We've had the great privilege this past ten days of having Dwight W. Burney Sr. as our guest. Some people may remember him as a former Governor and Lt. Governor of Nebraska. We know him as Dad or Grandpa.

Dad will be 92 on his next birthday, and he says, "I don't have an ache or a pain, isn't that wonderful!" He goes about life with a twinkle in his eye and an appreciation for all that goes on about him, giving piquant and good-humored advice to child and grandchild alike.

He had an opportunity this week, because grandchildren were checking in from all over, and he was some concerned about John's having over 100 students in his classes at U.N.L., because "he can't get to know his students" and Juli's announcement that she wasn't going to get married until she met somebody "as nice as Grandpa." He says, with a mock-serious face and that ever-present twinkle, "She'll have a little trouble finding somebody that nice!"

He has a philosophy about life that we'd all do well to emulate. It pops up all the time. Like when I showed him this letter from a distant relative agonizing over the problem of figuring out the heritage of the Burney family. He read it carefully, and then — looking at me with a quizzical expression — said, **"I don't really care about this. Who wants to be worrying themselves over a bunch of folks who are already dead. I'm more concerned about living."**

Then he added, "I don't worry about yesterday and I don't concern myself much with tomorrow. I just enjoy today!"

And enjoy today we did. We kept up a busy social schedule which included two visits to the Senior Citizens' Center for lunch. I don't know how it is in everybody's town, but in our town we feel that the greatest thing we've got going is our senior citizens, and the greatest thing they've got going is the Center. Not only are the meals delicious and nutritious, it is a good opportunity to socialize. Especially for Dad Burney this past week as he said, "Here's a place where there might be somebody old enough for me to know." And he met several old friends.

Dad doesn't do much reminiscing, considering his philosophy and all, but I truly love to hear about his past experiences, so sometimes he breaks down and shares memories with me.

In response to questions he said his dad didn't talk much, but had quite a sense of humor, and **"I've got reason to believe he thought I was just all right."** And his mother was not the prettiest woman, but "warm and loving." Pretty fine tributes.

He remembers that he was the first of the Burney boys to get to go to high school. And he rode a horse every day, six miles in and six miles out. "The neighbors used to say they could set their watches by me," he said.

He remarked about the different conveyances he'd ridden in his lifetime, "from a horse and wagon to a jet airplane."

He was anxious to get home. He and three friends play pool every day at the Polk Senior Citizen Center, and Dad and an "older man" usually "win quite a bit."

Dad likes to keep all his business tidied up on this old earth because he says, practically speaking, "When you're as old as I am, anything can happen." But we're not too worried. He and Grayce just got a new microwave by investing in some kind of money market certificate which won't mature for seven years. And you can be sure, Dad plans to stick around until it does.

"Juli Sings Blue Suit Blues"

October 1984

I'm one of those people who believe what I read, until I read something that contradicts it, and I tend to act on my beliefs.

I tell you this only to explain why my daughter Juli has three blue suits.

All the books I'd read about women dressing for success extolled the values of the skirted suit, particularly the sincere, blue suit.

To further imprint this image on my mind, I attended a business women's convention and as I sat with the officers at the head table, successful businesswomen one and all, I realized nine out of ten were wearing blue suits. I felt as if I were back in boarding school.

The books stressed that when you dress you are making a statement, and that people judge you by first impressions. In fact, no matter how wrong a first impression might be, people tend to never quite get over it.

So it behooves a person to follow this advice, unless that person is your daughter, an extrovert and an individualist, who's going to dress as she darn pleases. **"Theater people," Juli says, "do not conform."**

Not to be denied, I subtly gave Juli a blue suit. In fact, I didn't realize it until she pointed it out to me, but I may have overdone it. She opened a birthday present, which I'd cleverly found on sale, and said, "What a surprise, Mom, a blue suit." Her voice dripped with insincerity.

"You don't like it?" I asked, prepared to have my feelings hurt.

"Well," she said, shaking her head in bemused disbelief, "it's the third one you've given me."

Somehow, in my devious mother's mind, I'd lost track.

Lately, however, I'm having a change of heart about the sincere blue suit syndrome. I notice, for instance that Geraldine Ferraro never wears a blue suit. President Reagan does, Mondale does. Bush does. But not Ferraro. **Does this mean Juli might be a vice presidential candidate someday? Or that Ferraro is a theater person?**

Possibly.

On the other hand, it could mean that one does not have to wear a blue suit to achieve success.

What a mind-expanding thought. For Juli, it turned out to be a wardrobe expanding thought.

That is because while wandering through a store, I ran across my favorite kind of sale, a "20% off of 50% off" sale. And there, on the rack waiting for me was a bright green suit in Juli's size. I'm talking green.

Could I pass this up? Is the Pope Catholic?

Still, Juli is suspicious of anything I do along this line. She feels I'm trying to influence her. Silly girl.

So I decided it was a "new job" present, and showed up on her Lincoln doorstep. Her face showed shock as she opened the box. And I heard her telling her brother on the phone, "Guess what, John, things are getting worse. Mom's gotten into 'sincere' green."

Alleluia! After 40 Years,
Kip Quits Smoking

1984

I say this with absolute conviction. No one will ever dispute these words. If Kip can do it, anyone can.

I'm talking about quitting smoking.

Kip started smoking when he was 18 years old. He'd volunteered for the Air Force in World War II, and by the time he was 19, he was flying a B-17 with his own crew across the Atlantic Ocean to participate in war.

The Air Force gave the men smoking breaks and even provided the cigarettes. Little did they know that this seeming kindness might be more harmful to some of their young men than the war was going to be.

Kip's plane was shot up on his 17th mission and he came home with a permanently impaired right arm and an addiction to nicotine.

Only in that day and age, nobody knew how serious that addiction might be. Kip is now 60, and he has smoked for 42 years.

One does not quit overnight. In fact, as many times as Kip has tried to quit and failed, I'd begun to think he would not quit at all.

Not that he hasn't tried. Once he substituted chocolate covered peanuts for cigarettes and gained 40 pounds. That and his horrible disposition made me think he might live longer without cigarettes, but nobody was going to be too thrilled about it.

The doctor told him he was headed for a heart attack. So, he decided to calm himself down, he'd just smoke one cigarette a night. Well, as many of you know from experience, he was soon back smoking, only more cigarettes than ever.

That's what scared me. Every time he'd quit — and sometimes he'd try to quit by smoking later every day, and sometimes by trying cigars, or pipes — when he started again, he'd smoke more.

What got him to quit was a fluke. A blessed fluke.

He did not take kindly to turning 60. It just seemed to bug him. Without me ever saying a word, in fact, he decided to have a physical checkup. An unheard of event.

And the nurse told him that his lungs were much worse than they had been five years ago. One of the things that he'd always prided himself in was that, in spite of his smoking, his lungs remained the same.

That did it. He took Doc's advice and with proper preparation, he started chewing Nicorette gum, which you can only get by prescription. And he quit and hasn't smoked for three months. Not one cigarette. I'm really proud of him.

The reason I stress "with proper preparation" is that one of the articles we read on this method of quitting smoking said for people just to get the gum and think they will quit is like people who have diabetes just getting a bunch of insulin and thinking they have their problem licked.

You need to know how to make it work. It has to do with just chewing it a little, and releasing enough nicotine to get you over the jitters. Then stashing it like a chaw of tobacco and doing the same thing a little later.

Kip says a stick of gum lasts him about a half an hour.

The reason I'm especially proud of him was because the nurse called him two weeks after he'd quit smoking and told him she'd read the wrong chart on the breath test, and his lungs were still the same. (The blessed fluke.)

I was petrified that he'd start again. But the scare remained with him, even though it was a false alarm, and he's persisted.

In fact, he is in the process of transforming into one of those dedicated reformed smokers, and is yelling at all his buddies when they light up.

But he ought to know — nagging won't work. The smoker has to make up his own mind. Maybe it will take 42 years. But something will make them decide and that will be it.

And be prepared smokers, because that positive click in your subconscious, the one that will allow you to quit, can be brought on, I am told, by something so simple as reading a column.

Remember — if Kip can do it, anyone can.

Shoes On Your Feet And Food In Your Tummy

1985

"What are you complaining about?" said the craggy old cattle feeder, "You've got shoes on your feet and food in your tummy. A lot of people don't have that!"

The discussion started about the buying of Christmas presents, and how outrageous some of the costs are. It degenerated into a griping session with nobody finding anything much good to say about anything.

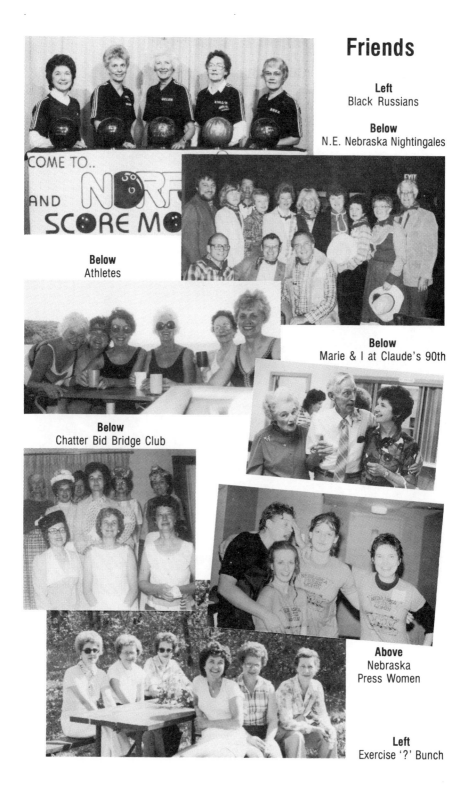

Friends

Left
Black Russians

Below
N.E. Nebraska Nightingales

Below
Athletes

Below
Marie & I at Claude's 90th

Below
Chatter Bid Bridge Club

Above
Nebraska
Press Women

Left
Exercise '?' Bunch

The Family

L to R
Lou Ann,
Chuck, Bill,
Tom, Kip, me,
John, Rob, &
Juli.

Left
Kate &
"Old Fraud"

Above
Almost perfect grandchild,
Kate.

Above
Governor Grandpa
& the Burney clan.

Right
The Burney kids
informally.

The Management Team

Below
Communicating

Above
At Work

Above
At Play

Below
Hartington
Centennial
1983

Below
40th
Anniversary

Below — Big Brother Vince

Below — In-laws Virginia, Pat & Kay

Left
Burney Men
Doc, Wid, Dad,
Don & Kip

Above — Governor Dwight & Grace

Above
Sister Connie
"The Jock"

Right — Rossiters
standing: Connie, Vince,
Lawrence & June
seated: Mary, Dad,
Mom & Ann
center: me.

But the above comment turned it completely around. We began to count our blessings, shoes and food being the first and probably the most fundamental.

Then we went on to wonder what it would be like to live in Poland now, with all the red giants breathing down our necks. Or in Afghanistan. Or Iran. Or Italy where the terrible earthquake took place. Or El Salvador.

All of our previous complaints began to look pretty foolish.

And the conversation came back to the subject that had set it off in the first place. Christmas presents.

"You know, the best present we could give would probably cost us nothing," said the wise one.

"What's that?" we asked dubiously.

"Ourselves."

"Think of what would happen if instead of a box with another shirt of pair of pajamas or tie, we gave to our loved ones a present of time. For instance, we could write a Christmas note saying, "I will be over and shovel your walks, or scrub your floor or something like that."

The possibilities are endless. What better present than a visit to a lonesome person. What better gift than the use of a skill that one person has for a person who does not have that skill.

In fact — we should do this all the time, but — especially at Christmas time. It would behoove us to give of ourselves to all of mankind — or at least that part of mankind we come in contact with. What a delight if we shook a little of the best of ourselves loose for the tired sales clerk, or the over-burdened shopper, or our weary friends and co-workers.

A smile here and a kind word there can work wonders. Try it and watch it multiply a thousandfold. And if it doesn't multiply — it'll make you feel better anyway.

All of which sends me to my files in search of an old poem by that ever-popular and not too talented anonymous, who nonetheless, says what needs to be said.

If you hear a kind word spoken, of some worthy soul you know,
It may fill his heart with sunshine if you only tell him so.
If a deed, however, humble helps you on your way to go,
Seek the one whose hand has helped you, seek him out and tell him so!

If your heart is touched and tender toward a sinner, lost and low,
It might help him to do better if you'd only tell him so.
Oh my sisters, oh my brothers as over life's rough path you go,
If God's love has saved and kept you, do not fail to tell men so!
**And if you get to feeling crabby and your wallet's feeling flat,
remember you've got shoes on your feet and food in your tummy.
And a lot of people don't have that!**

Infant Granddaughter Wins
Over Old Fraud

March 1985

From the first moment we knew that our granddaughter, Kate Johanna, was on the way, I was excited. Kip, the tough old bird, said I was "ridiculously" excited. Becoming a grandfather didn't thrill him. He took a "bah, humbug" attitude. "Just another kid," he said.

He didn't even get excited when John called to announce the birth. Of course, it was in the middle of the night, and he hasn't gotten excited in the middle of the night for a long time. After I hung up the phone, he sat on the side of the bed muttering to himself. When I said, with some enthusiasm, "Goodnight Grandpa!" he said, "Oh my God!" and fell flat. I think it was a prayer. Later, when people would ask him if he had a picture of his granddaughter, he'd say, **"Did you ever see a kid that carried pictures of her grandparents?!"**

All that changed this past weekend when Kate brought her folks up to get herself baptized. She took her grandpa in hand.

Babies, you see, don't really know anything. They don't know who they are or why they're here. They don't know the things waving about in front of them are their hands. They're just precious little blobs of humanity trying to figure things out.

To do that they stare at people's faces. They begin to recognize their friends, and they recognize voices. Some say they even recognize them in the womb.

Anyway, they look at you and make "ooh" faces and sense your love and respond to it, and that's what makes them grow up to be trusting human beings. They soon figure out grandparents are pushovers.

So it was that the first time Kate Johanna looked at her grandpa, she figured him out for the tough old fraud he was, and when she grabbed onto his finger and oohed at him he was a gone goose. "She is a cute little thing," he said, as if he were surprised.

He soon learned that if he propped her on his belly (he calls it a "slipped chest" and plans to get rid of it this spring), she'd burp beautifully. He thought this was a talent. It's true, not everyone can do it.

He went straight from "bah, humbug," to baby expert, insisting that he knew what Kate wanted better than her mother or her grandmother. For instance, she didn't want to lie in her basket while we ate, he said, she wanted to lie in the middle of the table so she could see us. That's exactly where he put her.

If she cried and we picked her up, he said, "That baby is never going to learn how to cry. She will never develop her lungs. You pick her up everytime she peeps."

But if she cried and we didn't, it was "Kate wants something! Better see what she wants." If she still didn't settle down, he'd say, "What are you doing to her anyway? I guess she wants her grandpa!"

Before the weekend was over, Grandpa Kip and Kate had become a team. Kate saw to that.

What A Way To Go, Doc!

February 1986

If there's somebody you love in this world, and you've put off seeing them because you think there's always going to be time, I encourage you with all my heart and soul to pick up your phone and make plans. Now!

Several years ago, in response to some intuitive force (I now think), the four boys in Kip's family decided to make time for each other. Up until then we'd been involved in raising families, and in careers, and it dawned on all of us that as much as we loved each other we weren't getting together much as a family.

Thus was born the "Burney Open," a high-spirited reunion in which the "boys" golfed and told stories, and the wives did whatever it is wives always do. It was a noisy affair because the Burney men are all chiefs, no Indians, and so everybody tried to run everybody else.

We didn't have any sense that we were running out of time when we started all this, because Burney men live forever. Look at Grandpa, who was then in his late eighties, and had two older brothers still going strong.

But we were. Four years ago we lost Wid. And the three brothers carried on, something like our cat with her lame leg. Not exactly right, but still managing. Then Don lost his wife, Pat. And now, this past week, we've lost our "Doc." Dwight W. Burney, junior, whom we also called "Junior," which seemed a bit ludicrous in view of his increasing importance as an orthopedic surgeon.

Doc did everything at full throttle, all engines open, full speed ahead. **He lived life with an infectious and irreverant enthusiasm.** He told old jokes so often we had them numbered.

He loved music. As a young man, he played trumpet with a musical group known as the "Tootin' Tantalizers" and he never quit playing it. He played at home along with big band records. He'd sit in church long after others left listening to the organ play its final hymn. He told his wife, Kay, "When I go, I want the trumpet music to blast so loud I can hear it through the box."

On his first trip to the hospital, a week before he died, his son, Dr. Dwight Burney III called to check up on him. It was the day the shuttle exploded, and young Doc was talking about how awful that was. **And the older Doc agreed it was awful, but added, "What a way to go."**

Typically, Doc insisted on going to hear a speaker he respected that last week, and went through his patients' charts. He joked with loved ones who worriedly checked in and protected everybody from his knowledge of what was happening. He just kept moving until what he knew was coming caught up with him. He died as he lived, throttle wide open, full speed ahead.

He died at Clarkson Hospital. "This is home to him, you know," Kay said. Every person there had their own story of Doc, his kindnesses, his warmth, his irreverant humor. He was surrounded with such an outpouring of love you could almost touch it. It enveloped all of us who kept his last vigil with him. Doc's family knew that he would want those who loved him to celebrate this life, not mourn his death, and that's just the way they planned his memorial. Pastor David Ruhe said, **"What a gift this man has been to us all!"** The closing Organ Voluntary, a "Trumpet Tune" by Henry Purcell, nearly took the roof off of the great church.

It reminded me of something comforting I read once, which compared dying to a ship sailing off into the sea. We stand on our side and watch as the ship spreads her sails and fades on the horizon, and we say, "There she goes!" But it is gone only to us. Because on the other side it is awaited with great joy, and a glad welcoming shout goes up when it appears on that horizon and the folks who've made the trip before cry joyfully, "Here she comes!"

In my mind's eye, Doc's ship soared into Heaven with that final trumpet blast, with joyous shouts of "Here he comes!"

What a way to go Doc. What a way to go.

Family of Sugar-Coated Hams

April 1986

Kip has always blamed me because our family is nine-tenths sugar-coated ham. But I have ample evidence, straight from Mesa, Arizona and his 93-year-old dad that our side of the family doesn't have to take all of the blame.

I admit, however, that the family tends to be — well — theatrical. Rob's just finished a one man show in San Francisco put on by Grandiose Productions, of which he is the presiding officer. He dispatches cabs and does a number of other things to put bread on his table, but he is an actor first and foremost and we've seen him occasionally on national television as an extra in such things as General Hospital.

While Bill's main business is at Bill Burney's Real Estate office Idaho Springs, Colorado (he thought up the clever name himself), he spends many weekends participating in melodramas and plays with the Maxwell House Players at the Indian Springs Resort in Idaho Springs, Colorado. And he is presently involved in a second made-for-TV (Colorado TV) movie wherein he plays the starring role of Coronado.

I asked him who wrote the script, and he said "We all do, it's sort of off the wall."

Then I asked the important question, "Do you get any money for this?"

And he said, **"Money, oh no, nothing like that. But sometimes we get awards.** And we have a great time. It's kind of like an American Monty Python."

John, our #3 son, has a doctorate in History, and teaches at the University of Nebraska. But the theater also runs in his blood. He played the lead in his high school plays, and has done some theatrical work since that time, and I understand his classes are sometimes productions. And Monty Python is his favorite personality. Need I say more.

Then there's Juli, and that girl has nothing but theater in her blood. She graduated with a degree in it, went on for graduate hours, taught it at Wayne State and is now working for the Nebraska Arts Council as an Artist in Residence while attempting to start a dinner theater in Lincoln. It makes us very nervous, but it could work for her (the dinner theater idea), because she's got great business sense, and is knowledgeable in every area of theater from the acting to building the sets to sewing the costumes. I can understand the acting. The business ability she gets from Kip. **But where she got her ability to**

build and sew is a mystery to me. At this very moment she's building an outside stairway in Lincoln for her brother John.

Our youngest sons, Tom and Chuck, have also shown tendencies to ham it up, but they've managed to keep it more or less under control. I suspect it to emerge, however, sooner or later.

The important thing for you to know is they can't blame it all on their mother. I've always suspected it, but the evidence came through for me this spring when we learned that Grandpa Burney was in the hospital because he had a nosebleed that wouldn't quit. He was fine, and made a fabulous recovery, but when we talked to Grayce, she said with a wifelike chuckle, "I know why he had that nosebleed!"

And when we asked why, she said, "Well, we had some professional belly dancers at the court here to entertain the people. Some people though they were indecent, and they just up and left, but your dad and I thought they were very talented and we sat in the front row."

I said, "You mean he got so excited about the belly dancers that his nose bled?" Knowing his sons, it seemed reasonable to me.

"No," Grayce said, "but when they asked for volunteers to come up and dance with the belly dancers, guess who was the only one who volunteered!"

It was 93-year-old Grandpa Burney, of course, who else? Don't you love it?

Grandpa looks kind of cross when we talk about it, and claims the belly dancing had nothing to do with his nosebleed, but then he gets quite a grin on his face and a person gets the notion he might try it again.

Road To Recovery — A Family Path Of Courage And Pride

1986

"Hi! I'm Rob and I'm an alcoholic."

"Hi! I'm Joan, and I'm Rob's mother."

It's been almost three years since I said those words the first time, but I can still feel their impact in my gut. Rob and I were at the Independence Drug and Alcohol Rehabilitation Center in Lincoln. A caring and tough counselor by the name of Carol Ann was officiating over a motley array of recovering alcoholics and the loved ones who'd come to be with them for a week of family therapy. The alcoholics ranged in age from 14 to 70; everyone from a teen-aged wife abuser to a respected judge. The disease of alcoholism plays no favorites. The average age, they told me, was 35. Rob was around 35 then, a veteran with an I.Q. that wouldn't quit, and a graduate degree. He figured he's been an alcoholic for 17 years.

We "families" were a diverse group, a microcosm of society. Before the week was out, we had become one family. We were joined by a single cause and mutual pain. We were there to support somebody we loved very much in beginning the journey to recovery from the ravages of drugs and alcohol addiction. Though we'd gotten there on what we thought was our own private road to hell — we'd actually traveled a similar road. We had all done our share of enabling by covering up and denying there was a problem.

For an alcoholic, denial is the name of the game. To get them to recognize the fact of their alcoholism, the people who live with them often do what we call an "intervention." They tell the alcoholic — in as loving a way as possible — what their alcoholism is doing to them, and to the people who love them. Betty Ford's family did this for her. So did Elizabeth Taylor's.

It is probably one of the most painful experiences in a person's life, both for the alcoholic and the alcoholic's family. And it is also the most heroic. It takes more guts than anybody even has, I think. You can only do it because you love a person too much to see them kill themselves.

But I want to tell you something. It is worth every heartache, every tear. Because it works. Almost always. It's up to the alcoholic, of course. We can't do it for them. We would if we could. When they recognize what they are doing to themselves and their families and take the twelve steps recommended by A.A., it is darned near miraculous.

So when I said, "I am Joan, Rob's mother," I said it with an enormous sense of pride. By the time I joined Rob for the week of family therapy, he'd made the turn. Considering the agony that goes into the painful introspection and spiritual awakening necessary for an alcoholic to begin recovery, the thing to do when someone has the courage to go into treatment is to cheer him on and sing alleluia.

God knows, it is tough. Going through the week of family therapy was one of the most profoundly emotional experiences in my life, and one of the most rewarding. We are a close family. We have a lot of fun, and do a lot of joking. But sharing at the gut level does not come easy for us. We protect each other from our feelings. Families need to share feelings. They need to know when there's hurting going on.

After we came out the other side of this, Rob told me that he would be pleased if I would write about our experience. He felt it might help other people who were mired in the progressive death that is the disease of alcoholism. Recovering alcoholics are dedicated to helping others. You will never in your lifetime find a more caring, or more effective group than A.A. And that goes also for Al Anon, and Alateen, the organizations for spouses and young people who live with alcoholics.

Nearly three years sober, Rob's now talking about how his life, lived one-day-at-a-time, is filled with the joy of "just living." He is working with young alcoholics and drug addicts at Pasadena Hospital. He loves it. He says, "Mom, I see me in every one of them."

I'm Joan. I'm Rob's mother. Alleluia!

Classmates Of 40 Years Ago
Still Special Friends

1986

"Anybody who would be out on a frigid night like this has to be either crazy or from the class of '46," said the tall farmer from west of town.

"Maybe both!" replied the several people sitting around the table at the Ten Pin Lounge. The class of '46. My class! A bunch of high spirited extroverts at whose graduation the faculty shed tears (of joy).

I've never been one to live in the past, but I thoroughly enjoy touching base with it. It's good for a person. One needs to keep in touch with where one's been to fully appreciate where one is.

Besides, there are no buddies like the ones with whom you went to school. We have the same frame of reference. We knew each other when. And we know underneath the polished adult exterior there once lived a scrawny scared kid, an exuberant clown, or a chubby struggling teenager, all trying to put up a brave front. (At times, I fit in all of those categories.)

We went to school during World War II, in years when President Roosevelt and Monsignor Lordamann reigned. Our boys did the work while their older brothers fought the war. Many of our classmates served in the Korean Conflict. Our class president, a warm and friendly young man named Ray Burbach, never came home. I suppose everybody feels this way, but I remember our class as having a special camaraderie and esprit de corps like no other.

Although we've gone our separate ways, it still gives me a warm

112

feeling to run into a classmate. There's definitely something special there. At least for me.

A reunion is the time to let that special feeling flow. You shed all the accumulated years of ups and downs, of laughter, sweat and tears, and for a brief time you wallow merrily in the days of yore.

You wouldn't want to stay there. Indeed, one of the prime rules for a reunion is that it shouldn't last too long because sometimes all that classmates have in common begins and ends in memories. But that's okay. That's fun, even. For every relationship that stays in the past, there will be those that you reestablish today. Mature relationships with "old" classmates are the most cherished of all.

And reunions aren't for everybody. Some are enthusiastic, like me. For instance, we've gotten letters and phone calls from Pat Hegert who lives in Florida, and Joe Hish who lives in Virginia, eagerly awaiting news of the upcoming bash. "We're coming!!!" they cry. And yet there are a few people who live right here who won't come. High school wasn't that great for them.

So what else is new? **Some high school memories are terrible.** It's a fantasy to think that the high school years were the best years of our lives. People who say that are dealing with a selective memory file. I remember the good times, but I also remember the insecurities, pain and terrible struggles with self-esteem.

That's why a reunion is so great. It enables one to scrutinize the past in the realistic light of today and to lay to rest the miseries.

One should attend a reunion with sense of humor at the ready. The ability to laugh at oneself and with others is a prerequisite. Put the past in perspective with the healing touch of humor.

'Twas a motley array of local members of the class of '46 who gathered last week to plan the July reunion. We laughed a lot. But it was difficult coming to grips with the fact that it had actually been 40 years. 40!!!

We certainly don't look it. At least, those of us gathered at the Ten Pin Lounge didn't. Of course, it was dark in there. And we really didn't have any reason to put on our glasses...

Kate And Muffin

August 1986

It was quite a transition. This past week I went from working in what Dr. Bigelow at Wayne State calls "the higher cognitive domain" to working in whatever domain one works in when one is caring for an 18-month-old grandchild.

We adore that little girl. And Kip and I had a great time with her. But every grandparent who reads this column will understand when I say after four days of "Gamma hold!" "Gamma ouside!" "Gamma pahk!" "Gamma juice!" "Gamma wock!" "Gamma book!" and "Gamma cows!" I was about "gamma-ed" out. If Gamma had any notion of not honoring one of the above imperious requests, a tiny "pweeze" would bring her around.

I came away from the experience with overwhelming admiration for my grandmother friends who take care of as many as three grandchildren at one time. I can't imagine how I raised six kids. **The Lord knew what He was doing when He gave us our kids while we were young.** The spirit is definitely willing, you understand, but the old body whines a lot.

And Kate was a good little girl. I didn't have to move a thing up, which amazed me. She would go up to the bookcase, shake her little finger at it, and say "Daddy. Books, no, no!" But she was busy. When she wasn't herding Gamma, she was herding some little (unbreakable) brass critters from table to windowsill and back again.

She was also occupied by her on-going love-hate relationship with Muffin, our three-legged cat. Muffin never gets far from Kate. The cat is as fascinated with the baby as the baby is with her. But she only allows Kate to pet her for a short time, then she gets testy and bats at her with her paw.

Kate is devastated and also outraged. She's always been under the erroneous assumption that Muffin will someday be her friend, and she will be able to haul her around like her scraggily stuffed kitten. Muffin has too much dignity to put up with that nonsense.

Kate shakes her little finger imperiously at Muffin and says, "Nauny (translate "Naughty"), nauny kitty!" Then she insists that Gamma join her in her outrage at this uncooperative cat. Gamma, being a little dotty, as most gammas are, shakes her big finger at the cat and also says, "nauny, nauny kitty!" We do that until Kate is satisfied that Muffin's properly chastised and then Kate goes huffily about her other important business. So does Muffin, with insufferable assurance, I suspect chalking up another one on Kate.

The cat and the kid were on the way to becoming fast friends before

114

Kate left, because "Gampa" showed Kate how much Muffin appreciated it when Kate would drop food on the floor while eating her own meal. Kate loved that game. So did Muffin. Gamma could have whomped Gampa.

John sent about a dozen books with Kate, but she only let us read two. Over, and over, and over. Bert and Ernie, and George the Curious Monkey. I'm afraid they'll turn up in my next speech.

Kate was with us so her folks could do last minute things in preparation to moving from Lincoln to Dubuque, Iowa (388 miles away) (I can get there in seven hours), where John will teach history at Loris College and Lou Ann will be nursing in critical care (intensive care/emergency, etc.) at St. Joseph's Hospital in the Mercy Health Care complex.

Kip and I hated to have them move that far away. I don't know about Muffin. She just sits in her chair and purrs.

Saying Goodbye To Grandpa Burney

March 1987

When we were in Phoenix a few weeks ago for what was to be our last visit with Kip's dad, our beloved "Grandpa," we had quite a scare. We hadn't even gotten unpacked when we were called to the hospital because Grandpa was being taken there. Kip's brother Don was with us, and it was a terrible time. Kip said, "Do you suppose we've come all this way and we're a day late?" We were shocked because Dad had been quite well.

I prayed with great intensity all the way to the hospital. "Not yet, Lord," I said, over and over. But even while praying, I felt selfish. Because Grandpa had been around for 95 wonderful years, and if the Lord called him home while the quality of his life was still so good, perhaps I should have been praying prayers of thanksgiving.

But I couldn't do that. And that night we were granted a reprieve. It seemed to me to be a miracle. Grandpa's pain went away. He'd just ridden his bicycle too much that day. We took him home from the hospital and talked and laughed and drank coffee and ate cookies till the wee hours.

The times we had together on that visit were touched with a heightened awareness of how we loved that man. We did a lot of hugging.

Grandpa and Grayce were glad to see us, but as usual, had a lot of things going on in their lives. We fit our farewells between a pancake breakfast and Polk reunion. Grandpa was excited about a local

115

pool tournament. In a competition with 40 other men, he'd made it to the play-offs. He was practicing for that.

We'd discussed at length plans for his 95th birthday party on June 14th, which is Kip's birthday. Grandpa was really pleased because EVERYONE was coming to his party. He knew he was much loved. He was a humble man, but had a sure sense of his own self worth. He once said with unassuming candor, "It seems as if nobody doesn't like me."

After we got home, we got a postcard informing us Grandpa had made the finals of the pool tournament, and ended up in second place. It seemed only a technicality of some kind (I don't understand pool) kept him out of first. He was pretty tickled about beating those "younger fellows."

On Sunday, March 8th, Grandpa gave a talk at the annual Nebraska Picnic in Phoenix. He told the gathered Nebraskans that they should live each day to the fullest, and not worry about yesterday or tomorrow, because today was all they ever really had. Grandpa truly lived that way. He said, "That's why I'm 95 years old."

Grayce said, "He looked so handsome."

On the morning of March 10th, Grandpa wrote Kip a letter and did his crossword puzzle. He seemed to be feeling fine. But at noon he felt a little sick and before the afternoon was half gone, he died, just as he would have wanted to without much fuss.

His grandson-in-law, Bill Burke, wrote from Belgian, "I would not say he's left us . . . he will continue to be alive as a model for my life."

And that says it all. Grandpa Burney is far from gone. **This fine, quiet, dignified, unassuming, extraordinary honest man has implanted himself in the hearts of all who knew him.** He had a unique relationship with each and every grandchild. They will always be guided by a few simple words, "What would Grandpa think?"

The family has been overwhelming gratified by the outpouring of love and affection from all over the state and beyond. We thank you. We have needed your support because, although we know we have much for which we can be thankful, we are devastated by our loss. We were so used to having him around. He never seemed old. His thoughts were always as young as spring.

Dwight Burney Senior had many official titles, some very impressive. But we suspect his favorite title was "Grandpa." And he was the very best. We will miss him.

Seeing The World Through The Eyes Of Two-Year-Old Kate

July 1987

Fascinated eyes watched as the fuzzy caterpillar inched his way across the patio. When it reached the garden hose and couldn't get over, a squeaky little voice started giving it encouragement. "You can do it, little caterpillar!" With a mighty effort, it finally made it over the hose, and the little voice cheered.

Then the little person who owned the voice, 27-month-old Kate Johanna Burney, scrunched down on her haunches and explained to the caterpillar that soon it wouldn't have to worry because it was going to be a butterfly. "And then," she said, nodding her head for emphasis as she made her point, "you can fly over the hose."

It is quite an experience to look at the world again through the eyes of a two-year-old. I can't even remember the last time I cheered a caterpillar over a hose. I renewed my acquaintance with Mother Goose, Dr. Seuss, Winnie the Pooh, Sleeping Beauty, and a multitude of other stories I'd once read to six little two-year-olds in succession many years ago.

I'd forgotten what quick change artists they were. How life can be so wonderful one minute and so terrible the next.

We all thought it would be a good idea if Kate stayed at Grandpa Kip's and Grandma Joanie's for a week while Kate's dad, John, flew into Chicago where he's working on a fellowship on French studies, and Lou Ann worked at her job as an intensive care nurse in the Dubuque Hospital.

It was fun to have her because she jabbers all the time and she's a good little girl. Her dad and mom have taught her the importance of cooperating and sharing, and — instead of a spat on the rear — if she sometimes forgets (as two-year-olds are inclined to do) she is told gently and quietly that it must be time for a "time-out." Grandpa, who was brought up in the "spat-on-the-rear-era" thought that it was ridiculous to reason with a two-year-old, but the fact is, it works. Kate hates time-outs.

The only time I had to use the threat of a "time-out" was when she wanted to stay with Bob Becker's chickens instead of going home with her grandpa. The thought of the time-out, AND Grandpa being unhappy, was enough to change her mind. Kate, who is no dummy, said, "We mustn't make Grandpa upset."

Only problem is that "sharing" seemed so reasonable to her that she thought it should work two ways. One day she disappeared and I found her in my office at my computer. She looked a little startled but was ready with a hasty explanation, "I'm just going to share this with you, Grandma Joanie."

Grandma Joanie explained that this was not one of the things we shared. Kate put her head down on the desk and said, "Then I will be very sad." (This usually gets Grandma Joanie.) But Grandma Joanie just said, "Sometimes Kate, we have things to be sad about in this world."

She understood because I heard her explaining it later to Muffin, our uppity cat. Muffin wanted to go outside and it was raining so she couldn't. And Kate said, "Sometimes, Muffin, we have to be sad."

Kate and Muffin established a truce, of sorts, on this visit. Muffin put up with Kate. We realize just how much she put up with her when Muffin walked out of the bedroom one day with a long-suffering look on her face and two necklaces wrapped around her neck.

Kate seemed to be having a really good time. And I think she did. But she missed her folks. One evening, as we were gathering up her multitude of books to head for bed, I heard her telling Muffin, "Soon I am going to go to Dubuque and see my mommy and then we will go to Chicago and see my daddy and then we will live happily ever after."

Chapter Four

"Animals are such agreeable friends,
they ask no questions,
pass no criticism."
George Elliott

The Birds and the Beasts

Chapter Four

One of the delights of living in the country is the cast of animal characters, wild and tame, that add richness and — yes — drama to one's life story. In addition to an ever-present, much-loved dog, we've always had a multitude of cats. It all started with one mangy kitten brought home for "just one week, Mom" by eldest sons Rob and Bill. It was a stray that baseball boys rescued and were going to take turns raising. That "visiting" cat started the Burney cat dynasty which was destined to populate Cedar County. The last of the line is the haughty Muffin, the three-legged "Theater" cat, rescued as a bedraggled kitten from a mud puddle by youngest son Chuck, and now ruling the household. In addition, we've had the drama of Esmirelda and her wild turkey commune, and the winter animal show put on by the deer gathering in our valley, and much, much more. Life would have been much simpler without our birds and beasts, but infinitely less fun.

* * *

Mystery Cat No Ghost

September 1973

I don't talk to my cats. Some people do, you know. Oh, I might say a word here and there, such as "Get off the table!" or maybe a friendly "Good Morning," but I do not carry on prolonged conversations with them.

And I've never particularly **wanted** to communicate with them. Until last week. And then I couldn't. You see, Kip came up to the house from packing silage and presented me with a problem.

"Joanie," he hollered, "I have a charity case for you." I hustled into the mud room (our back entry way) and discovered **him holding the ugliest, scruffiest looking yellow tiger kitten I'd ever seen.** "He just crawled up my leg down at the place and started purring in my ear," said the boss, and turned the skinny, wretched little critter over to me.

I took the poor little feller in and fed him, and he'd drink and yowl and drink and yowl, and his yowl was in a base voice that was almost four times as big as he was. It set your teeth on edge. Obviously he was trying to tell me something. When his tummy was all round and pooched out he waddled away from the milk dish, crawled up on my lap, and continued to caterwaul what must have been the saddest story I've ever not understood. Then he curled his pathetic little self up right in the middle of the slacks I was shortening and went sound asleep. What a relief!

When Kip came in we decided he was somebody's pet (elementary, my dear Watson, wild cats do not crawl up old bull-shippers legs on first acquaintance), and that he'd certainly been through some rough times. **He was a "personality" kitten. Some cats are.**

The kids were delighted (of course) when they got home from school. Just what we needed, another cat! They fixed him a special box and lavished him with so much attention that Cotton, our elderly house cat, took off in a huff. They made an unenthusiastic attempt to find out if anybody had lost him with negative results, and then dubbed him, "Maurice, the mystery cat."

He did not remain a mystery for long. A couple mornings later our neighbor, Hilary Hoesing was sitting in the living room having a cup of coffee with Kip (the kitchen table was occupied) and the kitty came zooming in the door, made a beeline for Hilary, jumped on his chest and started nuzzling his chin.

You wouldn't believe the expression on Hilary's face. His eyes nearly popped out of his head. You would think he was seeing a ghost. Turned out he thought he was. **"I'm seeing a ghost," he shouted, "this cat is dead."**

"He doesn't eat like a ghost," we assured him, but he remained unconvinced. "We ran over him with the pickup last week," he explained. "He was our favorite cat and everybody was upset. It was terrible! I even liked him, and I hate cats. He has personality." (See, I told you.) The cat was unimpressed with this tale of his demise, and just continued to purr away.

Anyway, so Hilary had son Jeff take him to the farthest corner of the farm and dispose of him. That was a week ago. What happened to the intervening week was obviously the subject of all the earlier meowing, and we can only guess at it. But the kitten, who's real name turns out to be Tiger, must have come back to life and made his way to the Burney household. A wise choice on his part.

That night a couple of ecstatic little Hoesing girls came to claim him and Tiger and/or Maurice the mystery cat went home. A cat with a distinctive personality, and eight lives to go.

Shame On You, Henry

January 1971

I don't know how you feel, personally, about hogs. It might not be a subject that you've given a great deal of thought.

Up until this winter, as a matter of fact, my feelings have been somewhat ambiguous.

They probably reached a low point when some of the little rascals got out and uprooted all my mums. But when my mums, thankful for any attention at all, not only survived but thrived, all was forgiven.

I've always seen definite advantages to them in the form of ham, pork chops, or whole hog sausage. However, my feelings have slightly polarized this fall. About hogs, that is! I hate them!

This reason, as is so often the case in a person's polarization, is one of their numbers.

We call him, among other things, Henry. **Even as a little fellow, Henry showed signs of precocious tendencies.**

Henry ALWAYS got out. The men could come in the house and give me solid assurances that the fence was finally hog tight, and Henry would be browsing in the front yard before they were through with their coffee.

As he got bigger, his techniques for escape became more of a puzzle, until one day, Buster, our hired man, spied him going OVER the top of the fence. Henry could jump!

But I still haven't conveyed to you the depth of my problem. One day, apparently when Henry the hog was on one of his forages, he noted the menagerie that inhabits our garage. A friendly hog, Henry, spying eleven cats and two dogs, thought, "What that garage needs is a hog." And in spite of the distinct hostility of the garage's residents, Henry made repeated attempts to join the group.

He developed a taste for cat food, enjoyed terrorizing the inhabitants, and learned that the best time to visit was when the less than friendly occupants in the house were not in. It never failed. When our vehicles were all gone, we would spy evidence of one of Henry's catastrophic visits upon our return home.

What was worse, because of the severity of the winter and the snow cover, we had for obvious reasons, supplied the cats with a powder room in the garage in the form of a box of cat litter. Unbelievably and to my absolute horror, Henry the hog has decided this is an excellent idea.

He breaks out of the most formidable surroundings, makes his way across the farm and avails himself of the facilities of our garage, including the powder room.

It will not take you long to figure out that this was, literally and figuratively, just too much.

One day when I was home without a vehicle I heard the wild commotion that heralded Henry's entrance on the premises. Aha! I thought, and raced to the garage door. Henry and I were going to have a showdown.

The most humiliating thing happened. The indomitable (?) watch dogs, scared out of their wits, (Henry is now huge) raced in the house and knocked me flat on the doorstep.

Henry, I could tell, was strongly thinking of following the dogs, ignoring me completely in the most humiliating way. Whoever heard of a house hog?!

I bellowed at him and he glared at me, picked up the empty feeding tray and shook it angrily.

Suddenly, I remembered a classical satire called "Animal Farm" in which the hogs end up as dictators, running everything. Henry's beady little eye had a strange look.

Enough is enough. I grabbed an axe from the corner of the garage, and took after Henry with shouting and yelling and wild threatening gestures with the axe.

I like to think Henry was thunderstruck. Never had he seen such an apparition. Here was this creature (me) weighing half as much as he did racing through the snow barefooted, wind whistling ominously through the holes of her jeans, pink and blue curlers flapping in the wind, sweatshirt bellowing out behind, waving a weapon and shouting at the top of her lungs, "Shame on you, Henry!"

I like to think, also, that if Henry had any ideas of taking over the farm, like the animals in "Animal Farm," he's given them up. He may still be running. (He MAY be back in the garage!)

Well, as far as that goes, all's well that ends well and Henry is going to end up as whole hog sausage at the next pancake and sausage breakfast at Holy Trinity. I donated him.

The thing that I WAS a little worried about was what the motorist thought that happened by as I was running wildly over the farm, waving that axe, and shouting, "Shame on you Henry!"

I sure hope he saw the hog!

The Taming of the Spook

November 1971

There is a rule in our house that no cats are allowed. Cotton the Great, our big white tom cat, is a frequent visitor, however, and Maurice, our fluffy teenager, has been known to sneak in. The other six cats that inhabit the garage are just allowed in on special occasions, (Cotton's birthday, etc.) and the dogs are let in only during thunderstorms.

In any case, they better not be in when the master of the house appears. If they are, a general uproar ensues, and we all get the lecture.

However, several weeks ago, we were allowed to bend the rule for a psychological experiment which we undertook. We were studying the value of heredity versus environment.

It started this way. I came home from town one day and heard the most pitiful caterwauling in the garage. None of our cats, raised with T.L.C. (tender loving care) would have any reason to sound like that. Upon inspection I found a terribly frightened little fluff of a grey kitten hiding in our garden tractor. She was unbelievably wild, and scurried off with her tail between her legs. There was no getting close to her.

Now we need another cat like we need a hole in the head, but you can see the opportunity here for scientific discovery. Of course you can!

Here we had a little scrawny starving wild kitten, who had obviously been raised in a state of perpetual fear and hunger. Would it be possible to use our environment, filled with the above mentioned T.L.C., to produce a reasonable facsimile of our lily-livered house cats.

The first problem was to catch her. We put chief scientific investigators Juli, Tom and Chuck on that job, and using lots of food and coaxing, they got next to the kitten. Project "Spook" was underway.

One day investigator Chuck brought Spook into the house. He headed for the nearest little dark place under the furniture that he could find, and we had a dickens of a time extracting him. Still scared spitless.

But to make a long story short, Spook gradually came around. Instead of slithering around the corners of the room, she began to walk straight through the middle with her tail up in the air and purring confidently the entire time. Half the size of any other cat in our brood, she is demanding twice the attention. As if to make up for lost time, she is nuzzling everybody and everything, and would rather purr than eat. (It took the kids three weeks to get a purr out of her.)

The crowning touch was the other night when she had the nerve to jump up on the couch and curl up beside the master while he was sleeping. We all waited with baited breath for the explosion when he discovered her there, but he just grinned. Then he caught himself and muttered something about "what is this silly cat doing here," but his heart really wasn't in it. **Spook just looked up at him and purred.** After all, even old bull-shippers should understand about kittens that are scientific experiments.

Saving Independent Pierre's Kittens

March 1974

After all that nice weather, everybody was a little startled last week to wake up to several inches of snow. But nobody was as startled as Pierre, our old mother cat. Apparently lulled into a false security by the warm weather, she'd had her litter of five kittens in the barn. She usually has them under the heat light in the garage.

Pierre is the most independent cat we've ever had. She is not even interested in coming in the house, as she has always considered it her job to personally rid the farm of mice and rats. And only if she is absolutely starved does she turn to us for food. She and I have always had a special relationship, however, nourished by the long summer evenings we spent sitting on the back step together watching our offspring play in the sun. But she asks no special favors and she grants none.

So the morning of the snow we were surprised to hear this imperious meowing at the back door.

"What does this black cat want that is yowling at our back door?" queried the old bull-shipper in none too friendly a fashion.

"That's probably Pierre," I replied cleverly, since she's the only black cat we have. "She must be starving to death is she's meowing at the door."

I explained to him that all she would do is come in, eat like crazy and then return to her brood. She is a very good mother. Reluctantly, he let her in.

And what does she do but walk right past the food and follow me into the other room, meowing her heart out.

I put her out, but at the first opportunity she raced back in, found me wherever I was and told me her sad tale.

I finally said to Kip, "I think she wants me to go down and get her kittens because of the snow."

And he told me that the kittens were just fine in the barn, that's where they belonged, and that I was to leave them there. I could see why Pierre wasn't pleading her case with him!

Pierre kept this constant barrage up all afternoon, and by the time we'd finished supper, she had me convinced. Kip happened to be sleeping on the couch at the time, so Chuck and I just decided to follow Pierre and see what she wanted.

Well, she led the way, you better believe, meowing orders loudly and waving her tail like a flag. She meowed us through a fence, into the barn, and up the steps to the loft, and there in a little hole in the bale pile were five long-haired little kittens. Three white, one black and one yellow.

Pierre was meowing and purring and meowing and purring. Chuck put the little balls of fuzz in the box we just happened to bring along, and Pierre jumped in after them, purring so loud I thought she would burst.

Then she nestled in among her kittens and allowed us to transport her back to the garage and the heat lamp, as if she were a reigning queen.

When Kip woke up from his after-supper nap, I told him Pierre had **made** us go down and get her kittens. He wasn't surprised. He said I'd held out a lot longer than he thought I would.

Then I caught him taking a peek at the kittens in their box and giving Pierre a pat on the head. One thing about old bull-shippers, their bark is worse than their bite.

Brave Puppy, Heroic Puppy...

January 1975

The New Year would have started out splendidly, what with both Nebraska and Notre Dame winning their football games, if I hadn't inadvertently made the whole family mad at me with my last column.

It wasn't what I said about them that irritated them, it was what I wrote about Puppy. I said he was cowardly. John, who is Puppy's greatest admirer, threatened to mount a protest and write letters to my editors if I didn't retract myself, and the other kids were equally angry.

You see, I'd forgotten about the Fourth of July.

Quite honestly, in regard to ordinary things such as prowlers and the like, Puppy hasn't (in my opinion) shown any outstanding heroism.

126

The kids have pointed out to me, however, that we've never had any prowlers.

But the thing is that Puppy is so friendly, that he will wag his way up to any stranger delightedly, and in all probability, if it were within his power, he would give them the key to the house and invite them in for a cup of coffee. That's the kind of a puppy Puppy is.

He will set up a brave barking protest if there happens to be a full moon, and he sometimes barks at passing horses (providing they are a safe distance away.)

His performance on the Fourth of July, however, even I will admit is incredible.

You see, every year he saves us from the fireworks. That's what he thinks anyway, and his performance has gotten to be the highlight of our Fourth of July celebration.

Whenever we light any of our fireworks, Puppy takes off after it, runs circles around it ferociously, and when it goes out he thinks it went out because he scared it.

Then he comes swaggering cockily back to us (if you've never seen a dog swagger, it is quite a sight) and revels in our praise and patting, only to be challenged by another burning fountain thing, or Roman candle, or whatever.

The reason that Puppy's actions are so impressive to us is that the other dogs we had went into hiding from the time the first firecracker went off (usually the first of June) until the last one went off (end of August). They were petrified.

So, in reviewing the case, I'd have to say that Puppy is not cowardly after all. He is dumb. (Only kidding kids!) I just hope we never have a real fire for Puppy to save us from. He'd be heartsick if we called in the fire department.

Good heavens, here I am on a cold, snowy day in January conjuring up memories of the Fourth of July. I've often thought that it would be more fun and safer to shoot off firecrackers on New Year's Day anyway, except that there might be some heads that could not stand all the banging around.

If that would ever come to pass, however, I am sure that Puppy would be ready for it. Brave Puppy. Heroic Puppy. Dauntless Puppy.

Pheasant And Deer "Quite A Sight!!"

March 1975

This week I had two great experiences on the same day. Lots of weeks, you know, a fella doesn't have any.

Both of them were visual and, of course, I have to share them with you.

The first occurred as I was drinking my second cup of coffee. I was gazing out the window in my usual morning stupor, when what to my wondering eye should appear but this beauteous sight. You will have to envision it mentally with me, because I didn't think about getting my camera, and if I had, there wasn't any film in it anyway.

Silhouetted against the morning sky, on the stark whiteness of a drift of new-fallen snow, stood the handsomest, most colorful rooster pheasant I've ever seen. I said to myself, "Myself, you are a lucky person. How many people can look out their kitchen window at such a sight?" The pheasant pranced and preened as if he knew I was watching, and then glided silently away at the approach of an oncoming car.

The second sight (great experience number two) was one I'd been waiting for all winter. Everybody had seen it. The neighbors had had to stop on the road for it. The schoolbus was delayed by it. It held Kip up on his way to a sale. (An ordinarily impossible task.) It was a visual experience that everyone was talking about.

"It" being our herd of deer.

Officially counted by the game warden at fifty-one (and unofficially as high as fifty-six) the deer seem to be watering in our creek and then foraging in all the area around us. Hence the frequent trips across the road, with ensuing stoppage (?) of traffic.

I'd gone to some effort to be where they were reported to be, and I was getting a little crabby about being the only one in the country that hadn't seen them. When it happened number three son, John, and I were driving down the road when we saw the first one. We were about to turn into our driveway when she caught our eye, not an eighth of a mile away. And we counted as one by one, follow the leader style, the beautiful creatures gracefully and effortlessly cleared the fence on one side of the road, and with one leaping bound, sailed across the fence on the other side. The trees on either side of the road made a frame for the deer, so that we couldn't see how many were coming, or where they were headed. We crept up on them (in the car) as they fluidly followed each other and counted twenty-eight. Until number twenty-nine came streaking across the pasture, a Johnny-come-lately, and I swear that his hooves barely touched the road as he cleared the fences. He was really moving, I mean she. We're told that there are two bucks, but we didn't see them. Of course, we don't know how many cleared the fence before we started to count, either.

But it was quite a sight, well worth waiting the winter for.

You know, we've been asked the question many times — by a popular farm magazine recently — and by our own selves at times. Why do people stay on the farm when the going has been so rough? And I imagine that there are as many answers to that question as there are farmers. Some people say it's a "way of life," and that doesn't adequately explain it either. But one day this past week, I added thirty more reasons to our list. One was a rooster pheasant, and the other twenty-nine were deer. Myself, you **are** a lucky person.

On Puppies And Pussies And People

March 1977

Cats always look as if they know exactly what they are about. Have you noticed that? Just this week I was driving through the streets of Hartington, which were piled high with snow. Walking along the top of one of the drifts was this black cat. He looked neither right nor left, but plodded purposefully along, as if he had an appointment (or a rendezvous) for which he was probably exactly on time.

That always impresses me. If a cat is in, he knows when he wants out. And if he is out, he knows when he wants in. Usually, either request is made just about the time you have comfortably settled in for a long winter's nap.

And a cat will decide he wants to mush on you when you are the very busiest, sitting on your papers or knocking aside your pen in the process. But if you want to pet him and he doesn't feel like it — forget it! He'll have none of that, thank you. You are not on his agenda for that minute.

Dogs, on the other hand, always are friendly, no matter what. When the weather is good and I head out for my nightly walk, Puppy (our old dog) is always delighted. He goes along, protects me from rampaging bunny rabbits, chases away any wild robins who might cross our path, and is a perfect companion.

Puppy will not eat when anyone is watching. He is too polite. Our cats, on the other hand, would knock over an old woman in a wheelchair to get at their food, and never give a backward glance.

I like them both, though. And feel that they have their place in the world. And it occurs to me that people can be almost divided into those categories.

There are the friendly Saint Bernard types who lop through life just hoping for a smile and a friendly face. Then there are the cat species — be they lions, tigers, or pussy cats, who rampage through life with a purpose, knocking down anyone who gets in their way, and pausing only when it suits them for a kind word or a little cuddling, but only if it suits them.

Probably the cat types are more successful if you measure success in worldly gain (and don't we all some times?). But if you measure success by a person's enjoyment of life and the things around him, I'd go with the puppies.

The thing is, because people (and cats and dogs) march to the beat of different drummers, they can't do too much about the way they are. Problem being that a lot of the time the "puppy" varieties waste time wishing they were "cats" and vice-versa.

Or — worse yet — waste even more time trying to change each other. "Why can't you relax like I do," a puppy personality will complain to his cat personality friend. And his cat personality friend will say "I wish you had more get up and go."

(Makes me think of that marvelous quote from somewhere, "My get up and go has got up and went!")

The moral of this story might be that cats may always know just where they are going, but puppies have more fun getting there. Then again, puppies may just end up some place else, wagging their tails behind them.

Cats Have No Family Planning

June 1977

The thing I don't like about cats is that they don't have any sense about family planning. You just get your cat population down to a decent size (one that will keep the mice under control and not knock anybody going out the back door down by their massive frontal attack) and the world conspires against you.

For instance, not two years ago we were down to three cats. The peculiar Spook, our lucky black cat, the amiable Maurice, and our mother cat, the friendly (!) Pierre.

But then Bernhard, the person, moved in, followed shortly by Bernhard the cat, and we acquired Chelsea, the city cat.

Bernhard the cat is a female, and she has almost no redeeming

features cat-wise. She is ugly, skinny, short-haired, and slightly cross-eyed. And she has kittens which look just like her, for the most part.

But Bernhard adored me, and would purr like a berserk outboard motor and rub against my legs. (Bernhard the cat, that is.) She would look at me lovingly with those crossed-eyes, and I would look at her and say in my crossest voice, "I do not like you Bernhard." **(This sometimes startled Bernhard, the bookkeeper, if he happened to be in the office.)** But it did not faze Bernhard the cat. She just stuck around and kept having kittens. And I'd feed her. She was the only thing around here who looked at me that way, even with crossed-eyes. And everybody needs love, you know.

But Kip says I have virtually set up a welfare station in my garage. He says what's wrong with the country is what's wrong with our garage. It would seem to be true.

Bernhard is a case in point. She had her kittens this spring in a maternity box in the garage, but after two days she moved them to the straw pile down by the feed yards. She evidently didn't like the attention the homely little things were getting. But just last week, she brought them all back and deposited them in the garage again. Then, she left.

And Kip raged. "See," he bellowed, "this was a perfectly good barn cat, and this is the time she would take these kittens out to learn to hunt, but why should she! She brings them up here and puts them on the dole."

But the worst of this whole situation is not the outside cats, it's Chelsea, the beautiful aristocrat from Omaha. She thinks she's a house cat. Several years ago I rid myself of house cats. Nobody could ever decide which cat was really the house cat, and so we'd end up with five or six in the house. Kip announced that either the cats went, or he did, and after a long discussion, we decided it would be the cats.

But Chelsea belonged to my sister, Anne. She'd originally been ours, however, and since I give a money back guarantee, she came home. This was after Anne discovered one of her kids was allergic to cats.

Chelsea came home with her own dishes, and explicit instructions from Megan (Anne's youngest) on her care. She was (supposedly) house broken. The only slight inkling I got that there might be a problem there was when Anne said (quickly and in passing) that she sometimes confused the bean bag chairs with her litter box. Well, turned out she confused almost anything with her litter box; the living room couch, an open drawer, laundry, whatever. Inside of a very few days Chelsea discovered that she, too, was an outside cat.

So, the upshot of the whole thing is that we now have not only our three original cats, but Pierre has five kittens, Bernhard had five, we have an additional teenager hanging around of Bernhard's, and one of Pierre's, and all are being presided over by the queenly Chelsea. Kip is threatening to leave and I'm considering it, too.

Feisty Cat Protesteth Too Much

September 1978

For the last twenty some years I've had a minimum of three mother cats in production. And they've had a minimum of two batches of kittens a year. And those kittens have numbered — remember we're speaking of minimums now — at least four to a batch.

So — I have dealt with, conservatively, some 500 cats. Now a person cannot get emotionally involved with 500 cats. But we have. And every time we gave a little fuzzy kitten away, it was an emotional wrench. And if one got run over, or caught in the motor in the winter, it was always a personal friend, and we had to shed a tear or two.

Frankly, it was getting to be a terrible drain.

So, these last two years I've made a concerted effort not to like any of the cats. I would feed them, but I would not get tied up in any conversations. (You may scoff at that, but cat-lovers know that cats are good conversationalists.)

There was only one cat that took my fancy, and she was as wild as could be. A fuzzy calico with big eyes and a foul temper. I didn't like her, of course, as I didn't intend to get involved. But I had to admire her independence.

The kids tried to tame her, but she mamed them a few times with her claws, and they gave up. Vicious little thing.

Kip was pleased with this turn of events. He has always disliked cats. It is only because he has great forebearance (and is gone most of the time) that we've had any cats at all. Also, he thought they were catching mice. When we had the onslaught of mice last year, he became further disillusioned, and the cats became even less popular.

Except, of course, this wild one. She had her allotted four kittens, and in a fit of domesticity, moved them in the garage. The boys fixed her a box, put the kittens in, and she moved them out. No one was going to fool with her kittens!

Whenever I went outside she would race around me hissing all the time. I decided she "protesteth too much" and so when I'd feed the cats, I would sit down by the food, and the only way for her to eat was to come right up to me, hissing all the time. Then one day I reached over and petted her head. Boy, did she bolt! None of that stuff.

But the twentieth time I tried it she actually let me scratch her on the head. One of my sons was working on her, too. She'd always been a challenge to him. And the other night he sat down on the back step, and she hissed right up to him, and let him pet her. Then she let him pick her up, and hissed some more, but she didn't try to get away. Now when I go to get the mail, she accompanies me, hissing all the way. But it's sort of a friendly hiss. And it loses its effectiveness when she rubs against my leg.

It's a good thing I don't like cats anymore, or I might be getting attached to her. Feisty little creature. She's sitting on the window-sill right now, hissing away. The way the world is today, you've got to appreciate her attitude.

Proof Positive — Pets Own People

December 1978

I have a theory that people do not own pets — pets own people. Witness the conversation I took part in just yesterday with an intelligent-looking store owner. Under discussion was one of the employee's couches, which said employee was thinking of having covered.

"We should have our hide-a-bed covered too," said the proprietor. "Our cat has ruined it."

Because of my developing theory, my ears perked up. "Your cat?" I queried.

"Yup," he said, shaking his head sadly. "Just ruined it. Clawed a big tear all across the front." Then he said there was no use getting it fixed because she'd probably just tear another one.

"I hate that cat," he said unconvincingly. **"If she wasn't so blamed cute we'd get rid of her."**

Then there is Louie, who rules the roost at my sister-in-law's house. Louie is a huge cat of unknown heritage who, if he decides he wants to go out, scratches on the furniture. Then if he decides he wants to come in, he wiggles the doorknob, which he can reach by sitting on the porch railing. He wants to go in and out a lot. And if scratching doesn't bring an immediate response, he tends to get a little testy and has been known to bite the master of the house on the rump, which is a little variation on the "biting the hand that feeds you" routine. This, however, always works — for Louie, anyway.

Puppy, our elderly dog, has his own unique way of running us. He jumps on the front porch windowsill and wags his tail against the window, setting up a fierce pounding commotion. If we don't immediately respond, he wags his head, which gives a kind of concert drum effect by banging the window also. He sometimes has with him our motley array of cats, who we suspect put him up to it. We are trained to rise from the couch or chair or wherever he's spotted us, go to the back door and either feed Puppy or play with him.

The problem is, he also wants to get in on anything extraordinary that goes on. So he sets up his disconcerting drumming display whenever we have company, and once almost totally disrupted a home Mass. Sometimes we just ignore him, and when we forget to explain to the company what's going on they think we're a little strange or else that we are keeping some very noisy skeletons, which we prefer not to discuss, in our closet.

Cats and dogs just don't choose anybody for their pets, however, and those of us who are among the chosen can take a little comfort from that. **People who put up with pets must be unselfish, softhearted, lovable, concerned about the other's welfare and maybe just a wee bit dumb.**

Just a minute, Puppy, I'm coming!

The Duck Round-Up

May 1981

It was an old-fashioned roundup with hooting and hollering, and even a little critter in trouble being saved by the good guys.

Only thing is, the scene wasn't out on the range and the critters weren't cattle. The roundup took place on the main street of Hartington and the critters were wild baby ducklings.

It all started in the morning, according to Cathy Lounsbery, although she didn't realize it at the time. As she came to work, she noticed a full grown wild duck flopping around like she had a broken wing. All this took place in the alley behind Lounsbery's House of Flowers. **Cathy, who is wise in the ways of wild birds as well as tame flowers,** said she had the fleeting thought that the bird must have little ones around. Wild birds often fake injury to lure possible predators away.

Cathy was not a predator, she was just a very busy flower lady with weddings and funerals galore and Memorial Day coming up, and probably a prom or two. She sure didn't have time to worry about a "dumb duck."

But she was not to be left in peace. A customer came into the store all in an uproar because there were baby ducks all over the street in front of Lounsbery's. The duck, who really was dumb, had led her little duck children through an opening between the buildings and out onto main street.

Now Cathy was distraught. She knew that the ducklings would not be long for this world on main street in Hartington. Times Square it isn't, but busy it is. So in true cowboy (duckboy?) fashion, she commandeered volunteers from the passers-by and surrounding business houses, and staged a duck roundup.

"I got a box to put them in," Cathy said, "but they were getting out and away as fast as we caught them, so I got another one and put it over the top."

Roundups, of course, are not without mishaps. One of the duck-lings fell into a basement window through the grate and had to be rescued.

The final number of ducklings was twelve. Where they came from and why nobody knows. It's almost certain that the wild mallard didn't hatch those ducklings in the alley. Though nobody knows that for sure either. One can hardly visualize her marching them into town from a surrounding pond either.

And where they've gone is just as mysterious. "I was standing there wondering what in the heck I was going to do with twelve baby ducks," Cathy said, "when this young couple volunteered to take them. They said they knew somebody with a game preserve." And so the ducks rode off in a car, presumably to a better life. "I'm not sure who it was that took them," Cathy said, "I was just glad to get rid of those silly ducks."

Good samaritan that she is, she was still worried about the mother duck. Cathy hoped that the mother duck understood her babies were headed for better things.

So, as in all adventure tales, the dust settled and life returned to normal in Hartington. It was a day like all days, filled with the events that altar and illuminate our times.

Well-Being Is Benefit Of Pet

June 1981

Cat lovers of the world, pet your kitty and beam. We have been vindicated.

A lot of people don't like cats. Some people hate cats. Cats don't care. It's the people who own them that most often come under attack.

And columnists who occasionally write about cats suffer mightily at the hands of the anti-cat faction. "If I see the word 'cat' anywhere in the first paragraph," growled one otherwise pussycat of a friend, "I just don't read that column."

With "cat" being the first word in this column, I've lost her already. Too bad. She's just the one who needs to read on.

You see, we who own cats (or dogs or other pets) may just be healthier than any of you. So there.

But you don't have to take my word for it. And Lord knows, why would you? **I quote from the June issue of Science Digest, wherein Dr. Aaron Katcher (appropriate name) says that new evidence shows that a cat, dog or other pet may actually help lower blood pressure, prevent heart attacks or toughen egos.**

In fact, he says, "We have found seven ways that pets increase well-being by decreasing depression and anxiety."

Now, I'm well aware that for my anti-cat friends, the sight of someone else's pet does not have this calming effect. In fact, I well remember the time that my above mentioned friend saw the beloved pet of one of our bridge-club hostesses cavorting over the dishes we were soon to eat out of. She almost had a heart attack on the spot. So, I'd say a significant study might be done by Dr. Katcher under those trying circumstances.

The recent TV special about the woman who owned 62 cats (give or take a few) even turned MY stomach. If Katcher's theory works according to numbers, her blood pressure must be zero.

Extreme cases aside, people who have pets consider them companions. Our old dog, Puppy, and I have had many a meaningful conversation as I take my nightly walk. Puppy thinks I'm brilliant, and leaps with joy at anything I say. The cats come along, too, but they are aloof and disdainful. But they do Puppy and me great honor by escorting us.

Katcher says pets also make people feel safe. They are pleasant to pet, and take people's minds off their troubles. They are also a stimulus to exercise. They help children become more "fully human" and caring for a pet is good for them.

When our grown kids come home for a visit, Puppy is the one they come to see, along with their favorite cat. For years we could hardly give a kitten away, because each new family was painstakingly divided among the six kids, and nobody wanted to give up his or her kitten. We once had 36 cats (outside) before Kip lowered the boom. We started dispersing them regularly. Many farms in Cedar County have less mice today because of our prolific cats.

It makes me feel good to think that we may have a part not only in lowering the mice population, but in lowering the blood pressure of the dear folks upon whom we unloaded (I mean "to whom we generously gave") our multitude of kittens.

If my anti-cat friend is still with us, I'm sure she'll be calling any moment for a cat. I suppose, though, I shouldn't hold my breath.

Tears Leak For Deer

March 1984

I cannot describe my feelings as I watched the lone hunter tracking across our pasture with his bow and arrow at the ready. My feelings were so mixed as to be painful.

You see, every morning we have had our own wildlife show just by looking out our picture window. Our red house sits on a hill, and overlooks our valley, in which the Bow Creek winds its way through wooded areas and meadows.

Responding to some kind of schedule for the day that is instinctive, as many as forty deer run and leap and saunter and just generally flow from their night habitat, which is downstream to our bluffs.

It's a breathtakingly beautiful sight.

We worried with them during the sub-arctic weather because the snow cover was such and the cold was such that they couldn't find an open space on the creek to get water.

They actually came into our cattle yards and drank out of the heated cattle waterers. And for food, they gathered around the haystacks in our neighbor's fields and in ours.

I have interviewed conservationists in years past who tell me that it is not good when the deer bunch up like this. A disease could wipe them all out, for instance.

And they've also told me that "harvesting" wildlife is a necessity. They need to be hunted. It's part of an important cycle. They love wildlife more than most, and they tell me it is essential that the herds are thinned out for their own ultimate good. And I believe them.

So, intellectually, I am on the side of the hunter. And emotionally, I am on the side of the deer.

The bow and arrow season lasted until the end of December, and the young men given permission to hunt on our farm were relentless. But the lonely figures would come and go, with no deer in tow.

There is an immense dignity that surrounds this bow and arrow hunter. It seems fairer, somehow, than the long-range rifles. It's an elemental contest, pitting the prowress of man against the illusive beast.

I began to look at the scene out our picture window as an ongoing drama. And as days went on, I felt less fear for my deer.

The last day, however, the hunter was wiser. Dressed all in white, he awaited the deer in the trees. I didn't know he was there, but the deer sensed something wrong.

Kip called my attention to it. "Look at the deer milling around," he said. "Something's wrong, must be a hunter in the trees."

And thus it was, after shooting many arrows into the air and having them fall to the earth he knew not where, our hunter actually bagged his deer. And the lone figure came back across the field with deer in tow.

So the hunter was happy, and the conservationists will be happy because the deer dispersed. They scattered.

No longer do they prance across our meadows in the morning. Intellectually, I think that's good. That's why I can't understand the tears leaking out of my eyes as I write.

Alarm Cat Relieves Stress

April 1985

People have strong feelings about cats. I know cat owners who think their cats are little four-legged people. On the other hand, some friends have told me they hate cats. "If I see the word 'cat' in your column, I just quit reading," they say crabbily.

It takes courage for me to share a cat story. I realize I will lose some readers after the first few lines. Nonetheless, pets are supposed to be good for stress, so maybe columns about pets will also relieve stress. I think you might enjoy hearing about Muffin, our three-legged alarm cat.

As a scruffy little half-starved cat, Muffin was saved from drowning in a mud puddle by our son Chuck, who nursed her back to life. She was half the size of the other farm kittens. Knowing Muffin wouldn't make it through a winter, Juli took her to Wayne State College where she was teaching.

Surrounded by theater kids at Wayne State, Muffin began to think of herself as an entertainer. **Theater people do not conform, and neither do theater cats.** Like theater people, she knows how to get attention and is mischievous. She is a beautiful cat, and she enters the room at just the right moment, poses herself center stage and preens. She appraises her audience with expertise and instinctively rubs up against the person who likes cats least. How do cats know that?

She's in our house in spite of Kip's injunction against house cats. We came back after a trip to find Muffin welcoming us at the back door. Juli had moved to a cat-less apartment, and Muffin, several light-years in development from the wretched half-drowned kitten of yore, had moved in and taken over.

An accident which left her with a paralyzed back leg did not diminish her good opinion of herself nor leave her with any less character. Theater cats have grit. Alternately haughty and loving, she has woven herself into our lives, and in spite of some misgivings on our parts, assumed the duties of alarm cat.

If we aren't up with the sun in the morning, she feels it's her duty to wake us. She comes in with soft little mewing sounds which become increasingly strident as the morning goes on until she ends up in a full yowl. We don't know why she does this, but it gets us up.

She also sounds the alarm when anyone drives in the driveway. With some kind of a sixth sense we do not understand, she will jump off the perch of her choice, race out to the back door, her bum leg flying in the wind. We know that within minutes the doorbell will ring.

She's totally independent. If we want to hold her on our laps, we can forget that. She has other important business. But if I sit down with something important to read or sew, she jumps up and curls herself right in the middle of my important business and purrs. In this way she effectively slows down my life.

I think stopping to pet a kitten is about the same as stopping to smell the roses. My cat-hating friends don't know it, and since they haven't read this far they won't get mad if I suggest it, but what they need is a cat.

Wild (?) Turkey Part of Wildlife Show

May 1985

"There she is!" Kip said with some excitement. There she was, sitting on the side of the fence around our well. "She" is a crippled wild turkey that has adopted us and seems to think she is a pet. I have named her Esmirelda. She's a lively old broad deserving of a little respect.

If we gobble at Esmirelda in a friendly fashion, she looks at us appreciatively and gobbles back. She has taken over. She ignores the cats and traipses up and down the lane between the houses and the barn on some schedule known only to her. The pilgrims never saw a turkey like her. She's had some TLC from our neighbors along the way and become quite fat and sassy.

We could hardly wait to show her to daughter Juli when she wandered through on the way to do an "Artist in Residence" stint at Santee.

"What do you mean, wild turkey?" she said. "That's a tame turkey if I ever saw one." We explained the distinction. **The turkey is not so much wild as she is free.** She goes where she pleases. If anyone takes a shot at her, she reverts to wildness in a hurry. She gets mad.

You might think it doesn't take much to excite us, but that wild turkey is an example of why I may never be able to move out of the country. Some critter is always wandering through, and I love it.

Everyday we see a wildlife show. Esmirelda joins a cast of performers. In fact, she often crosses paths with the rabbit couple responsible for the little bunny family in our pfitzers. **Deer crisscross the meadow below the house, the neighbor's guinea hens visit occasionally, a prairie chicken sometimes walks with the turkey** and because of the mild winter, we have more pheasant than we have seen for a couple of years. Bit players include an occasional raccoon, skunk, fox, and coyote. (We aren't crazy about all of them, you understand, but every show has to have a villain.)

The birds, who seem to bellow loudest in the spring, provide musical accompaniment.

One morning we looked out our picture window, and there in the alfalfa field, having a chit-chat, were a pair of pheasant, the turkey and one of our neighbor's guineas.

Credit for Esmirelda's presence and the wild turkeys that dot the countryside is due the Nebraska Game and Parks Commission. Their work to stock the area has been such a success that in 1982 we had our first turkey hunting season.

This is a natural area for wild turkey. The rolling hills and wooded areas make a perfect habitat for many types of wildlife. In the early 1800s, wildlife abounded. An ancient history book says wild birds were so plentiful they blackened the sun when they went into flight.

By the turn of the century, civilization, drought, harsh winters, prairie fires and unrestricted hunting had taken a severe toll and wildlife had "nearly or altogether disappeared."

We'd like it if nobody shot the crippled turkey who's adopted us. She goes well with our crippled cat. I understand, because it's been explained to me numerous times by my hunter friends, that prudent hunting is good for wild birds and beasts. It spreads them out, so it keeps them from getting too inbred. It keeps the population down so there's enough food and cover for those who survive. But anyone can see none of the above applies to Esmirelda.

The Goose Patrol

May 1986

It may come as a surprise to some, but it comes as no surprise to me that the army has enlisted a Goose Patron to guard 30 sites run by the U.S. Army's 32nd Air Defense Command in West Germany.

I had an experience with a gander that has forever made me wary of geese. I have no doubt that a web-footed brigade would do wonders on guard duty.

My experience took place at Brooks golf course in Okoboji. Though I enjoy it, I'm not good at golf. So when my three golfing co-horts and I came up to a lake that my friends cold easily hit over, I — being no fool — decided to go around. Unfortunately, at the edge of this lake there was a mother goose busy hatching her young. My ball landed about five feet from where the picturesque and kindly-looking goose had her nest.

I didn't think twice as I headed for it. Considerate person that I am, I parked the golf cart some distance away in order not to scare the mother goose, grabbed my club and jauntily strode toward the ball.

In a briefer time than it takes to tell it I was not so jaunty. I was running pell mell for the cart, chased by an enraged gander, who was honking at the top of his lungs and out to do me bodily harm.

I jumped in the cart, and he all but jumped in with me. I was shouting (my golfing partners told me later), "I'm going, I'm going!!!" But the gander was unforgiving. I floored the gas pedal, but the golf cart was not speedy, and the gander stayed with me for what seemed like hours.

It did not help that my so-called friends thought the whole scene was so funny they were rolling on the fairway. Nor that the team of men golfers coming down the other fairway were convulsed with laughter.

The experience remains etched in my memory.

The humiliation of it recedes, however, as I contemplate 900 of these squawking waterfowl on guard duty. Gaggles of geese, in platoons of six to forty, will take up posts.

I can testify personally that the idea of goose guards is not as ludicrous as it might seem to some. My personal testimony in their behalf probably would not carry much weight. But history does, and it shows that geese have been used as guards for centuries. They have an acute sense of hearing, and when startled they sound the alarm by hissing, honking loudly, and flapping their wings.

In 390 B.C., a goose patrol saved Rome by raising a noisy commotion as the Gauls approached the city walls. Europeans use geese to guard their homes to this day.

It makes sense. And what is more, according to the Time Magazine, the entire goose patrol will cost the Army about half the annual tab for a single trained guard dog.

Tall Turkey Tales Continue

September 1987

I told you I would not write about turkeys any more. But, let's face it, I lied.

I was really glad I made that promise right after I made it because I didn't want to share with you the fate of Esmirelda and Tom's first five babies. I thought you probably had enough problems of your own.

The computer was still warm from exulting over their birth when some predator got to them, and the little ones disappeared. Esmirelda was all beat up. She must have put up quite a fight. But all that was left of the baby turkeys was a pile of feathers.

I was furious and also distraught all out of proportion. After all, they were just turkeys, and one way or another they will someday disappear. Perhaps even down some human gullet. However, I wasn't prepared to face their early demise. They were so tiny they barely made a mouthful for whatever critter got to them. Perhaps it was a coon, perhaps a fox, perhaps a coyote, we do not know.

A reader friend who lives near Sioux City called to warn me about this. She informed me her turkeys were being eaten by coyotes. She said she's had some success raising baby turkeys by taking the eggs to an incubator and then keeping the little ones in a pen.

We have no pen suitable for turkeys. We thought Esmirelda and her babies would be safe because they stayed right next to our house. But they weren't, and Esmirelda went all around the house calling for her babies. It was very sad.

Then, to my concern, Esmirelda also disappeared. I assumed she was in mourning, or she'd just gotten disgusted and moved to someone else's house. I wouldn't blame her.

But no. Several weeks later, joy of joys, she pranced by our house with five more baby turkeys. Esmirelda was not to be deterred. She simply went into hiding, laid a bunch more eggs and had another family. What a trooper!

Our joy was compounded by the fact we had two more wild (free) turkey hens come to live around our place, bringing with them their five babies. You think I'm not tickled?

Every morning Esmirelda, her two lady friends and their combined families of eight (Esmirelda's five are now down to three) saunter up to our house and make the rounds. The five older turkey children are almost grown. Esmirelda's are still small. But they seem to enjoy each other's company. They have become a turkey commune and travel together.

What tickles me is what they are doing when they take their morning saunter around our house. They are gobbling grasshoppers. I hate grasshoppers. Usually, this time of year, they mow the pasture next to the house and the grasshoppers come in and wipe out my flowers.

Not this year. **The grasshoppers provide a gourmet breakfast for the turkey gang.**

And you would love this picture. Every morning, after eating her breakfast, Esmirelda sits on the patio in the sunshine with her three little ones snuggled under her wings. They are so cute. I am overwhelmed with pleasure. It's that picture I had to share with you.

I will try not to write about turkeys any more. But I won't promise. Obviously, I can't be trusted.

Chapter Five

*"When the student is ready,
the teacher will come..."*
Ancient Axiom

*The mind stretched by an idea,
will never return to its original shape.*

Education

Chapter Five

The problem with education is that the more you know, the more you know you don't know. So, if you're really paying attention, the more education you get, the more you need. My life has been greatly enriched by the teachers who've passed my way, and not all of them have had a lot of letters after their names. Indeed, one of the wisest was my friend Ferdie Pietz, our local philosopher and auctioneer, whose "formal" education stopped at the third grade. My curious need to know was undoubtedly fostered by my parents, Emmett William and June E. Rossiter, and the rest of my family. I can only guess what my mother might have accomplished had she lived in this era. She was a musician and a scholar who could discuss philosophy with Lawrence, banking with Vincent, and sports with her grandsons. But she married my wild and totally chauvinistic Irish father, who dramatically influenced the world of Independent Banking by the words he wrote on his green ribboned typewriter. My brothers, Lawrence and Vincent, and sisters, Mary, Connie, June and Anne have all been education addicts. My little sister Anne and I are workshop junkies, and will doubtless have as our epitaph, "Where do we sign up?" Problem is, when we suspect we have learned something, we have this great need to share. Some of what I suspect I know, and how I got to know it, I share in the following essays.

* * *

The Graduation Owl

May 1971

In a dusty back corner of our kitchen closet resides a paper owl. He lives in a shoe box, and at first sight, his flattened body and dismembered parts don't amount to much. But, when you unfold his round fat little self, assemble his spectacles, wings, feet, graduation hat and diploma, and place him in the center of the dining room table, he assumes an air of great wisdom.

His wise old eyes survey the whole scene, the newly scrubbed rug, the freshly picked flowers, the unusually dust free room, and seems to find wry amusement in what is taking place.

The owl and I have presided over three high school graduations. I must say, the owl has worn better than I have. A little scotch tape, and he looks better than ever. It would take much more than scotch tape to take care of me, although the scotch part isn't a bad idea.

The owl knows that for all the jolliness and festivities, mothers shed secret tears at graduations. The frantic and uncharacteristic cleaning is just to cover, and when the many activities that engulf the parents of seniors calm down, mothers become aware of a large lump in their throats that just won't go away.

It's kind of like the first time your kid graduated into the deep water of the swimming pool. Although we can still yell encouragement from the sidelines, the kid now has to do the swimming on his own. It's a proud feeling, but a scary one.

The graduates themselves have mixed feelings. They've worked long and hard for this day and eagerly awaited it. And now they wonder what the hurry was.

There is such a vulnerability about these beautiful young people, as they march proudly, resplendent in their caps and gowns. They seem to be marching into their future in this sad old world with a gallantry that portends great hope for the rest of us.

No place is this vulnerability more evident than in the classic graduation pictures. Not yet fully mature, yet no longer young, they proudly look out on our world.

The pictures themselves are a sign of the times. No. 1 son, Rob, sports a crew cut. Bill's, the now, is a little longer — and if John, our present graduate, hadn't been wearing his glasses, his hair would have flowed gently over his eyes. Seven years hence, when youngest son, Chuck, graduates, there will probably be no face visible at all. Only hair.

However that may be, the owl and I will be officiating somehow, that's a comforting thought. So, good luck graduates, wherever you are — and God be with you. With that combination you can't lose.

And congratulations parents! We've survived another one.

And if I sometimes feel like it would be nice to dismember my own parts, fold up my round little body and crawl in the shoe box with my owl to await the next high school graduation, I shall dismiss the thought as unworthy. As the motto of my class of '46 stated: "There's more beyond." — And how!

What Is A School?

November 1972

It seems to me as if I've been going to school for at least a thousand years, five hundred of them this fall. But the fact that I am a late bloomer, so to speak, education-wise, has given me the opportunity to have a unique viewpoint of the exciting things that are going on.

The trend toward individualization, for instance, and the stress of spotlighting strength and minimizing weakness. **Saying to the student, every student, "You are Somebody."** (Nobody ever said that to me in school, they said I was dumb in math and couldn't spell...and they are still saying it.)

So, I've been trying to figure out how to share with you some of these exciting things without boring the socks off of you and sounding preachy. Allan A. Glatthorn's "A New Catechism" states it beautifully. Some of you may have seen this, but I think it bears repeating.

Who is a Pupil?
A child of God, not a tool of the state.
Who is a teacher?
A guide, not a guard.
Who is the faculty?
A community of scholars, not a union of mechanics.
Who is the principal?
A master of teaching, not a master of teachers.
What is learning?
A journey, not a destination.
What is discovery?
Questioning the answers, not answering the questions.
What is the process?
Discovering ideas, not covering content.
What is the goal?
Opened minds, not closed issues.
What is the test?
Being and becoming, not remembering and reviewing.
What is a school?
Whatever we choose to make it.

From a teacher's standpoint, the things that are going on in education are very stimulating and a little frightening. Because a school board can make decisions and an administration can issue dictums and rules. **But if anything is going to happen in the classroom, there** is only one person that is going to make it happen. **The Teacher.**

Now, I'm sounding preachy. But I've studied these things from the viewpoint of a parent, and from the viewpoint of a school board member, and from the viewpoint of a student and from the viewpoint of a teacher.

And I've seen the beautiful things that can happen to students who are encouraged and allowed to prove that they are somebody, and that they are important. That the teacher cares!

I've also seen the havoc that can be created by the negative downgrading approach. It is up to us — parents, teachers, school board members, students, citizens — to see that the positive approach always happens and the negative approach never does. Because wherever you live, my friends, that last statement of Glatthorn's holds true:

What is a school? Whatever we choose to make it.

1973 — A College Degree — Finally!

May 1973

By the time you get around to reading this column, I will have graduated from college! **Although it is definitely an exhilarating feeling, it is also peculiarly embarrassing to graduate at 44.**

For one thing, it's the graduation talks. All that business about leaving the sheltered world of college and going out and facing life falls on jaundiced ears. (Mine!)

Then, it's the ambivalent feeling I have about degrees. Although I've worked my tail off for this one (figuratively speaking, unfortunately) I am not all that impressed. I think the reason is that I've watched the Wizard of Oz too many times.

Do you remember that poor straw man who went through so much heck just because he wanted a brain? Then the Wizard ends up handing him a diploma, saying something like "Where I come from, they use these instead of brains."

And I think we've all run into people like that. Lots of letters behind their names, but no knowledge of anything really very important or practical, such as how to get along with their fellow man.

We also know, at least I do, people who haven't had the opportunity for education beyond the 8th grade. But when it comes to passing out summa cum laudes for sensitivity, awareness and practical knowledge, they will be the ones that get them from the Teacher up there in the sky.

So, in spite of the fact that I've been wearing my cap and gown around the house for two weeks now, I think I have my achievement in the proper perspective.

But if I'd been inclined to get chesty about it (which for me would have been quite a trick), I took care of myself in my own Klutz-like fashion. Coming out of the chapel after the thanksgiving service, resplendent in cap and gown (so I thought), I was sweeping majestically down the steps when the flowing sleeve of the gown caught on the railing, causing me to stumble awkwardly down the remaining stairs. The story of my life.

I am graduating from and have taken the major portion of my courses with Mighty Little Mount Marty, and am grateful for their firm and uncompromising guidance. However, I have actually matriculated in six colleges. (Matriculated simply means to enroll, but when one graduates one says matriculate, you see. It has only one advantage and that is that it sounds a mite indecent.)

I spent my first year at Duchesne in Omaha. (Which is now defunct but I didn't have anything to do with that.) Then after the kids were all in school, I started taking a few courses here and there. Besides my work at Mt. Marty, I've taken Extension courses from the University of Nebraska and the University of South Dakota, summer sessions at Yankton College, special music workshop at Mary College in North Dakota, etc., etc.

But I never thought I'd ever graduate. And now I have! By golly! Son of a gun! Land a goshen! Whoopee!!! So, come by, y'all, and see my diploma. It's hanging right over the sink so I can watch it while I'm doing the dishes.

Ten Commandments For Meetings

My least favorite thing to do is go to meetings. That's not true of a lot of people. For some folks, meetings are their natural habitat, they enjoy them. **It seems to me if they don't have a meeting to go to, they call one.** Meetings being necessary, it would be easier if one felt that way.

I ran across an article in our National Federation of Press Women magazine, which if its suggestions were followed, would probably cut down on meetings by fifty percent, and on the length of meetings that much or more. And it just might be that we meeting haters would learn to like them. Well, we'd go anyway. It's called the "Ten Commandments for Meetings," by Lt. Col. George C. Wallace. It was printed in an Army Logistician magazine, and originally outlined while the writer was "attending a two-hour meeting that should have lasted

not more than 30 minutes."
Here they are:

1. Don't have a meeting unless it's necessary. Perhaps the information can be exchanged through phone calls.

2. Determine the purpose of the meeting. Will it produce a decision or provide information?

3. Prepare a specific agenda of key issues and distribute in advance.

4. Invite only those individuals necessary to accomplish the purpose of the meeting.

5. Determine who will chair the meeting. One person cannot control the meeting and actively participate at the same time.

6. Never schedule a meeting for the last hour of the working day unless absolutely necessary.

7. Make administrative arrangements. Should it be a sit-down or stand-up meeting? (Stand-up meetings save a lot of time!) Should it be a round-table discussion or classroom lecture? Have handouts and guidelines available if necessary.

8. Start on time. Latecomers will get the message.

9. Conduct the meeting in a firm, business like manner. Maintain control, summarize frequently, and cut off long-winded speakers when they have made their points.

10. At the end, sum up the conclusions, decisions, and follow-up actions, and circulate copies of the minutes if available.

Of course, all of these things are easier said than done. There are meetings and meetings. Some meetings are really just disguised social events. In our "out in the country club" for instance, we sometimes call a meeting to order and never remember to adjourn it. Just slips our minds.

And some meetings, if you insisted on starting on time, you'd be very lonely. Nobody's there. Of course, if you started on time a few times, they would be.

Also, it's hard to cut off a long-winded speaker. Especially if that speaker is somebody important. I remember a panel discussion a friend of mine was trying to chair. There was a Lt. Governor, a congressman, a senator, a distinguished columnist, and the president of an organization. None of them had much sense of time. And they were all interesting. It's just that the meeting began to look like it would never end. I guess a pre-planned signal would have worked here. Like you'd hit them over the head with a ball bat when the time was up.

In any case, meetings are a pain, but they are a necessary evil. They make the world go round. And round. And round. And round.

Gossip, The Snake That Poisons Everybody

February 1982
I've needed to write this column for a long time. **I've avoided it because the subject is unpleasant, and because I am just as guilty as the next person.** But it's a subject which I think it's necessary for all of us to look at — once in awhile. And maybe do a little thinking on.

I'm talking about gossip. Gossip is very interesting, and even worth repeating when it's about someone you don't particularly care about. It's when it hits close to home that you recognize it for the monster it is.

And let's face it, most of us gossip. In fact, according to one of the multitude of psychology books I've delved into, **all gossip isn't harmful. There's good gossip, and there's true gossip.** And people sometimes behave better than they otherwise would because they want to avoid gossip.

But there's the gossip that comes from an unknown source, with questionable facts, that is malicious.

They say people repeat that kind of gossip because by putting other people down, it makes them feel bigger and better. The people who have troubles of their own point the finger at others in order to cover theirs up. I suppose there's some truth in that.

But it's also true that without any malicious intent, people can misconstrue something they've seen, or misread a fact, and they can start a small story that will be blown completely out of proportion.

We've all played the gossip game where somebody whispers something into the ear of the player at one end of the line, and sees what kind of a crazy interpretation comes from the person at the other end after it has been whispered to each person. It's always wild and often very funny.

The problem is when it happens in real life it can do lots of hurt, and it's not funny. And it's always been with us. In 700 B.C., a fellow by the name of Hesiod wrote: Gossip is mischievous, light and easy to raise, but grievous to bear and hard to get rid of. No gossip ever dies away entirely. If many people voice it, it too is a kind of divinity."

Living in a small community is wonderful. I would not live elsewhere. But because we know each other so well, gossip gets to be a problem sometimes.

Long ago I cut this quote from some place, I don't remember where.

"The Snake That Poisons Everybody!"

"It topples governments, wrecks marriages, ruins careers, busts reputations, causes heartaches, nightmares, indigestion, spawns suspicion, generates grief, dispatches innocent people to cry in their pillows. Even its name hisses.

"It's called gossip. Office gossip. Shop gossip. Party gossip. It makes headlines and headaches. Before you repeat a story ask yourself:

Is it true? Is it fair? Is it necessary? If not, SHUT UP!"

Which brings to mind a verse by Ogden Nash:

"There are two kinds of people who blow through life with a breeze,
And one kind is the gossipers, and the other kind is the gossipees."

It would do us well to remember that there's a fine line in between. I've added a couple of lines to Nash's poem —

"Remember when a story comes round, and the gossiper you be,
To handle it with loving care, and shake it carefully,
To sift the lies and venom out, and let only truth fly free,
Cause the next time a story comes this route, you might be the gossipee."

The Stumbling Blocks And Walls Of Life

January 1983

I have a relative who used to be a terrible sport on the golf course. It was so embarrassing. He'd rage and holler and throw his clubs.

Then one summer he came up to visit and reluctantly we went out with him to play golf. And we had a wonderful time. He was relaxed and peaceful and just had fun.

"What happened to you?" I asked. He knew what I meant.

And he said, with a relieved sigh, "I just finally figured out that I was a rotten golfer. I'll never be anything else. So I would either have to quit playing or just decide to have fun."

And he decided to have fun.

I'm with him. What a sensible decision! He recognized one of the walls he had to deal with in his life and he sat down in its shade, so to speak, and was having a picnic.

The way I see it, we have two things that get in our way when we are deciding on our goals in life: stumbling blocks and walls.

Stumbling blocks are the worrisome things that come up that we can turn into stepping stones with perseverance and work and desire. Sometimes they are the Lord's directional signals. They say "slow down" or "try harder" or "detour."

Walls are something else again. They are the things we cannot do anything about, such as getting an irreversible disease, like diabetes. Or being crippled in an accident. Things with which we have to learn to live.

They can also be, in a very real sense, talents we would like but we just don't have. Accomplishments we aspire to for which we haven't a shred of innate ability. I could name four. How about you?

Face it! We each have our own set of talents. But sometimes we'd sure like the other fellow's. And we try so hard!

It won't work. **It's tough to admit there are some things we are not,** that we have our own personal walls. So we just bang our heads against those walls like a bunch of dummies. You know what we get? Headaches.

A good example of what I'm trying to say would be a baby learning to walk. The baby has stumbling blocks, literally. And if the first time that little tyke got up and fell down he said, "Well, that's it for walking!" he'd spend the rest of his life crawling. But a baby is persistence personified. He turns those stumbling blocks into stepping stones and not only learns to walk, but he runs and skips and jumps and roller skates. And that's what happens if we are persistent in the things we have the talent to do.

But suppose the baby says then, "Well, now that I've learned to walk, I guess I will learn to fly." Whammo! The kid has hit a wall. Human beings do not have flying equipment. Persistence won't help.

Well, there are some accomplishments in life which some of us do not have the innate ability to achieve. We'd just as well try to fly!

Unlike some of you, for instance, I will never win a math contest, par the golf course, sew a jacket, paint a picture, win a drink for four strikes in a row at the bowling alley. Things like that. Some of these things I don't try. Some I accept mediocrity and just have fun, like my nephew.

It's like the old saying, "If at first you don't succeed, try, try again. **But then if you don't succeed, try something else. Don't make a darned fool of yourself!"**

Assuaging The Itch Of Knowledge

June 1985

Five days a week, during the month of June, I'll be going to classes at Wayne State College, all day long. I'm working on my Masters in Psychological Counseling, and have been for a while now. Maybe all my life. It's lousing up my golf and making my friends crabby. "Are you ever going to quit going to school Burney?" they say.

It's a good question. I don't know. And I'm crabby with myself about it. A person should be able to let up. **But I have this urge within me, like an itch I can't scratch, to learn as much as I can cram into my mind about — well — my mind. And yours.** And Kip, bless his heart, familiar with the gleam I get in my eye when the itch strikes me, says "Go for it!"

The itch started to act up when I volunteered for the two years of training in Family Ministry under the auspices of the Archdiocese of Omaha. I learned with proper training you can be a lot of help to people when they need you. A lot of what you do is advise people to go to counselors. Counselors can do wonderful things.

So I got this urge to know what those counselors knew. I don't mean I want to go into the profession. I've got all the professions I can handle. I just want to have knowledge. If an opportunity arises, I can be part of the solution, not part of the problem. And I wanted to reinforce what I was saying in my columns and my speeches.

And just think, I could analyze all my friends. The lucky rascals.

So I'm working like a fool, but I love it. I feel right about it. The sponge of knowledge is assuaging my itch. The other graduate students and the instructors are marvelous characters. Column material abounds.

And I'm only kidding about analyzing my friends. I've tried that and if I'm not careful, I won't have any friends left. They tend to tell me to stuff it.

Seriously, the one thing that is repeatedly enforced is the importance of family and friends in our lives, and the love of those who are closest to us. A kindly reader sent me a poem about such things, which I've been wanting to share with you. This is a good time. It explains a lot of things, I think. Including why some people get an itch now and then.

No title. No author. It goes like this:

"...If nobody smiled, and nobody cared and nobody helped us along,

If every moment looked after itself and good things always went to the strong,

If nobody thought just a little about you and nobody cared about me,

And we stood all alone in the battle of life,

What a dreary old world this would be.

Life is sweet, just because of the friends we have made

And the things which in common we share.

We want to live on, not because of ourselves, but because of the people who care.

It is doing and giving for somebody else, on which all life's splendor depends.

And the joy of this world, when you've summed it all up, is found in the making of friends."

Nontraditional (Meaning "Old") Student Graduates Again

December 1986

"It was a day like all days, filled with events that alter and illuminate our times...and you were there."

Some of you may remember the show that ended with those ponderous words. It was called, I believe, "You Are There," Alister Cooke (or however he spells his name) was the host. (I think.) It supposedly reenacted days in history just as they happened. I liked the show a whole lot and the above quotation is forever implanted upon my brain.

It popped up as I was thinking about this column which will end one year and begin another. Across my mind marched a multitude of events — events which certainly altered and illuminated my times and some of which also affected yours. Looking over past columns, I see I have waxed eloquently, and not so eloquently, on a variety of subjects. We've been through a lot together. I rambled on to you about things I considered amusing, ranted about the explosion of the Challenger and poured my heart out about the death of our beloved Doc. Nothing alters one's life as much as the death of a loved one, and many of us have had to deal with that in this past year. Sometimes it seems as if we're constantly going through some stage of the grief cycle.

In the illumination department, this has been a year to end all years for me. A year of classes and tests, and testing myself. I celebrated these illuminating events on December 20th, when I graduated from Wayne State College with a Masters of Science in Education, with

155

my field of study being Psychological Counseling. **I don't even pretend to be modest about this accomplishment. I've never worked harder, nor deserved anything more.** And I've loved almost every minute of it. **Almost!**

Getting a Masters should be illuminating, it is only right and just. I've been educated and humbled and confused and enlightened and depressed and uplifted...and that's just by my fellow classmates. Two of them, Wayne's Marlene Uhing and Norfolk's Jean Doyle, were hooded the same day I was. Friendships made in counseling classes are special. Counseling classes are intimate, and for the most part, caring. The best of them become a semester long group session. One develops a comaraderie, an esprit des corps. It's like going through the war together.

The professors were an education in and of themselves, never mind what they were teaching. I took some fourteen classes with six different teachers. Their teaching styles were as varied as were their personalities. I watched carefully, trying to incorporate into my own being the things I thought worked especially well. One cannot really copy anyone else's style, but one can incorporate positive things into one's own.

One thing I've learned from my years of speaking and writing classes is the importance of listening carefully and heeding constructive criticism. If I get comments on a speech, and 400 people say it was wonderful, but three people have some criticism, I enjoy what the 400 people say but I look carefully at the criticism. And I learn and learn.

I see people go straight up in smoke when they're criticized, especially people who are new to a job. It is painful. But going up in smoke is a mistake. **Experience the pain and then get on with evaluating the criticism.** Evaluate carefully and evaluate sensibly. Consider the source. Dismiss what's not pertinent, and get on with the learning.

Part of success in any classroom is understanding what the teacher wants from you. Because I wanted so badly to learn what makes people tick, I studied with a passion and soaked up most classes like a sponge. And I enjoyed. However, the class on tests and measurements I never did like. Never! I learned — but if I had taken it first, I would have never taken another class. (That's what I mean by "almost!")

And so — life goes on. We look over the past year, learn from it, and start another one with enthusiasm. It was a year like all years, filled with events that alter and illuminate our time...And we were there.

Every Job Includes Some 'Manure'

February 1987

When our eldest son graduated from the University of Nebraska, he claimed that it said on the bottom of his diploma, **"This diploma guarantees the graduate will never have to clean out the hog house again."**

When our second son decided to give up farming and feeding, one of his reasons was he hated hauling manure.

Interesting thing was, when they got out into the world, they discovered that no matter what kind of a job a person has, there's always going to be some manure. That is, there is almost always some frustrating element in any position that equates to hauling manure.

The point is, no matter how much people like what they are doing, they usually have at least one thing to gripe about. City people with great jobs hate the traffic. People love their own jobs, but can't stand the person at the next desk. A teacher loves teaching, but hates lunchroom duty. A homemaker loves cooking, but hates doing dishes. Such things.

The problems mount when we spend so much time dwelling on the negative that the "manure" takes over and we forget the good parts.

There's ways we can evaluate this. Make one list with all the positive things about your life. Make another with all the negative things. Do this when you're calm and can be rational and realistic. If the negative aspects of a job, for instance, outweigh the positive, then it's time we were making some plans to change.

But if we mostly like what we're doing, then we just must decide to be philosophical about the parts we don't like. We can choose to do that, you know, or we can choose to whine around. We have the mental power. It happens in our heads. We choose to respond positively to life or we choose to make ourselves miserable.

To be fair, sometimes the item "Need to Eat" makes the whole list idea completely irrelevant. One of the facts of life is we have to make a living. But even then it's an attitude thing. Our task is to make the best of the situation, to (as the old song said) accentuate the positives and eliminate the negatives, as much as possible.

It's as important for people who are retired. **I guarantee you if you get up in the morning and say, "Well, this is going to be another miserable day,"** it will be. But if you get up and say, "I've got this day just once and I'm going to make the very best of it," you will do that too. If you simply start replacing the negative thoughts in your head with positive thoughts, you will have an enthusiasm for life you never dreamt possible.

However, if you're truly miserable at your job, if the manure is overwhelming you, seriously contemplate changing. Don't just blow up and get mad and quit. Plan your future realistically, looking at your marketable skills. Set goals for yourself. If you don't have marketable skills, opportunity awaits in all the terrific college outreach programs. Get busy and get some. Don't allow yourself to wallow in misery.

However, chances are when you make your lists you'll be surprised at how many positive things there are. Perhaps you really like your town, the people you work with, or even — praise Heaven — your job.

I know people who complain bitterly about what they're doing, but I know and they know they would be miserable doing anything else. If truth were to be known, they even like the stress. They just can't admit it or they wouldn't have anything to complain about.

Whining is boring. Take the people who keep harping on getting old. So what. Who isn't? George Burns said, "Some people practice being old. They groan when they sit down, they groan when they get up and pretty soon they've got it made, they're old."

Mark Twain had it all figured out. He said it's all mind over matter, if you don't mind, it doesn't matter.

Chapter Six

"Age is mind over matter,
if you don't mind, it doesn't matter."
Mark Twain

"Countless intellectually vigorous lives may have
atrophied on the mistaken assumption that
old age brings an unavoidable mental decline."
Psychology Today

Aging

Chapter Six

A sense of humor is essential to withstand the heat from the growing number of candles on your birthday cake. My interest in the newly discovered truths about how older people can remain young in spite of a number of years, has been fueled by the flame of those candles. As you can tell from the "keeper" essays included here (which pop up every year around the time of my birthday), I have become more militantly anti-aging with each year. You may think my outcry against accepting the vicissitudes of age without a battle has a ring of she who "protesteth too much." Just don't bet on it. I have a feeling that the new generation of increasingly vigorous and intellectually active elderly is going to be heard from. As far as the candles are concerned, you just watch our smoke. Read on . . .

* * *

If You Don't Mind, Age Doesn't Matter

October 1983

It's all in your attitude. "Age is a matter of mind," said Mark Twain. "If you don't mind, it doesn't matter."

And I don't mind. I consider having another birthday infinitely preferable to the alternative. Thus the news that I will be 55 years old on Sunday, October 30 does not depress me totally. Just think: The big double nickle. The speed limit.

It is a worthy enough occasion to make me feel I have the right to ruminate a bit on life. (Cows ruminate by chewing their cud, people ruminate by pondering.)

What I've ruminated up is that I can no longer deny I am middle-aged. Up to now, I've avoided the thought. **In fact, I'm still wondering what I'm going to be when I grow up.**

And I don't feel, mentally, any different than I did when I was 35. Or even 25. I don't know how a person who's 55 is supposed to feel, but I suspect everyone feels just as I do, about the same as always.

Erma Bombeck says that most middle-aged women are so confused about their identities and under so much stress that they can be found under their kitchen sinks, in a fetal position, nipping at the vanilla.

Occasionally, that thought occurs to me.

But I firmly believe, as with all else in life, we must accept growing older with a sense of humor. No use whining around about it.

Of course, it is true that after 40 the body just gets to be something of a maintenance problem. The eyes go first. That's a blessing. The Lord, in his wondrous wisdom, makes the eyes go first so you can't see what's happening to the rest of your body. Everything seems to develop a vague ache, and if it doesn't ache, it probably doesn't work.

One mustn't ponder on those things, however. If I've learned anything in 55 years, I've learned that it sometimes takes a real effort to enjoy life. And the secret of staying young at heart is maintaining enthusiasm.

So, if you can't think of anything to be enthusiastic about, it's up to you to find something. It's an awful thing to waste life by moping about in self-pity. It makes one curl in oneself and be a joy to no one.

Enthusiasm, on the other hand, begets enthusiasm. It is seductive.

If being 55 were going to depress me, which it (almost) doesn't, I would just have to consider what a lucky person I was. I have a husband who's still my friend, kids whom I love fiercely and who are more than interesting, a family who has been supportive no matter how silly I get, and friends who are warm and caring and fountains of enthusiasm in their own right — all those things. And I also have the creek to walk, merry-go-rounds to ride, songs to sing, coffee to smell, loved ones to hug.

But it's up to us to grab on to life and live it to the fullest. **Make things happen — don't wait around and feel bad because they didn't. And don't wait until tomorrow. Today is all we ever really have.**

Here's an example of how this works. If you're going to have a birthday and you're sure everybody will forget it and you know that will make you feel bad, help them remember. Put up signs. Make phone calls. Write a column.

It never fails. I'll be waiting by the mailbox beloved family and friends.

Bumps On The Road To Maturity

October 1984

Most of my life I've strived to gain some semblance of maturity. I've accepted the definition of experts that "Maturity is ability to assume the responsibility for your own actions."

And just when I've reached a plateau and I feel I've attained that enviable position, I do something really dumb and figure out that in my heart of hearts, I'm trying desperately to find somebody to blame it on.

Then a beloved relative gave me an article from an Al-Anon bulletin which defined maturity in another way. **"Maturity is the growing awareness that you are neither wonderful nor worthless."**

We (my beloved relative and I) were both delighted with this definition. Perfection is, after all, not a human attribute. Accepting that fact, we go a long way toward accepting ourselves for what we are, mentally and physically. It produces a comfortable self-esteem.

The article goes on: **"Maturity. . . has been said to be the making of a place between what is and what might be. It isn't a destination, it's a road.**

"It is the moment you wake up after some grief or staggering blow and think "I'm going to live after all!" It is the moment when you find out something you have long believed in isn't so, and parting with the old conviction, find out you are still you.

"The moment you discover that somebody can do your job as well as you can, and you go on doing it anyway.

"The moment you do the things you've always been afraid of.

"The moment you realize you are forever alone, but so is everyone else, and so — in some ways — you are more together than ever.

"And a hundred other moments when you find out who you are. It is letting life happen in its own good order, and making the most of what there is."

A comfortable and wise way to look at maturity. It is not a "destination," but a "road."

The road is sometimes bumpy. I'm sure each of you can look back in the last year and find times when you were admirably mature and times when you were not so admirable.

For instance, I felt tremendously mature when I realized I'd conquered my fear of flying. And when Kathy Wintz and I survived getting through New York's Kennedy Airport carrying all of our luggage and neither of us panicked or bawled, I was sure I could handle anything in a mature way.

But when I got off the plane in Sioux City, Iowa after a trip to Montana and found my car wouldn't start and I kicked the car, I realized I'd hit a bump on the maturity road.

This is a pattern with me, I have to admit. I am most mature about things that would bother a lot of people, but machines that don't work drive me crazy.

Ann Landers says, "Maturity is the ability to control anger and settle differences without violence or destruction. Patience and willingness to pass up immediate pleasure in favor of a long-time gain."

I'm working on it. Realizing it's a road, not a destination, helps. I will pat myself on the back for the times I demonstrate matureness, and understand myself a little better when I do not. I am not wonderful, after all. Neither, and you can bet on this, am I worthless.

It's a realization we can all live with. Maturely.

Age Wrinkles Skin, Not Minds, Souls

October 1984

This is probably the best news I've ever shared with you concerning mankind. Especially if you are — well — mature.

According to the latest research, "Intelligence does not decline with a person's aging."

I just celebrated my 56th birthday. I'm glad I did because it means I'm still around. A lot of people aren't. And age has never bothered me. I keep too busy to think about it. Yet, I can hardly believe I'm 56. When did that happen?

"Sunrise, Sunset" as they sing in Fiddler on the Roof, "Swiftly flow the years. One season following another, laden with happiness and tears."

But enough of this maudlin blathering.

Here's the good news: "The new research challenges beliefs long held by scientists and the public about aging and suggests that, among people who remain physically and emotionally healthy, some of the most important forms of intellectual growth can continue well into the '80s.' The '80s!

It also suggests that declines in intelligence can be reversed and that "earlier notions about the loss of brain cells as a person ages were in error."

But listen up, my friends, because a lot of what happens is up to the person doing the aging. To quote the experts, **"Countless intellectually vigorous lives may have atrophied on the mistaken assumption that old age brings an unavoidable mental decline."**

And to quote George Burns, "I see people who the minute they

163

get to be 65, start rehearsing to be old. They practice grunting when they sit down and practice grunting when they get up, and by the time they get to be 70, they've made it — they're a hit — they're old now!"

The eminent researcher on aging, Warner Schaie, said, "The expectation of a decline is a self-fulfilling prophecy."

Our key mental faculty, called "crystallized intelligence" continues to rise over the life span of healthy people. Crystallized intelligence is a person's ability to use an accumulated body of general information to make judgments and solve problems.

In practical terms, crystallized intelligence comes into play, for example, in understanding the arguments made in newspaper editorials. Or writing newspaper editorials. Or columns. We fondly hope.

There is a slight, but much slighter than we used to believe, decrease in what is called "fluid intelligence," the set of abilities "used in seeing and using abstract relationships and patterns." In other words, in remembering things like names or phone numbers, or playing chess. "At worst," the experts say, "this is a nuisance." People learn to compensate and it presents "no real problem for daily living."

We maintain these factors according to all the eminent researchers and George Burns, who is eminently old, in this way:

"Being mentally active. Well-educated people who continue their intellectual interests actually tend to increase their verbal intelligence through old age.

"Have a flexible personality. A longitudinal study found that those people most able to tolerate ambiguity and enjoy new experiences in middle age maintained their mental alertness best through old age.

"Staying socially involved. Among those who decline, deterioration is most rapid in old people who withdraw from life."

I am sure you can come up, as I can, with great examples in your own town, neighborhood or family. I have three lovely friends who are 80ish. When they were 75ish, they all went to town and got their ears pierced. They bowl (beat me) and are so feisty that you stay out of their way if they've got a bone to pick with you.

Ignore that old saying, "Life begins at 40." That's nonsense. Life begins every morning when you get up. Enthusiasm is the key word. People do not grow old by living a number of years, they grow old by deserting their ideals and giving up their enthusiasm. "Years just wrinkle the skin, but if you give up enthusiasm, that wrinkles the soul. There's no excuse for a wrinkled soul."

So let's get our little wrinkled butts in gear and go for it! As George

Burns says, "With a positive attitude and a little bit of luck, there's no reason you can't live to be 100. Once you've done that, you've really got it made because very few people die over 100.

Age Smooths Life's Sharp Corners

August 1984

When you get past 40, the wisdom of the depression days becomes a lesson in living, "patch it up, wear it out, make do or do without."

In one sense, life becomes a challenge: keeping all the parts in some semblance of a working order.

But in another, life becomes more enjoyable. It's a mellowing out process and I see it in a delightful way in all of my peers. (And myself.)

We'd all do well to live our lives according to the Serenity Prayer. You know it well. "Lord, give me the serenity to accept things I cannot change, the courage to change the things I can, and the wisdom to know the difference."

The hardest part is "the wisdom to know the difference."

You learn the hard way. When you're young, with the arrogance of youth, you sometimes look at someone else's problem and you say "I certainly wouldn't ever put up with something like that!" And then it happens to you. And you find out you put up with it.

And you look at the crosses some people have to bear. And you say, "I don't know how they stand it. I would never be able to survive that burden." And then that burden happens to you. And you survive.

And when you're young, you pray for things that become not so important as you grow older. As a kid, I prayed for material things. A new bicycle. Things like that. And my prayers were "deals." If you do this Lord, I'll do that. Payment on fulfillment of contract type of things.

I'd fuss about getting no answer, and my mom would say, "You got an answer, Joan. It was 'no!'"

The hardest thing in this "wisdom to know the difference" is the recognition you have no control over any other person. Just yourself. So no matter how smart you think you are about running everybody else's life, you're never going to get to do it. It's not your job.

Oh, we try. We know better, but we don't want people to make the mistakes we've made. We can't stand by and watch it happen. Oh, what a pain it is.

But there is no gain without pain, and you can't take the hurt out of life for others. You can cry with them, and pray with them, and

165

laugh with them. But you can't keep them from learning the hard way the "wisdom to know the difference." Just as we have, and continue to do.

There's a wonderful quote by Marcel Proust. I think it's wonderful anyway. When I look back and realize that some of the problems I thought were insurmountable have somehow gotten behind me, it helps me realize that I'll get through whatever is happening today, or is coming tomorrow. Because one does, and with the proper perception, one can get through them with some degree of enthusiasm.

Here 'tis: "We do not succeed in changing things according to our desire, but gradually, our desire changes. The situation we hoped to change because it was intolerable becomes unimportant. We have not managed to surmount the obstacle, as we were absolutely determined to do, but life has taken us around it, led us past it, and then if we turn round to gaze at the remote past, we can barely catch sight of it, so imperceptible has it become."

Experts Say We're Aging Better

At 70 years old, Christopher Isherood wrote the following: "If I had known when I was 21 that I should be as happy as I am now, I should have been sincerely shocked."

Most of the people I know who are rolling into their fifties, sixties, and seventies could make that statement. We are having a great time and don't feel nearly as old as we expected to. When we were kids, 30 seemed ancient. Now it seems everybody who's older is younger than they used to be when they were older. If you know what I mean.

For instance, the members of our bowling team, the infamous and noisy Black Russians (named after the drink, not the communists) range in the above mentioned age groups. I'm 58 and am almost, but not quite, the youngest. (By a mere and unimportant six months.) But when we get beat, which we often do, we get beat by teams who have members vigorously marching through their eighties.

There's nobody younger than octogenarian Jessie Dooley when she goes through all kinds of bodily gyrations to guide her bowling ball into the pocket for a strike. (And she gets them, too.)

The good news is that according to the latest issue of Psychology Today, it's not just that we think we feel younger because we have an older perspective, we feel younger because we are younger. "The attitudes of a 70-year-old today are equivalent to those of a 50-year-old a decade or two ago," say the experts.

Research has revealed that "healthy older people can maintain and enjoy most of their physical and mental abilities and even improve in some areas." And adds, "Because of better health care, improved diet and increasing interest in physical fitness, more people are reaching the ages of 65, 75 and older in excellent health. Their functional age is much younger than their chronological age." (See, I told you.)

The growing presence of healthy, vigorous older people is beginning to overcome the stereotypes about the elderly. Increasing numbers of older men and women are enrolled in colleges and universities. Gerontologist Barbara Ober says, "Older people make excellent students, maybe even better than 19- and 20-year-olds." Also younger people may have higher highs, but older people have more satisfaction because they "tend to judge their lives in more positive ways."

And — listen up you young squirts — many of the problems we associate with aging are not the result of age, but of disease, abuse and disuse — factors often under our own control. It's the old "If I'd known I was going to live this long, I'd have taken better care of myself" realization.

Wouldn't we all? This is a digression and nobody young will probably pay a bit of attention to it, but one of the things I did as a kid that I wish now I hadn't done was get a deep tan every summer. So now the skin covering my vigorous and otherwise healthy body, sprightly intellect and enthusiastic soul is beginning to look like a raisin.

No use crying over spilt sun beams. The important thing (at any age) is to stay active and feel useful.

Retirees should not vegetate but decide how to use their skills and pursue their interests. Bowl. Make plans. Take control. Studies show even people in nursing homes are happier if they have some control, such as choosing a plant or selecting which night they prefer to go to a movie.

And don't be afraid to try new things. Or even keep trying old things. Why not? Researchers talking about physical and mental fitness say people rust out faster from disuse than they wear out from overuse.

Use it or lose it. Okay?

Common Sense, Humor Best Allies

June 1986

"There you'll sit several hours, growing tenser each second,
fearing your fate will be worse than you reckoned,
till finally Miss Becker, you beckoner, beckons . . ."

There are two things that make life enjoyable as one grows older and one's body gets to be something of a maintenance problem. One is common sense and the other is your sense of humor.

With that in mind, I'm going to take you from Dr. Seuss's humorous approach to the problems of aging to Dr. Robin West's common sense approach to worrying about it.

Sometimes both worries hit at once. For instance, we're beset by aches in strange places and can't remember where we put our glasses so we can read the labels on which medicine one must take for which ache. We find ourselves saying, "Not only is the body going, the mind is going!"

Seuss's new book "You're Only Old Once," subtitled, "A Book for Obsolete Children," takes a humorous look at the horrendous process of going to the doctor for a complete checkup. How many of us, young and old, have not sat in a doctor's waiting room worrying and waiting "till finally Miss Becker, your beckoner, beckons . . ."

And longingly dreamt of living in a place where . . .

"everybody feels fine at a hundred and three
because they chew nuts from the tutt-a-tutt tree.
This gives strength to their teeth, and length to their hair,
and they live without doctors, with nary a care."

But, unfortunately, we find ourselves sitting . . .

"in the golden years clinic on Century Square
for spleen readjustment and muffler repair."

And about forgetting things. Occasionally (like often), I've forgotten something and somebody's said "It's Alzheimer's!" I haven't laughed. It's scary.

But according to Dr. Robin L. West, as quoted in a recent Ann Landers column, **"that's an inappropriate mindset." We've always mislaid things and forgotten things. But when we're young, we forgive ourselves and say it's caused by memory overload. Which is exactly what it's caused by when we're older.**

Anyway, if you're worrying about it that's a good sign.

Landers adds this comforting thought, "People who are facing Alzheimer's or senility are almost never aware of the symptoms. In fact, they are the last ones to realize that they are not behaving normally.

Besides, numerous studies now show that a challenged brain simply never quits learning. You can improve your mental capacity at any age by keeping your mind busy. The following exercises challenge different mechanisms in the brain and are good for all ages:

— **Practice foretelling the future, anticipating the way things will go.**

— **Use mental imagery to imagine yourself doing something well before you do it.**

— **Challenge yourself with new experiences.**

— **Learn a foreign language.**

— **Be sensitive and aware of little things around you.**

— **Do something physical to music.**

— **Challenge yourself mentally with crossword puzzles or mental skill games.**

Remember, "Age is a matter of mind. If you don't mind, it doesn't matter."

Chapter 7

"If you don't like the weather,
wait a minute..."
Somebody

"Everybody talks about the weather,
but nobody does anything about it."
Charles Dudley Warner

Weather

Chapter Seven

The following essays were chosen for their variety of weather reports. From sun-lit summer afternoons, to blustery blizzards, to gooey, glucky mud, to sumptuous Indian summer days, to the terror of possible tornadoes, to creeks careening out of control in a spring gully-washer, we have enjoyed and endured and survived. Through these essays we relive those days, as I give you Mother Nature in all her moods.

*   *   *

School Kids Move To Town In Snow Of '69 (But Pick Pillow Is Left Behind)

March 1969

I've moved to town for the fourth and last time. The fourth because of the mud and predicted snow, and the last because the owner of this house, the sainted mother of myself and six other characters, the grandmother of 49 assorted grandchildren, and the great-grandmother of 16, give or take a few, has decided to return from Florida for some mad reason and will arrive next week to take possession of what's left of her house.

It is really a shame because **I've just mastered the art of having everything I need in the place where I am NOT.** Sometimes pairs of things, such as shoes and gloves, are distributed equally between the places, rendering themselves completely useless.

At any rate, town is not a good place for me with my weakness. People. Especially people with coffee. I am a hopeless addict.

Then there is this other thing: I can't sleep. I have a pillow which I call my Pick pillow, without which I am nothing. It is full of goose feathers and was given to us on our wedding day, along with a mate, by Mr. and Mrs. Bill Pick, Sr. It is an unfortunate fact that Mr. Burney,

171

whom I also acquired on that unforgettable day, I can do without, at least for a few days especially since he is still shouting marching orders via the telephone but **without Mrs. Pick's goose feathers, I cannot sleep.**

I am sure that she plucked these feathers from her own private geese, and if any of my Pick friends know otherwise, I hope they won't tell me. I only feel pity in my heart for these poor youngsters that are growing up on the hygienic foam monstrosities that represent our modern day pillow.

I remember Mrs. Pick fondly for another reason, and I include this for that 25 years ago fans, for we aim to please. When we were in grade school in the dear old Holy Trinity School, that has since gone to its eternal reward, Mrs. Pick used to bring a huge cake made in the shape of a Santa Claus, at appropriately enough, Christmas time.

It used to be a real highlight, though I was always a little sad to see Santa disappear piece by piece down our little gullets.

It impresses me even more, in retrospect, because there were no cake mixes in those days. I guess I should make up my mind, for I suspect I can't have the cakes and goose feathers I remember while taking advantage of the cake mixes, dryers, etc., etc. But isn't it lovely to have memories to crawl into once in awhile to escape from the realities of today!

The Pain Of Rain NOT Falling On The Plains

July 1972

Think carefully. What would be the most ecstatic thing that could happen to you in the middle of the night in mid-July?

If you answer "Rain!" you get 100%. And if you are a farmer, I bet you answered rain.

But for those few of you who might have other answers, I will explain.

Rain in the middle of July in Cedar County has been almost unheard of for the past few years. We've watched our cornfields curl and our pastures dry up and dry thunderstorms come and go. And somehow our spirit sort of dries up too.

This year looked, until last night, like it might be more of the same.

And Kip has become such a pessimist about it that he is afraid to let himself believe that it even might rain. Last night, for instance, he and another farmer friend were watching the clouds pile up around

172

us and listening to the thunder rumble, and this is the way the conversation went:

"Probably just heat lightning."

"Yup, it's going to the south again."

"Going around us for sure."

"Yup, going to miss us again." Or something like that. On and on it went. And I thought it looked like it might rain.

So, in the middle of the night when I awoke to the unmistakable pitter-patter of little raindrops, I was just delighted. I poked the Old Bull-shipper and said ecstatically, "It's raining!" He grumped and snorted and finally grumbled "It won't last."

But I went back to sleep feeling just great. At least we were granted a reprieve. No curled up cornfields for a while.

And sure enough, when we got up in the morning we'd had an inch of rain. And what is more amazing, Hilary Hoesing, who lives south of us, also got JUST an inch. The reason that's amazing is because we've lived side by side for over twenty years and he's always gotten a half inch more rain than we have. That is, that's what he's claimed. Whether Kip telling him we'd just had a half an inch (a cheerful falsehood) had anything to do with it or not, I'll never know.

I just know it's great to get up in the morning and talk about last night's rain. (Farmers just love to talk about last night's rain.)

And this is the first time in several years that we've been able to do that in July. So now you know. If you hear raindrops in the middle of July, that somewhere there's a farmer smiling.

Snowed In — Winter Of '74

November 1974

Well, here we are — snowed in. And I'm out of eggs, butter and milk. How dumb can I get? I heard the weatherman say that there was a 70% chance of snow, but he'd been saying that about rain all summer and it never got here. And not once did it cross my mind that the first real snow of the season would be a blizzard. Who thinks of things like that when they are running around in a sweater on a balmy Indian-summer day?

And we didn't just get an ordinary blizzard. We got one of the wildest drift-raising blizzards many of us have ever seen. **All the neighbors agree with us that they've never had more snow on their places and that they've never seen drifts this high.**

George Huerta Romero, the Mexican exchange student who is stay-

173

ing with us, had never seen snow before. Oh — he'd seen it on the ground in the California mountains, but he'd never seen it coming out of the sky. The more it snowed and the more it blew, the bigger his eyes got. He bundled up and with the boys and Kip, went out in it to get hay to the cattle and when he came back in out of that wild storm, he just sat on a kitchen chair, a short Mexican bundle of clothes, and shook his head. When he finally got his voice back he said, "I could never believe this, I theenk." **What he didn't know is that we could hardly believe it ourselves.**

This much moisture is good news and bad news. The ground isn't frozen yet, so a lot of it should soak in. That's the good news. The bad news is that the ground isn't frozen yet, so a lot of us are going to sink in with it.

From what we've heard, the snow plows are having a devil of a time because they've got ice under the snow and mud under the ice. We have a hill that we have to go up immediately after turning off of Highway 15. That is, we have to go up it if we can. Lots of times we can't. The plows spent hours trying to open it going up — and when they couldn't, they came around at it from the backside and tried to open it going down, and got stuck. Gives you some idea of the condition of the roads.

So, if this column isn't in the papers, you'll know why.

Anyway, when you finally make your mind up that you are snowed in and there's nothing you can do about it, you sort of settle down and relax. Kip, of course, didn't give up going to the sale until the last minute. He much prefers getting snowed in someplace else. Then, the only reason he gave it up is that they called off the sale. **He said he could understand them calling off school for a blizzard but he never would understand calling off a sale.**

So, we did our usual blizzard things. We made popcorn and fudge (we gain a lot in the winter), and played pool and chess and poker and used up all the butter on the popcorn. Fortunately, I found some of the butter seasoned salt from my Weight Watcher days so we didn't have to quit making popcorn. But it doesn't work too well on toast or pancakes.

Problem is, the winter of '48 keeps running through our minds. You remember, the one where it started snowing the first part of November and we were snowed in until May. The rare times the road was open, you went to town and back fast because two hours later it would be blown shut. Should we have a replay of that, George will go home to Mexico, an expert in pool, chess, and cards, and say in perfect English, "Boy, have I seen snow!"

Burneys Mount Rescue Missions —
Birds, Beasts And Amorous Pheasant

1974

Dreary day marches relentlessly into dreary day, and it would seem a good time to review the high points of the past winter from the viewpoint of rescue missions accomplished right here on the Burney farm.

A tiny snow bird was the first victim of the winter to come our way. Tom found it in a lifeless condition and cradling it gently in his hands, brought it home and put it in a shoe box and fed it with an eyedropper. I was sure that the shoe box would be its final resting place, and when I came home from town one day and found our boring house cat, Muffin, sleeping contentedly by the shoe box, well — I thought Muffin was its final resting place.

Fortunately for happy endings, I was wrong. Tom had let the little fellow fly out of the house when he found it perched on a lamp shade singing its little heart out.

The second rescue mission was something of a replay. One of our steers fell through the ice into the lagoon. This is not an aesthetic experience for anyone, even a steer as number two son can attest to. Last year he fell in pulling last year's steer out. Since he (Bill) was in anyway, he pushed him (the steer) out from behind. This year, however, he used the tractor and a chain, a method which he heartily recommends.

The third victim of winter was a robin, a fat little fellow with a bad wing. He was hobbling around out in our yard, which is suicidal for four reasons, all of them cats.

I slipped out the back door to avoid the cats, and tried to catch the robin before they did. He remained one hop ahead of me, however, and I slithered and slid around like a clumsy oaf, trying to explain to the dumb bird that I was after him for his own good. He didn't buy that, of course, but my clumsy presence did force him to fly up into the honeysuckle hedge and then out into what had to be safer territory.

Our fourth rescue effort didn't even get off the ground, so to speak. It was a rooster pheasant that Kip spied sitting dejectedly outside of our bedroom window. He was the most pathetic sight I'd seen for some time. (The pheasant, not Kip.) His head drooped dejectedly and his whole body registered despair. He looked forlorn and bedraggled. Here was a bird in need if ever I'd seen one.

So I loaded up with food to tempt an ailing pheasant and headed out to do my good deed. The Florence Nightingale of the animal kingdom.

But I no more than got out the door when a dramatic transformation took place. **Right before my eyes, the ailing bird became a kingly creature. Head snapped up and jerked excitedly from side to side.** Whole body became erect and majestic. With sudden decisiveness, he started to prance across the field.

I couldn't believe my eyes. Kip looked across the field and started to laugh. "Your poor pheasant was in need all right, Joanie," he said, and following his glance I could see for myself what he meant. Because standing on the top of the dike were a couple of hen pheasants, coy as could be, and our boy was headed straight for them.

It was comforting in a way. Because, you see, snow on the ground notwithstanding, it was a sure sign that spring is here.

Snowed In Blues

For A Cattle Sale-Oholic No Risk Is Too Great
December 1975

Do you feel as if you are about to come down with a case of the screaming meemies? Do you suspect your children are growing horns? Is your spouse getting irritable or — more to the point — irritating? Do you have a tired back, tired eyes and tired blood?

Is it iron deficiency anemia? No!! It's the "snowed in" blues.

We've been snowed in for the better (?) part of two weeks and I knew we were in trouble when the kids started listening to the radio hoping they wouldn't call school off.

We're getting a little tired of each other. We've played pool, Yahtzee, poker, Monopoly, bridge, chess, gin rummy and the piano. This may sound to you as if we are passing the time amiably, but we are a family in which nobody loses gracefully (except at the piano). Somehow, they even seem to get to shouting and yelling over the 1000-piece jigsaw puzzle we're putting together on a card table in the living room.

It boggles the mind to think what kind of shape we would have been in by now, psychologically, if Kip hadn't managed to get to three cattle sales. He had to risk life and limb to do so, of course, but when one is a cattle sale-oholic, no risk is too great.

Because I know what a problem that is. I've tried for years to get a Cattle Feeders Anonymous started. I thought the victims of this

176

disease (and there are a lot of them in this area) could call each other when the market was too high, or they felt a terrible urge to go to a sale in the midst of a blizzard. Then they could talk each other out of it.

Now the reverse happens and they encourage each other in this feeder's folly. But they are a hardy lot and seem to survive. I think they must have a large guardian angel assigned to them. Probably one wearing a cowboy hat who has a little sinus trouble, so as not to be bothered by constant exposure to the pungent smells that cattle feeders seem to enjoy.

Whether the rest of us will survive if the winter keeps up like this is subject to doubt. I've talked to some of my friends in the neighborhood who've been snowed in with a whole passel of little ones underfoot. Their voices are getting shriller everyday.

One pointed out that it isn't as bad to get snowed in after Christmas because new games and toys are in abundance. But by now everything is worn out or broken up and they are having the uneasy feeling that before long they will be worn out or broken up also.

I have a trick I do to make the winter bearable when it is — in fact — not. When we have a particularly bad moment — as when the weatherman smiles cheerfully into the TV camera and points to the incoming snow front and I have an uncontrollable urge to break his face (poor fellow), I simply lean back, shut my eyes and conjure up a favorite summer memory.

I will imagine myself bouncing in an innertube on the waves of Lewis and Clark Lake with a bottle of pop in one hand, looking at a fleecy cloud sail across the blue sky.

Or sitting on the sand around a roaring bonfire roasting marshmallows and singing songs.

Or sitting in a boat in the middle of the lake with a fishing pole in one hand, soaking up the hot summer sun.

Now that you have the idea — try it. Think of your favorite summer memory. If you are a golfer, drag out the feeling you had when you made your longest putt. If you are a gardener, remember planting the seeds in the warm earth. Shut your eyes and relive it — and see how the tension eases.

Bad memories work also. Negatively, of course, but we are merely looking for relief. I remember standing in the line at the "Worlds of Fun" in 100 degree heat for 45 minutes to ride on the sky ride. That almost made the blizzard palatable.

We store up these memories consciously in the summer, having had many years' experience with wild Nebraska winters. For instance,

I say to the kids — when we're bouncing around in the innertubes — "store this memory up, we'll need it this winter." It not only helps in the winter, it adds a degree of awareness to the enjoyment you are experiencing at the time. Try it — you'll like it.

1978 — The Year We Finally Had Enough Rain

August 1978

Ferdie Pietz, my good friend and our local auctioneer-philosopher, took me aside at the grocery store the other day and imparted some wisdom.

"When you go home, young lady," he said, "just look around. You've never seen it look like this, this time of year." (The reason he is my good friend is he always calls me "young lady.")

Anyway, Ferdie, who's going to celebrate his 50th wedding anniversary very soon, said that he's never seen it look this good either. And he has a few years on me.

So, since I always do what Ferdie tells me, I came home, parked on the hill above our little red house, and I looked around.

Ferdie was right. This time of year I've never seen it like this. Usually, everything would be brown and dead-looking. There would be a good reason for that . . . it would have been dead.

And the creek would have been barely a trickle, probably dry.

And the cattle would have been standing on near-barren pastures. And dust would be blowing. And my flower gardens, such as they are, would have been sparse and anemic-looking.

But what to my wondering eye should appear but lush looking green! A flowing stream. Cattle standing in pastures belly-high. A pastoral scene so luxuriant-looking it takes one's breath away.

And my flower gardens are incredible. Blooms tumbling all over each other. Sweet alyssum actually growing out into the yard and between the cracks in the sidewalk. Double petunias vying with bright red geraniums in unbelievable abundance as they reach toward the sky.

The whole thing, of course, is that we got an unheard-of eight inches of rain (or more) in July. The earth has responded in gratitude and awarded us with an abundance of flora. **We must drink it in visually, and record this year in our hearts. 1978 . . . the year we finally had enough rain.**

Ferdie's words come back to me again: "We probably aren't going to see anything like it again."

I refuse to think about that as I sit on my hill looking over our beloved valley. I think only that this is the way it's supposed to be. A little like the Garden of Eden, certainly. Before the blamed serpent got in the act.

As if to bring me back to reality, a grasshopper jumps in my window. And a corn borer moth flutters by. So...the blamed serpent is doubtless, in his own way, still in the act.

But nothing can take this perfect time away from us. And during future droughts and parched Augusts, we can say to our grandchildren: "You should have seen the August of 1978."

And they can say, bored to death, "Yes, Grandperson, you've told us about that before!"

And we'll forgive them if they're bored. Cause they can't possibly know what it was like. We can only hope that sometime in their life they'll experience this kind of day, and they'll have somebody like Ferdie Pietz to call it to their attention.

And Then Came The Mud, The Mud, The Mud!

March 1979

And then came the mud! It's been one of those winters, but we could see the light at the end of the tunnel. Or, to be more accurate, two dry tracks on our country road.

We don't ask much, you understand, and the two tracks signified to us the beginning of spring, and the end of what's seemed to be the longest, and coldest and meanest winter we've had since — well — last winter.

Now, by two dry tracks I mean just that: two ruts down the center of the road which bear one vehicle in some degree of safety. Woe betide anyone who strays from those ruts. But then, as the days linger on, the ruts become so deep that straying from them becomes well nigh impossible.

There's always the chance that you might meet a car, necessitating moving to the soft shoulder. How does one do this? Verrrrrry carefully.

Also along this route there remain some large mud puddles where the road doesn't drain and the drifts are melting inward instead of down the ditches.

179

These are a challenge. One must get up enough speed to plow through them, but not so much that they go careening out the other side.

All of this is possible and the need to get to town or just get out, makes most farmers and farmers' wives masters at negotiating the roads.

Until, that is, it starts to rain. Then the tracks fill up like rivers and the large mud puddles become bottomless pits. Gravel seems non-existent, and when one starts to slide on the slithery mess, one just keeps sliding. At least one of our cars ended up hind-side backwards on the bottom of a steep hill.

The grown-up child who put it there hadn't driven in mud for some time. Kip claims that after all the drought years we've had, some of our kids hadn't ever seen mud. But in this case, she confused her father's shouted orders for ice as pertaining to mud. "I thought I wasn't supposed to put on the brakes," she said in her own defense.

"That's ice!!" shouted her father. **He thinks if he shouts it will somehow be an order which is indelibly imprinted on their brains.**

Anyway, she didn't (put on the brake, that is) and careened from one side to the other before making a circle and sliding into the ditch on the wrong side backwards.

One needs to put on the brakes in mud and with mud tires, the car will grunch grudgingly to a halt, allowing one to creep onward. "Creep" is the key word here. This is just in case you city folks decide to pay us a visit.

My advice is, however, not to travel the country roads unless you are very, very sure that they are passable. Most of them are just barely so, but some of them won't be for a long, long time. And then it's wise to have a four-wheel-drive vehicle of some kind.

As I'm writing this, the weather forecaster has just announced that we might expect snow showers later today. Here we go again. We've already shoveled enough mud out of our garage to build a dike. A person could get upset, get upset, get upset, get upset, get upset!

Enjoy Soul-Satisfying Spring

June 1979

Everything is lookin' good! I griped so much about the weather and the roads last winter and this spring that I thought I owed Mother Nature an apology and a vote of thanks for these last few days.

I can drive down our gravel road with nary a rut to impede my progress. I can look out my picture window and see nothing but lush green pasture and rich black cornfields with the corn just starting to show in the rows. There isn't a snowdrift or an ice patch in sight.

We had some snowdrifts which I thought would surely last until July. They are gone, gone, gone.

"This is why I like this country," a friend of mine said, "because when we get a good day we appreciate it so very much."

This is, without a doubt, the most beautiful time of year. With the lilacs in bloom, their delicate scent greeting you at every turn, and the green so fresh and — well — green.

I know, I know. In the fall I say that's the most beautiful time of year. I like summer too. And even winter, right at the beginning anyway. But right now, spring is the best, and it will not be here for long.

So, get out and enjoy. Take time to smell the lilacs. Eat strawberries. If the people who grew and picked and sold strawberries knew how much joy they were giving us strawberry lovers, they'd have to feel good.

I am slightly allergic to strawberries, but I eat them anyway. Gorge on them is a more accurate description. Then I itch and scratch happily away. Sometimes the pleasure is worth the pain.

I have a friend who gets deathly ill if she eats highly spiced foods, but she is plumb nuts about Mexican food. And sometimes she just can't stand it any longer, so she goes out and has some anyway. **Once in awhile," she says, holding her aching tummy, "a person just has to do it!"**

I'm not condoning this, you understand I think it's dumb. I also think it's very human. We're not perfect, you know, any of us. So if we accept that, we will forgive ourselves for our occasional foolishness and spend most of the time being sensible.

In any case, there are a lot of things to do in the spring which will neither make you itch nor your tummy ache. Take a long soul-satisfying walk with the animal or person of your choice.

Go fishing. If you don't like to put worms on the hook or take the fish off, just go and hold a pole like I do. There's something soul-satisfying about fishing.

Sit on your porch and watch the people go by and smell the lilacs. There's something soul-satisfying about sitting on a porch. Worst thing that happened in architecture was the disappearance of the front porch.

In fact, there's something soul-satisfying about spring. Excuse me while I munch on another strawberry, scratch a slight itch, and lean back and enjoy.

Thanksgiving '79 — House Guests Become Hostages

November 1979

The snow descended in huge flakes, making the world beautiful but rendering the vehicles of man impotent.

No car would move, four-wheel-drive vehicles slowly ground to a stop, and even tractors floundered in the gathering flakes, hampered even more by the soggy ground underneath.

Kids slithered or were pulled in from schools and jobs, everyone arrived after somewhat harrowing journeys on icy highways.

Many a Thanksgiving gathering, however, had people missing, scattered all over the snow area in an attempt to get home.

And others celebrated with strange meals, since gatherings around here are often cooperative affairs, leaving one family with all the salads, one with the pies, and one with a gigantic turkey.

Our gathering was actually enhanced by the storm, since we insisted our snow-bound hired man and his wife come up the hill and join us.

Country roads were impassable, leaving some families, like my friend Marge Seim, with gobs of cooked food and no company, and all her company in town with no cooked food.

Frustrating to say the least.

Funny thing, wasn't but a few hours after the kids nearly broke their necks to get home that they realized we were snowed in and they couldn't get out. From then on, every effort was made to counteract Mother Nature's dictum. Only loud noises from the father of the family kept them from heading out in the full blast of the blizzard just to see if they could get out.

Finally, on Thanksgiving night, after the boys opened the roads and moved a few drifts, and the roads froze, Kip said, "I guess it's time we released the hostages!"

182

And five young people scattered to the four winds. Kip said, "I can't remember ever being so antsy when the roads were bad!"

I reminded him of the time he took 13 runs at the Marsh hill to get us to town and ruined the transmission in the process.

"Yup," he said, and forgetting the whole premise of his argument added with some pride, "but I got out!"

People don't really change, they just get older and forget a lot.

Hail The Size Of Tennis Balls

June 1980

I never really believed the stories about tennis ball sized hailstones until Mother Nature played her destructive game and I saw them bouncing around our front yard.

It was fifteen minutes till five o'clock on Friday the 13th. Appropriately. I know the time because I was just backing the car out of the garage to get my columns to town to catch the mailman at five o'clock.

My deadline for my columns is actually Thursday, however, Friday is the absolute last minute. So, I am usually heading into town at fifteen minutes to five to catch the mailman.

I have never seen it hail like it hailed that late afternoon. It was as if Mother Nature had gone on a rampage and was waging war on the earth. I watched as our windows got broken and the little flowers I'd so carefully planted in our gardens got obliterated.

We launched a heroic and stupid effort to save a baby kitten, but other than that we just sat and watched, horrified.

The poor cattle were racing back and forth looking for protection when there wasn't any.

It lasted a long time; I think twenty or thirty minutes. Needless to say, I didn't get my columns in the mail. Someone measured one of the hailstones at 4½ inches around.

At that, we were on the edge of the storm. More damage on one side of our farm than the other. Still not as much as the farms to the west of us received.

Just before I headed to town with my columns, got cluncked by a hailstone, and pulled back into the garage, I was holding forth to whomsoever would listen in this house about how silly it was to be superstitious about Friday the 13th. "That's just a bunch of bologna," I said. "After all, your dad and I got married on the 13th, we live in 13 county, everybody in the area has 13 on their license plate. Actually, it's a lucky number."

183

I still think that's true. I could have been (should have been) on the road when it struck. And when I was bemoaning the state of all my flowers to my cousin who lives up the road, she said, **"How would you feel about 1800 acres of cropland?"** But she added, **"If we had to have something, this was 100 percent preferable to the tornadoes those poor people got in Grand Island."** And it was.

The Year The Bridge Club Got Snowed In

February 1982

Blizzards spawn adventure, of a sort. Problems crop up that would boggle the minds of our pioneer forefathers. For instance, they never had to worry about the gas running out, to say nothing of running out of Pampers. And they certainly didn't have a bridge club that spent the night.

My brother and his wife, who live in rural Yankton, had two grandchildren visiting when the blizzard hit. Although one does not choose to get snowed in with grandchildren, when it happens, one copes. My sister-in-law is one of those rare people who can make almost any situation into an adventure and even a festive occasion. They were getting along fine, until their gas tank was empty. Well, there's no getting gas in a blizzard, so they ended up winding their way through the snowdrifts to stay at a neighbor's home. **"It's something to move in with the neighbors anyway,"** said my sister-in-law, **"but imagine moving in with your grandchildren."**

A grandchild was the problem in a rural Hartington home, too. A friend of mine was babysitting just for a day when in came the blizzard. Her kids couldn't get their kids, so she settled down to cope also, but she ran out of Pampers. ("This wouldn't have happened in our day," she muttered.)

She was able to scrounge around and find some ancient diapers, but the problem was ancient diapers call for rubber pants.

Of course, one can improvise. Possibly plastic bags would do the trick. They turned out to be too narrow one way and too wide the other. In desperation, she was just starting to experiment with Saran Wrap when it occurred to her that her neighbor might have a pair of rubber pants left over from yesteryear. A phone call brought an affirmative response, so Grandpa hopped on to a tractor and forged the drifts in the blizzard to get them. Greater love has no man...

When we had children, we were very careful about traversing one-way roads, that is, roads with only one way carefully carved out by our knights in shining armor, the snow plow operators. **But with no "responsibilities," we apparently get dumber. That's why the bridge club ended up snowed in at our house.**

We'd actually ridden with two couples from town to our neighbors, the Millers, who live two miles west of us. When the wind came up, we made a dash for home, but we didn't quite make it. It took a kindly neighbor, Dennis Arens, a snow blower and a shovel to get us home, and that one-mile trip took an hour. The town folk stayed here, needless to say.

That's the third time this year I've learned my lesson about being out on lousy roads when the weather is erratic. One-way roads become no-way roads in a hurry when you've got 18 inches of loose snow and the wind suddenly comes up.

Fortunately, the warm weather we've just had has put a crust on the snow, and though the wind has done its best to disrupt the snow since that time, it's pretty well settled.

So now we've learned again. We'll fill our tanks with gas, our cupboards with Pampers, our shelves with groceries, our minds with common sense, and be prepared for the rest of this wild winter.

But remember, "If we had no winter, the spring would not be so pleasant; if we did not sometimes taste of adversity, prosperity would not be so welcomed." AMEN!

Taking It Out On The Poor Weatherman

April 1982

Weather forecasters, beware! Your lives may be in peril.

Ancient instincts even now may be boiling up in your listeners. Winter will not wane, and your popularity is skating on thin ice. We are well into spring, and the view outside my window would be more appropriate on Christmas Eve. Enough, already.

In ancient days you would have been long gone. According to the books and articles in my own personal archives, there is good evidence that it was a common practice to kill the messenger who brought bad news.

People who dispense news for a living always have had to put up with this phenomenon. There seems to be an inability to distinguish the reporters of bad news from the people or things that make bad news happen.

Egyptian pharoahs, Greek kings and Chinese emperors are reputed to have made a common practice of executing the messengers who brought bad news.

In the second book of Samuel it says that David had an Amalekite killed because he brought him the news of the death of Saul.

Sophocles wrote about a sentry who had to deliver bad news to King Creon and said, "But we knew you had to be told the news and one of us had to do it. We threw the dice, and I lost. I'm no happier to be here than you are to have me. Nobody likes the man who brings bad news."

In fact, there are those who think it would be better to keep bad news from others. In "Anthony and Cleopatra," Shakespeare has Cleopatra say, **"Though it be honest, it is never good to bring bad news."**

We can't help ourselves. We prefer good news. Adlai Stevenson said in 1958, "You will find that the truth is often unpopular and the contest between agreeable fancy and disagreeable fact is unequal. For, in the vernacular, we Americans are suckers for good news."

Nonetheless, we have to be prepared. And the true forecast, no matter how peculiar to the season, is necessary.

"There is nothing as powerful as truth," said Daniel Webster, "and nothing so strange."

But our taste of spring was so brief. We'd hoped for more. Patrick Henry spoke to that point, and though he was not talking about the weather, he might have been.

"It is natural for man to indulge in the illusion of hope. We are apt to shut our eyes against a painful truth," said Henry, and going on at some length about it, he concluded, "I am willing to know the whole truth, to know the worst, and to provide for it."

And so are we. But we don't have to be happy about it. So if we have the desire to bash a weatherman in the head as the snow continues to fall, perhaps it will help to know that it comes of an innate instinct deeply rooted in our subconscious.

Perhaps before this column even hits print, they will have changed their dour faces to smiling ones and be predicting warm weather and sunshine.

Suppressing our ancient instincts to "kill the messenger," we would do well to remember the hapless sentry of Sophocles' tome. Forecasters doubtless feel "I'm no happier to be here than you are to have me."

186

Don't Wait Until 'Some Day,' Do It Now!

June 1982

Summer is upon us, and it behooves a good columnist to remind her readers to take time to smell the roses. Sometimes a little reminder is all a person needs.

Because you know as well as I do that before we can even blink an eyelash, summer will be over. And we will be muttering to ourselves about all the things we meant to do but didn't.

For instance, if we aren't very careful to work it in, Marie Huck and I will not have had our picnic at Butterfly Creek, a sassy little stream that meanders around someplace south of Stanton. We crossed it in the middle of a blizzard two years ago and because Marie is a butterfly nut, and I love little streams, we both agreed that come summer we would come back and have a picnic. We haven't done that yet. Surely we will this summer.

And if we don't steal the time from whatever dumb thing it is we have to do, our exercise (ha!) club will not get to the lake for their annual wilderness appreciation day. We've already missed the lilacs because we were all "too busy." **Lilacs don't wait for anybody. One has to make time for the lilacs, or one is the lesser for it.**

And if we aren't careful, we'll never work in that hot dog at the ball game we promised ourselves, and we'll never see the warm smile of appreciation on an elderly friend's face when we take her a jar of fresh homemade chokecherry jelly.

We will have planted the flowers in our yards and around our gardens and tended them with great business, but if we don't have the time to sit in the sun and admire them, we will have missed the whole point. One of Mother Nature's greatest wonders is a sunny summer day. But if we don't sit down for a minute and let that sun seep into our soul, what good does it do her — or us?

"I can't do these silly things," you say. "I'm a busy person!" I know. I say that too. But then I look at my bulletin board and on it I have a little poem that I cut out of my friend, Gwen Lindberg's column many months ago. She borrowed it from somebody else. And she listens to the words too. I know.

187

When I Have Time

When I have time, there's a poem to be written, a song to be sung.
When I have time, there's a child to be led, a prayer to be said.
When I have time, I'll tell you a story, I'll visit a friend.
Alas, time is gone.
The poem's unwritten, the song unsung.
The child grew up to be a man, the prayer went unsaid.
The story's untold, the friend is dead.
For what momentous affair did I neglect,
A poem, a song, a child, a friend?
Was it a dirty dish or an unmade bed?

I thought you might like to have this for your bulletin board too. Together, let's make up our minds to celebrate life this summer, my friends. We still have that precious commodity — time. And summer stretches before us with glorious opportunities. **Let's not wait for when. "When" is now!**

Fall Freeloading On Gardener Friends

October 1982

The coming of frost is almost a blessing to some of my friends, whose vegetable gardens have been producing at such a staggering rate that they are almost inundated with canned and frozen goods and sick to death of canning and freezing.

I admit I have a little pang of guilt when I stop at my friend Helen's house. She lives in town. I load up on tomatoes and take them to the country. By rights, it should be the country lady unloading on the town lady.

Their bountiful gardens work to my advantage. **I don't have much of a garden. But I don't have one purposely — just for my friends. What would they do with their surplus if they didn't have me around to gobble it all up?"**

One has to develp patience if one is leeching off of one's friend's gardens. One will probably not get at the fruit of their vine until one's friends have had their fill. It's a small price to pay. In a good year, like this year for instance, it is not long before one's friends have their fill. Tomatoes and green beans and cucumbers and zucchinis appear miraculously on my kitchen table. It's wonderful.

I've had my try at gardening in a big way. One year I planted 40 tomato plants. Fortunately for me, the cattle got out and trampled

188

most of them into the ground.

Once I put a garden in so early in the spring that I was the laughing stock of all the "good" gardeners. "You silly fool," they scoffed and derided, "everything will freeze!"

By some miracle we had no late frost that year and everything grew. Needless to say, I had the first cucumbers in the neighborhood. I could hardly wait to distribute them to my unbelieving gardener friends. My family never saw a cucumber, of course. First things first.

However, that silly garden began to flourish and grow and grow and flourish. I began to panic. I love to plant, and delight in the first fruits of my planting, but I'm not crazy about the continual harvesting. I felt trapped by this crazy garden. I considered letting the cattle out to trample it or a pig or two to root it up. Finally, in a kind of desperation, I just let the weeds grow so I couldn't see it anymore.

You're shocked! So am I. It's disgusting. But one has to recognize one's weaknesses and work with them. I am not the world's most enthusiastic gardener. In fact, if I can manage it, I'm not a gardener at all.

But come harvest time, I am like the grasshopper who fiddled while the ants were at work. I don't have any freshly picked vegetables. I love freshly picked vegetables.

So I hang around the houses of my friends looking forlorn and neglected until they take pity on me. "Would you like some tomatoes?" they say.

"Would I!" I cry, jumping up and down like Snoopy doing his dinner dance. Then I take out the huge shopping bag I've hidden on my person and say more decorously, "Perhaps just a few!"

Snowbound In '83 And Loving Every Minute

December 1983

Strange things happen at our house when a blizzard sets in. Kip gets wilder and I get calmer. As we begin to realize that this time the weathermen are right, the men around here get restless, then unhappy, and proceed right to miserable. They know the work a blizzard entails, and that is part of it, but that isn't all. Men can hardly stand being snowbound.

First, the cattle sales are out. One can't get out of town, much less to sale barns. Kip begins to experience withdrawal symptoms. He starts to pace from window to window, listening to weather reports as he goes.

And it gets worse, and even going to town is out. So bowling and gin rummy with his cohorts in the geriatrics league is out. And the pacing becomes frenetic.

And still it gets worse. Until even going out is out. The men are stuck, as it were, in the house. Snow has swirled in "humungous" drifts around every door. Wild frustrations set in. **Although this has happened almost every winter in our life on the farm, the men can't seem to believe it.**

On the other hand, women nestle in when a blizzard hits. In the first place, hearing the forecast and believing it, they've laid in enough supplies to survive for a couple of years. They put on a pot of soup, bake cookies, and hum merrily.

As snow flakes pile upon snow flakes, they take out their knitting, clean out drawers, read books, and just enjoy the momentary, complete respite from the intrusion of the outside world. Can't go to meetings. Don't have to worry about unexpected company. What a delicious feeling.

Blizzards always seem to strike around holidays and that's the worst thing. Two years ago, you will remember, a pre-Thanksgiving blizzard hit just as all the kids were trying to get home. We had family coming in from four directions and it was a very frightening time.

Daughter Juli slithered in from Vermillion, South Dakota on solid ice and had to be helped out of ditches several times. Almost everybody had to be pulled up the hill on our country road. Finally, they all got home and I breathed a sigh of relief.

With this whole tribe of young adults, we had a very merry Thanksgiving dinner.

But all of a sudden, for them, reality set in. They were stuck at home. I mean, they really wanted to get home, but they certainly hadn't planned on staying home. Home is just a fuel stop. And they began to pace like caged animals, along with their father.

Many of you know exactly what happened. They worked just as hard at digging out as they had digging in. Kip's basic rule that nothing moves away from home until the cattle are taken care of got him enthusiastic help in that department, and then, with snow blower and loader, they hit the road.

By nightfall on Thanksgiving Day, we were again alone, with the cats gnawing contentedly on the turkey bones and Kip participating in his last choice of something to do, playing gin rummy with me. (In 10 years of playing, I owe him $86.30.)

So you see, strange things do happen during blizzards. Too bad you can't stop by.

The Joys Of Popcorn

November 1984

I was awakened the other night by a howling wind and an intense desire for popcorn.

It sounded as if we were having a blizzard, and for the thirty-seven years of our married life, we have munched our way through every blizzard. When the wind cranks up outside, someone automatically goes to the kitchen and cranks up our battered old cornpopper.

In the early years, we popped corn in an iron skillet, shaking it vigorously back and forth on the stove. The sound of the scraping of the pan was soon lost in the crescendo of joyously popping kernels. Until the popping would slow down, and the shaking. Carefully the popper would remove the lid, and "ka-pow!" a couple of kernels would fire away. It never failed.

Then we'd pour the melted butter over the top, wave a salt shaker over all, and dig in.

The smell would permeate the whole house, so people would rise out of every room and head like zombies to the kitchen.

Other favorite popcorn memories flood in. A movie is not a movie without popcorn. I usually say I don't want any, and then eat all of Kip's. I say that because I'm always intending to diet, and I never do.

Kip's on to me, however, and he buys me my own whether I claim to want any or not. Who can resist popcorn?

Almost nobody, it would seem, because Americans eat some 500 million pounds a year, according to a Reader's Digest article.

It is also claimed that eating popcorn has a therapeutic value, and the American Cancer Society (Illinois Division) lists eating popcorn among its recommended non-carcinogenic activities, along with sitting in the shade and having a good laugh.

Popcorn dates back thousands of years. Archeologists excavating in Mexico unearthed preserved cobs. American Indians presented it to Pilgrims as a gift.

And it's becoming sophisticated. From the favorite caramel corn to chocolate popcorn, 65 flavors have been developed, including jalapino, strawberry, amaretto, pizza, clam-chowder, watermelon and licorice.

Just plain old popcorn is irresistible to me. In fact, time and weight and health considerations have made our popcorn plainer rather than fancier. We no longer pile on gobs of melted butter. Nor do we wave the salt shaker over the top with such vigor.

It makes no difference. If I were to isolate the elements of my life which have made living enjoyable through the years one would be popcorn. It would include the smell of popcorn wafting through the house, and the memory of a whole houseful of kids munching away. The fierceness of the blizzard paled in significance, always, as we warmed ourselves on huge bowls of popcorn in the coziness of our snug little red house.

Three cheers for Orville Redenbacher.

Cross Your Bridges — Tomorrow They May Be Gone

December 1984

Except for one startling exception, the view out my office window this morning would be a perfect one on which to peacefully meditate — a pastoral view of calming serenity.

I write on a crisp wintery day, looking out on hills that stretch as far as the eye can see, a subdued patchwork quilt of grays, golds and browns. A tinge of white frosts my picture. I am thankful it's just a tinge. In past years it has been mountains of white, and Kip's beloved cattle, who are now munching peacefully in snowless feed yards, were up to their bellies in snow which foretold the mud and yuk to come.

And past years were nightmares for travelers during the holiday season. We spent many days of the holidays with fear clutching our innards as loved ones traveled the roads.

Not so this year. Fall has given us some perfect days, and we greet each one incredulously. "Can you believe this day?" we say to each other, reveling in each as if it would be our last because we truly believed it would.

And with a decent November under our belts, we consider the possibility, the wondrous possibility, that we may be in for a mild winter. We're entitled. It's about time.

My suspicion of Mother Nature and all her tricks is heightened by the startling exception to the calming influence of my view.

This is because the eastern end of my view is a bustling flurry of activity. Cranes and trucks and earth moving equipment and men and giant hunks of steel are working together to put to rights Mother Nature's last rampage.

While the whole view has always had a calming effect on me, this "exception" is a lesson in humility. I would have bet my last nickel that the last time they put in this bridge it was there to stay — a huge steel bridge firmly implanted with all kinds of safeguards.

One should never bet one's last nickel. **The gentle pastoral view Mother Nature is allowing me to enjoy today is the scene of the violent flood I wrote about last spring.** As we drove home from Norfolk on that day, Kip, awed by the rampaging of our meandering formerly-peaceful creek, said, "Well, one thing we can be sure of is that bridge won't go out."

We got home in time to watch it go, bombarded by the power of the water and the huge logs it carried with it. Unbelievable, but it happened. It took Mother Nature about half an hour to wipe out what it's taken man months and months to rebuild. That's the thought that keeps me humble.

The creek is now a trickle, and a passing stranger might think it's ludicrous to put the massive steel bridge over this gentle stream. Not us. Because we know that hopefully not this spring, maybe not even for fifty springs, but some spring, Mother Nature is just going to get her ire up and have at it.

The lesson I learn each morning as I look out my window is to enjoy each day as you've got it. **Hug your loved ones, drink in the sunshine, cross your bridges.**

Nice Winter Leaves
Northeast Nebraskans Nervous

April 1987

The little portion of northeast Nebraska that we call home has had a winter to end all winters. That is, we've had no winter at all. Even this past week when much of the county was wallowing about in snowbanks, all we had was rain, rain, rain.

And we're worried. Mother Nature is not to be trusted. **We say to each other, "We're going to have to pay for this!"**

It's pretty silly. Of all the things we choose to worry about, perhaps the dumbest is the weather. Worry never changed the path of a single cloud, diverted one snow flake, or stopped even an evening's breeze.

But worry we do. The talk around here — before it rained six inches — was that the mild winter probably meant we were going to dry out this year. "Now," said the friendly fellow who filled my gas tank after I'd slithered and splashed into town, "I suppose we should be worrying about it being too wet to get the crops in."

I suppose we should. On the other hand, will our worrying change a thing? Of course not. We could certainly think of jollier ways to

193

use our time.

Admittedly, some people seem to be born with more worry bones than others. I have a dear and beloved friend, Shirley, who is a world class worrier. If they have gold medals for worrying — she would have a wall full. I've been on her about it so much that now she worries because she worries too much.

I realized something interesting about my friend, however. For her, talking her worries out is an effective outlet. She has them, why not get them out in the open. When things get tough (as she knew they would!) she just gets in there and pitches in to take care of everybody. When it counts, she's a doer, not a worrier.

But there are those poor souls who are not only worriers themselves, but aren't happy until they get everyone around them worried too. These often well-meaning types will come up to you on the street and say, "You should get more rest, you look terrible," when up to then you felt fine.

They are the people who say, "I think you need to hear this for your own good." Believe me, you don't.

They like to be the first with the bad news, especially if it concerns you. I'm convinced these are not unkindly people, they just need to feel important. Perhaps they need affection. When they approach with some unsavory news or morsel of gossip, we should hug them. Very tightly.

The toughest worries to pare down to size are worries about our kids. When your kids are little, the worries are little too. Unfortunately, you don't appreciate that until they get big, and the big worries start.

A phone call from a grown kid with a truckload of problems can wipe out a parent's perfectly lovely day...or week...or year...or lifetime.

The fact is, parents don't have much more responsibilities for what their grown kids choose to do with their lives than they do for what Mother Nature chooses to do with the weather. You may find that hard to believe. But it makes a lot of sense, and it should be a relief. We can love them, cheer them on, but once they are adults, we can no longer assume the responsibility for their choices, anymore than they can assume the responsibility for ours. (Which is a relief to them, too!)

That's enough about worrying. I look out my office window at a picture of pastoral serenity and beauty. The sun is shining brightly, the skies are blue, and the grass is greening up. I can hear the meadowlarks a'singing in the trees.

We're going to have to pay for this!

Chapter 8

"The trouble with being a good sport is that you have to lose to prove it."

**The real test of golf and life is not
keeping out of the rough...
but getting out after we're in.**

Sportsmanlike Conduct?

Chapter Eight

For a person who is an admitted non-athlete, sports have been a big part of my life. I have followed the careers of my five sons through a variety of endeavors in high school and college, and even now am enduring the agony of having a coach or two in the family, and several referees. (No mother should ever have to watch a son referee.) Kip, the friendly cattlefeeder, is a born-again golfer. And even Juli, our one and only daughter, the sensible (?) theater person, has succumbed to a passion for softball. Through it all I trumpet my message that "It is just a game," and winning is NOT the important thing, learning teamwork is. I believe this in my heart of hearts. However, in my body of body, I turn my meager and feeble efforts toward bowling with the "Black Russians" and golfing on a team with my friend Darlene, and I truly want to win. Besides, I love the camaraderie, the esprit des corps. So these sports essays are a mixed bag, lambasting the rude sports fan, sympathizing with referees, and sharing the sad tales of my own lust after the thrill of victory, while dealing with the agony of defeat.

* * *

Wid Misses Football Game, Joan And The Marges Win At Races

October 1973

This week I'm going to tell you the true tales of events that happened to two Super Sports Fans. One would gladly commit a major crime to get tickets to a Nebraska game, and the other heads for the horse races whenever she puts $2.00 together.

They are similar in their commitment to their respective sports and in their knowledge of the specifics involved. Their stories, however, differ. One is sad, and the other is happy.

196

The first involves Super Football Fan, a man with whom we are relatively well acquainted, Kip's brother, Wid. He traveled to Lincoln a week ago Saturday to see his beloved Cornhuskers play. He thought he had a ticket awaiting him, but when he got there there was none.

So, with all the zeal only a super fan can muster, he made a beeline for the stadium, parked in a $3.00 parking lot, and set out to buy one of the tickets that are always being hawked before the game.

However, if you will remember, that day was a perfect day for football. Apparently, everyone decided to go. There weren't any tickets available. Not one. So super fan stood sadly on the sidewalk, his hopes to see the game gradually fading to despair, and watched the happy throngs make their merry red way into the stadium. Then, having no alternative, he returned slowly and sadly to his car.

It was blocked in. He couldn't move. So, with the crowds cheering and the bands playing just a stone's throw away and with the smell of popcorn in the air, our frustrated super fan sat in his car all afternoon, dressed in red from head to toe, and listened to the game on the car radio. Only a fellow fan could fully appreciate his frustration. I guess you all know now, this is the sad story. I will pause while you wipe away a tear.

The other story, revolving around Super Horse Racing Fan, Marge Seim, occurred just last week. Three of us, two Marges (Seim and Miller) and myself (middle-aged type women), journeyed to the races and under the direction of Marge Seim, we spent all afternoon winning something on every race. After the first race we never opened our billfolds, just collected our winnings and bet them on the next one.

We had a system that involved a blue sheet and a green sheet, the World Herald predictions, the predictions on the program, an elderly man sitting next to us, and a horse racing lady with whom he was acquainted. We bet on the surest thing, according to all our information, usually bet on him to place, and although we made very little money, you would have thought from our exultation and exuberance that we were going home owning a piece of the track.

It was great fun. The only glaring error we made was in not taking the horse racing lady's advice (through her elderly friend) when she told us one of our sure things wouldn't come in. That race, she cautioned, was fixed. We couldn't go against the system, and that horse had four first places according to the above mentioned sources. So, we bet it anyway, but darned if he didn't start out last and manage to maintain that position for the rest of the race. I wouldn't say that the race was fixed, but what does it mean, anyway, when the jockey is dragging his feet on the ground?

It was probably significant that the most money we made was

on the last race, when I mistakenly bet on a horse we'd picked in the race before. Number 7. In the last race he was a nothing, and nobody would go in with me on my mistake. Of course, he won. So, our combine ended up winning $1.40 apiece, and I ended up with $11.40.

That's why this, Sports Fans, is The Happy Story.

Off To The Races With Grandpa Burney

1979

"Goodness is seductive" sayeth the sages. So are the horse races. Not for everybody, of course. But they are for me and for Grandpa Burney. The difference is I bet on the favorite to show (come in third) and Grandpa bets the long shots.

And Grandpa figures out his own bets by some kind of intellectual process. I pick up hot tips in strange places, like the rest room at the Marina.

Grandpa thinks it's boring and possibly un-American to bet like I do. He thinks one has to "win big" to enjoy the races. I don't care. The important thing to me is to get my chubby little middle-aged body to the pay-off windows. If my horse pays only $2.20 on my $2.00 bet, it makes no difference. I go to the window as if I'd just won the Daily Double.

Grandpa Burney, who is 87 years old and has only one vice (the horse races), also occasionally bets his age. This, to my mind, makes as much sense as anything. However, it is difficult to bet 50.

I never lose at the races, even when I lose. It's because of my philosophy, which you might enjoy using yourself. I go to the races planning to spend $18.00 for an afternoon's entertainment. Two dollars per race for nine races, right? And so, if I only lose four dollars, I end up making fourteen.

We have a combine of middle-aged ladies who attend races in a group, pool all our knowledge and bet accordingly. We get so excited when our horses win (and since we bet on the favorites to come in third, they often do), we make spectacles of ourselves. And, we also create a false impression. Because we win often and cheer a lot, people think we know something.

It was on one of these forays that I ran into the lady with the hot tips in the rest room. A lovely blond sat in the corner of the lounge area reading a racing form. Racing forms, for the uninitiated, are newspapers that tell all about a horse's performance, in unintelligi-

198

ble rows of figures with confusing designations. They are great for keeping an ice cream cone from dripping on your lap at the races.

I said to my friend, Marge Seim, who was with me, "Don't let me forget to place the bet on two and eight in the Daily Double for Max." **Max, my banker nephew, with the great financial genius all bankers have, was betting his age,too.**

The lovely blond (with the racing form) said something to the effect that it would be a miracle if those horses won. Marge and I looked at her with sudden respect and advanced on her like a couple of vultures. Here was somebody who KNEW. And we coerced her into giving us the winners for all the races.

We didn't know what she knew, but since we knew nothing, where could we go but up?

"Anyone who believes someone who says they have a hot tip is crazy," said the lovely blond, giving us the hot tips, which we believed.

At any rate, to make a long story short, we took her advice on many a race, and she was right on most of them. In fact, if we had wheeled one of the horses she told us was going to win, we would have won nearly two thousand dollars on an exacta. We didn't, of course. We don't know what "wheeled" means.

This very day, Grandpa and I are leading each other astray, and heading for the races at Atokad in South Sioux. I'm having a little trouble, however, convincing him that we have to spend some time in the ladies' rest room at the Marina.

Golfing In Self-Defense

1980

People who don't golf, think golfers are crazy. They're right.

I'll give you a case in point. Friends of ours came from Denver on a blistering hot summer day, the temperature soaring over 100 degrees. In spite of this, we golfed.

We were miserable, but having a great time, if you can understand that. "I don't think we'd get much sympathy from anyone if we died of a heat stroke on the golf course," I said.

"That's right," they chuckled, and grabbed their drivers to tee off.

Then there was a day in early spring which was acting like winter. My friend, Darlene, and I headed out to the golf course. It is not easy for us to clear the decks so we can play during the day, so we play — no matter what the weather is. This day we were on the first green and it started to sleet. **I mean, as we were putting, little ice crystals**

199

were pelting down upon us. Did this stop us? Are you kidding?! We just added another sweater to our already bulky attire and forged onward.

I took up golf about three years ago. I did it in self-defense. It was either that or spend our twilight years watching Kip and his golf cart go off into the sunset (or the sunrise or the mid-day sun) without me.

I didn't like anything about golf, with one exception. **I liked the camaraderie displayed by the golfing people.** I liked the esprit des corps the golfers seemed to enjoy, and the way they sauntered in off the course tanned of visage and with their hair tossled by the wind. I thought that was great.

I didn't like the fact that golfers used a different language. It was immaterial to me if they hooked or they sliced, or they faded their shot around a dogleg. I didn't care what kind of critter got in their way. So what if they got a birdie or an eagle? What were they doing on the golf course anyway? But with five boys and one husband playing golf, you can bet that in the summer golf language was all I heard.

And I certainly didn't think it was too intelligent to take two hours a day (or more) and spend it trying to hit a stupid, little round ball around a pasture. Couldn't they be improving their minds?

I would watch them go off and cheerfully settle down with a good book. Didn't I have the best of things after all? Well, you can bet your life I did.

But I don't anymore. Because one day I hit that ball and it went flying up in the air, and I was hooked. I play golf poorly, but I play it whenever I get a chance. I don't know why. All of us have a touch of masochism in us, I guess.

One day, by sheer accident, I got a birdie myself. Not the kind that flies about, you understand, but the golf kind, which is one shot short of a par on a hole.

Kip said it just proves the old saying "Even a blind sow will sometimes find an ear of corn." Which gives you some idea how he feels about my golf.

So, if you go by a golf course and see a bunch of loonies out there in the broiling sun or the freezing cold, flaying away at that little white ball — especially if one is a short, pudgy middle-aged lady — think kind thoughts. They need all the help they can get!

Gander Threatening To Lady 'Jock'

June 1981

The title of this column could be, "I Was Attacked On Brook's Golf Course."

Little did I know that my sincere and dedicated efforts to please my husband would lead me to be a victim of this vicious attack.

It all started out innocently when my sister-in-law, Kay, invited me, Barbara Marsh and Darlene Miller to her cabin at Okoboji to play a little golf.

Now — I have often expressed the opinion in this column that golfers are crazy. **The fact that I have become one has in no way altered that opinion.**

Anybody who would play golf in wind so strong that their ball blows off the green; in sun so hot that the part in their hair burns; in rain; in sleet; in weather that no other circumstances could force them out, as we have, is a little nutsy.

But I am what you might call a shotgun golfer. I was forced into golf by a love affair — my husband's with the golf course.

Kip is very patient with me, but he desperately wants me to improve. He says the secret is to "practice, practice, practice!!" And he'd appreciate it if I did most of it without him.

So the idea of getting me on a golf course, without having to assume any responsibility for me, really appealed to him. He sent me off with lots of good advice ("don't take so many dumb shots!") and his blessing.

We went at golf with a vengeance. We even started out with the resolve of walking at least 18 holes a day. **We were, no doubt about it, a bunch of middle-aged lady jocks.** I tried to cover up the fact that my feet were doing a "Snoopy" on me, screaming in dire pain at the rest of my body, which was having fun. You see, my golf shoes don't fit and I'm too tight to buy new ones. The weather got a little precarious and so we decided to rent carts. This decision was fortunate for my feet and, as it turned out, for the rest of my body too.

Those of you who have played the beautiful Brooks Golf Course at Okoboji know that it has water hazards. (I'm finally getting to the attack.) Those vicious little lakes and streams have a magnetic attraction for balls. A wise lady golfer who has tiny drives does not attempt to hit over the lake, she goes around it. Especially after watching her three companions plunk their balls into the lake.

Having done this, and feeling quite virtuous about my decision, I headed cheerfully for my ball, admiring two darling geese as I walked in their direction. Not to bother them too much, I left my cart and walked to my ball.

It was then that I noticed one was a lady goose sitting on some eggs, and the other was a gander. Something in the way they were hollering at me (the geese) broke my concentration on my ball, and I looked up to see the gander coming at me with his neck bowed and mad. I mean, I'm talking MAD. I literally ran for my life.

With unseemly haste, and most unceremoniously, I leaped into the golf cart intending to speed away. **Golf carts do not speed.** I darn near jammed the accelerator through the floor and the gander threatened to crawl right in the cart with me. My friends said I was yelling, "I'm leaving, I'm leaving!" at the top of my lungs.

It wasn't a pretty picture, but must have been funny to them because they, of course, were rolling on the fairway laughing hysterically. Only the fact that I put a decent distance between his lady and her eggs made the gander give up the chase.

Thereafter, the jokes at my expense were, I thought, a little tasteless. But one had the ring of truth. **I may never get a birdie or an eagle, but I darned near had a goose!**

Trying To Bowl Like 90-Year-Old Tina

December 1981

My friend, Tina Perk, bowled 90 last week substituting in a league. So did I. There's only one little difference. Tina will be 90 years old on her next birthday. I just turned a hale and hearty 53.

Tina's also been a great bowler in her time. I've always been lousy. Tina has no illusions about how she should be bowling at 90 years of age. She says with a sassy grin, "I do well to pick up the ball!" Everybody loves her.

I still have a vision that someday I might bowl a 200 game. I have all the attributes necessary: good health, two arms, two legs and a bowling ball. I have dedication and I concentrate. I concentrate so hard my head hurts. I still bowl 90. Nobody loves me.

Why do I keep trying? I don't know. There's a multitude of us out here, you know. Bowlers who just keep pegging away in spite of our horrible inadequacy.

Perhaps there's something masochistic in our makeup, and we derive pleasure from our suffering. We certainly have to put up with embarrassment, ridicule, snide remarks and open hostility. (And that's just from our team mates.)

But I think it's because we love the esprit des corps that team sports generate: the camaraderie, the laughter and gaiety of all these women flexing their athletic muscles in open combat.

We are not deterred by the fact that when we flex our muscles, nothing happens, oh — maybe a few tears.

I've done some thinking on this, and it seems to me that the toughest thing people have to do is admit that there are some things that they are not, and will never be.

For instance, I've always wanted to be a big bosomed blond soprano, singing at the metropolitan opera, and I'm an alto. Of course, those that know me well, blabber-mouths that they are, will tell you that neither do I have the other attributes mentioned. However — I could dye my hair, and augment my figure by garment or surgery — regardless of all that, I could never sing soprano. I've tried it. I sound like a chicken caught in a lawn mower. Ask my choir.

The point of all this is that perhaps that I should realize that even though I have all the physical attributes and accouterments necessary to bowl (shoes, ball, etc.), I do not have the inner talent necessary, the God-given ability.

Then again, maybe it's the way I approach it. Two lurches and a lob would not be classic form I am sure. Maybe it's because when my straight ball doesn't work, I switch to my curve ball, which doesn't work either. Maybe I try too hard.

Our good friend, Ab Mauch, is a superb bowler and gives lessons. He suggested I take some. "What do I do wrong?" I asked with a whine.

"Everything!" he replied. Perhaps that should tell me something.

Ab is not the only one who's suggested lessons. So have all the Black Russians. That's not as ominous as it sounds. **The Black Russians are my team. We chose the name because we ascertained that we did better after we drank the drink.** We didn't bowl better, you understand, we just "did" better.

At any rate, I'm considering it. I don't know if a person who's bowled with two lurches and a lob can change her style after forty years, but it's worth a try.

It's either that or back to trying to sing soprano.

Why do I have this feeling that someone's going to send me a bottle of blond hair dye?

Dumb Little Voice Undermines Bowling

February 1982

Take my bowling. Please.

I am the fifth member of a team called the Black Russians. It's not called that because of any subversive communistic tendencies, it is called that because the members of the team are fond of the drink of the same name, and have been known to turn to it in times of trouble, which — when we are bowling — are numerous.

The members of the team are nothing if not erratic. **I wish that were "erotic" as in "sexy" but it is "erratic" as in "eccentric" or even "irregular."**

Like our top bowler went into a slump this year and it's lasted from October until now. And our other top bowler bowled 86 yesterday.

It is some kind of humiliation to be the bottom bowler on a team where the top bowler bowls 86. Then, of course, she bowled a 178. Twice as much. You figure it out.

Some people call the fifth member of a four member team a substitute. That would hardly be accurate with the Black Russians. The other four members are mostly gone. They are the travelingest bunch. Being a substitute on that team is a permanent job. Sometimes even when they are here, they're gone. But they bowl anyway.

The point of all this is that I — the bottom bowler — was going to really show them this week. I read this article and I had it all figured out. The article said that the reason anyone has trouble in sporting events is because they fail to recognize a valuable fact, and that is that in order to succeed at anything one has to be only one person.

What am I talking about? Well, this isn't going to be easy to understand, but this is the way I figured it out.

Most of the time, when you are participating in any sporting event, you have two voices running around in your head. One is telling your body what to do, and the other is questioning the fact that your body can do anything. In other words, when you're getting ready to roll the bowling ball — say — at a difficult spare, one voice is bossing your body around so that you can actually go through the motions, and the other is criticizing. Saying, "Boy, I'll never be able to pick that spare up!" And so you won't.

The man who wrote the article said that you have to get rid of the second voice. The critical one. The only way you're going to excel is if you're just operating with one voice — or one mind — **with no dumb little voice undermining your effort.**

And the way to do that is to concentrate totally on what you are doing. Now, I'm talking CONCENTRATE. So hard that the sniping little critic in you doesn't have a chance to get a word in. And to do that you have to take up your whole head with what you're doing. You have to look at your spot so hard you have no room for anything else, and be aware of its triangular little shape and the board that goes out from it. In golf, it would be total concentration on the ball, the letters on it, the dimples by the letters, etc., etc.

I'm convinced that the article is right but this column does not have an ecstatically happy ending. **You see, if the little critical voice has had free reign for a multitude of years, it doesn't shut up so easy.** However, believe me (my dear Black Russians), it will work eventually. I know it will! I mean — you have heard this before, but you've never heard it uttered so sincerely — wait till next week!

And The Black Russians Bowl On — And On

January 1983

Well, what can you expect from a permanent substitute? So what if my average is 126 and I only bowled an 87. Do they have to make a federal case out of it?

I bowl for the fun of it. The camaraderie. The esprit des corps. **Unfortunately, I think by the time I got done last Tuesday, my des corps had their esprit sagging.**

Years ago I read in some scholarly psychological tome that a person had to do something completely frivolous and totally irrelevant on a regular basis if that person was to maintain a degree of mental health. And you know how I feel about mental health!

Too bad for my bowling team, the Black Russians, that I've chosen bowling for my winter frivolous and irrelevant activity. In summer, as we all know, it's golf.

But golf can be experienced without inflicting oneself upon a team. Although I do. **Because it's hard to have any esprit des corps with oneself.** But we only play team golf briefly in the summer. Perhaps it has something to do with the fact that some poor soul is going to be stuck with me.

Bowling, on the other hand, is primarily played as a team sport. Occasionally we practice on a Saturday, but most of the time we are girded in our Black Russians T-shirts, and we are in mortal combat. Well, maybe not mortal, but combat without a doubt.

The Black Russians march (stumble?) into battle on Tuesday afternoon. With our little hearts beating wildly we do our warm-up exercises (breathing) and set out with high hearts and great expectations. Once we had the high series. We never quite got over that. We always think that could happen again.

We once called ourselves the "Free Spirits." That name seemed to have the dash and verve that we felt our team deserved. Then the other teams started making cracks about how "uplifting" that name was. And it dawns on us that we had innocently purloined the name of a famous bra.

With an average age of — never mind — (some of us have illusions that we're younger than we are, you see) we play against some wonderful teams, some of whose members are in their late seventies. They beat us.

As an incentive to do well, we penalize ourselves twenty-five cents for bowling below our average. And if we bowl below 100, we have to pany one dollar. If everybody gets a strike, except one, it costs that one a dollar. Then we go out and eat at the end of the year. The way I'm bowling this year, we're considering a trip to the Bahamas.

If You Value Your Marriage —
Don't Take Lessons From Your Spouse

June 1983

Heed this well! If you value your marriage, never take lessons from your spouse in any sporting endeavor. Especially golf.

Golf becomes addictive, but when you are learning, it is the stupidest game in the world. You take this long stick and strike at a defenseless little white ball with enough severity to send it flying through the air. Why? Nobody really knows. **People say it's just a game, and then play it as if their life depended upon it.**

And something happens when a husband is trying to teach a wife. About the 100th time he says "You aren't keeping your head down!" the urge to kill supersedes the urge to hit the ball. And the long stick becomes dangerous.

A case in point would be last Wednesday, when my friend, Darlene, and I were racing around the golf course as is our custom. We were slowed to a snail's pace by the saddest sight in the world. A handsome young couple, the husband of which was trying to teach his wife to play golf. We watched with great sympathy, having barely survived this kind of experience ourselves.

206

About the fifth hole, the young wife waved us through. Her husband was no place in sight. We thanked her and asked, "Did you lose your husband?"

And with a sigh that came from the bottom of her toes she said, "I wish!"

I learned to play golf in self-defense. It was that or watch Kip fade into the golf course in the spring and not come out until fall. (Between cattle sales, of course.)

I will never be good, but I feel that I've reached the only goal I ever had for myself in sporting endeavors, I've become adequate. But I'd never made it to even that stage with marriage intact, if I hadn't gone to a professional to learn the basics. I think husbands try to teach everything at once. Professionals just concentrate on one or two things at a time. And husbands want you to learn right now! Impossible.

It is amazing the people who are addicted to this silly game. Now — if you will excuse me — I have to put on my little socks with balls on the back and head for the course. **(To give you an idea of my ability my son Bill says, when Mom hits the ball, we yell "Two!")**

Poem Lambasts Obnoxious Sports Fan

November 1984

I ran across the poem in a South Dakota newspaper at a particularly appropriate time, because I'd gone to a sporting event and had my ears assaulted by an obnoxious fan — and he was yelling for our side.

I couldn't believe that this raging maniac was the same person I knew as a reasonable human being outside of the sporting arena. He flayed out at the coaches, the referees and the kids with equal passion. If I had been a mother of any of the above, I'd have hit him over the head with my purse. . . or if I'd been close enough and Kip had not physically restrained me.

Just the thought of fans like this makes my blood boil. They ridicule and deride, they bellow and bluster, they scream about sportsmanship and display none.

It goes way beyond the normal bounds of emotional enthusiasm and occasional understandable bursts of frustration.

I am, of course going to share the poem with you. By that old reliable "anonymous," it speaks volumes and needs resurrecting. It's written about a boy, but applies to daughters as well.

"He Means A Lot To ME!"

Please don't curse that boy down there,
He is my son, you see.
He's only just a boy, you know,
He means a lot to me.
I did not raise my son, dear fan,
For you to call him names.
He may not be a super star,
It's just a high school game.
So please don't curse those boys down there,
They do the best they can.
They never try to lose a game,
They're boys, and you're a man.
The game belongs to them, you see,
You are just a guest.
They do not need a fan like you,
They need the very best.
If you have nothing nice to say,
Please leave the boys alone.
And if you have no manners,
Why don't you stay at home?
So please don't curse those boys down there,
Each one's his parents' son.
Win or lose or tie, you see,
To us they're number one!

The Snow Birds Return To Find Black Russians At The Bottom

April 1985

Kip came home from his obligatory morning trip to town to have coffee with the boys and said, "The snow birds are returning." We were pleased. It's a sure sign of spring.

The snow birds he's referring to do not have wings. They're friends who've wintered in warmer climates. Every winter a portion of the population of every midwestern town heads south. These are the lucky people who've retired, or have saved up enough money, or who still have borrowing power. They're able to go forth to avoid the rotten weather. They come home tanned and rested and greet all of us pale faces without a twinge of regret. This was a mild winter and we hardly suffered at all, so we took some comfort in that. But, usually we're plowing out from under snow when they return and green with envy.

What brings this all up is that among the snow birds who've return-ed are members of my bowling team, the Black Russians. And all of the returning members came back with the same questions. "What is our team doing at the bottom?" And then they look at me.

Those of us who are left behind, and that's mostly me as the fifth member of the team and permanent sub, are hard put to explain. We've bowled our hearts out. Concentrated on our spot. Thought positive thoughts.

Perhaps, for me, it's an identity crisis. I'm always subbing for somebody different and I never know who I am. I've never had the luxury of developing the rhythm you get from the secure knowledge that you are always the first up, or the anchor man, or whatever. It's comforting to be able to follow the same bottom up to the lanes.

This past week was perhaps the worst. My opponent was my friend, Myrtle Miller, and she is eighty some years old. She's a darned good bowler and she whupped me right into the ground.

I had a lot of fun, and didn't bowl too badly, you understand. But she bowled better. And I said to my team, **"You know, you have to give Myrtle credit. She does a great job for being eighty. I sure hope I can bowl that good when I'm eighty years old."**

"You can't bowl that good now!" they said with just a hint of disgust in their voices.

You might wonder what keeps a non-athlete like me humiliating herself like this year after year. Well, I'll tell you. It's the camaraderie. The esprit des corps. Before I took up golfing, I used to watch the girls come in laughing with wind-blown hair. I wanted to be one. How did I know most of them were miserable? Same with bowling. I'd see them after bowling having their soda pop and laughing over their game. How would I know it was to keep from crying? I wanted to be a part of that. I thought even if I wasn't good, they might let me on their teams if I was fun.

I explained that to the Black Russians. They said I wasn't that much fun! Oh well. Golf season's almost here. At least I'll get a tan.

Kip Strews Joanie All Over The Course

May 1985
Picture this. Me, strewn over the hillside on number one fairway at Hartington Golf Course and Kip merrily driving away in his golf cart.

209

It was bound to happen. For several years I've barely gotten my derriere settled in the seat before he races to his next shot. It's a wonder I don't have a severe case of whiplash. Complaining brings a degree of insincere contriteness, but no improvement.

Kip plays golf in a hurry. He taught me to not take time to look at the birdies or smell the lilacs. "Hit the ball and run," is his motto. He bought clubs for me so we can play together, but now he has a problem — occasionally, we have to play together.

The obvious thing to do, since I sometimes hit the ball as many as four times to his one, is to teach me to hit it in a hurry. He doesn't really care where it goes, or what my score is, as long as I don't hold him up.

Part of the hurrying is due to the fact that we often play golf in the evening, after the various leagues have gone around, and we are determined to finish nine holes even if we play the ninth hole in moonlight. We've done that. It's a form of insanity.

On this particular occasion, however, it was Sunday afternoon. The course wasn't crowded. Perhaps that's why I hesitated that fatal moment before plopping down (or attempting to plop down) in that cart.

I couldn't believe it when the cart roared off. One of my feet was on the floor of the cart, my derriere was poised to descend, and the other foot was still on the course. Most of my body was still with the foot on the fairway. I was set for him to go forward, and he did a quick turn and headed across the course. I did an inelegant kind of split, tumbled on my face and rolled on my back in time to see him go over the hill. **Had I not let out a shriek of outrage, there is a distinct possibility he might never have missed me.**

He wheeled around in a hurry, I can tell you. "I was just going to help LeRoy find his ball," he said, realizing I was furious and hoping my sense of humor would come to the fore.

I wasn't talking. When I'm mad and not talking, there's going to be a reckoning somewhere down the line. I inherited my dad's wild Irish temper, and although I have it under control most of the time, when I blow, I blow.

I saw a look of fear come into his eyes. "I didn't mean to do it!" he said. "You can't think that I meant to do it!"

I'd hate to tell him what I was thinking. I was thinking I wanted to bop him over his head with his precious golf clubs. I was thinking it would serve him right if I'd broken my neck. I was thinking of the headlines: "Burney Spews Wife on Golf Course, Breaks Her Neck!"

Then, of course, I had to laugh. Don't think he's off the hook, though. One of these days I'll be driving that cart.

Family Of Football Enthusiasts
Can't Share Mother's Feelings

February 1986

I think everybody in the world is aware of the fiasco called the Super Bowl in which the Chicago Bears demolished the New England Patriots. If I'd been the New England Patriots quarterback, I'd have gotten the ball and then faded back to pass, and then dropped further back to pass, and then mingled with the crowd and gotten the heck out of there.

I don't like professional football. It's watched in my house all the time, but not by me. Even if I'm in the room where it's going on, I do not watch. I read or write or study and completely ignore it. I don't know who's playing or what the score is, and I don't care. My family of avid sports fans cannot understand it.

Even I got caught up in the frenzy that surrounded the Super Bowl. I couldn't have ignored the game if I'd wanted to because we were in the car on the way home from Omaha when it was played. I was trapped with no diversionary tactics available. I can't read in a car, I get car sick. Anyway, it was too ridiculous not to listen to.

Kip bet on the Patriots because he liked their style. He wasn't too worried because he had a 10-point spread. That is, he wasn't worried for a few minutes. He was in his glory the few seconds they were three points ahead, but he soon was reduced to incoherent mumbling.

Son Tom was in a state of ectasy. He's been a loyal fan of all the Chicago teams since he was 3 years old, and after suffering with them through many losing years, he's finally come into his own.

Tom (who like his mother is involved in a lifelong battle with calories) said it seemed unfair to sit in front of his TV set with a diet drink and carrot sticks and watch a 308-pound guy named "Refrigerator" become famous.

The reason I don't like professional football is it is so vicious. I've heard people interviewed about what goes on in those piles, and it hurts even to watch. To my mind, chicken that I am when it comes to inflicting pain upon myself, I think a person would have to be crazy to play — or on drugs, which we understand has sometimes been the case. It's ironic that the very success of some of the players makes it possible for them to afford to destroy themselves with drugs.

I think those of us who are — well — more mature, can be glad we were raised in an era when the "social" drugs were not available, when pot was something you cooked in and grass grew in your yards.

I didn't even smoke or drink ordinary stuff when I grew up, and it wasn't because I was health-conscious. No, come to think of it, it was because I was health-conscious. Our dad was very strict and un-compromising, and he let it be known if we smoked or drank, he would be hazardous to our health.

In any case, I wish the professional athletes well. Maybe it's worth it to get all busted up for a lot of bucks. Maybe it's even fun to watch. But me, I'm going back to being a non-watcher. It doesn't hurt.

Referees Face Brutal Barrage

March 1986

Pity the poor referee,
If he pleases you, he doesn't please me.
If he calls it my way, you think he can't see.
His job is as thankless as a job can be.
Pity the poor referee.

Sports fans can be unreasonable about everything, but never so much so as when attacking a referee. In the heat of battle, I even find myself, sweet person that I claim to be, shouting at the poor fellows.

I know a certain amount of this is understandable and even expected. I am appalled, however, at how ugly some fans get. They cast aspersions on the referees' parentage, make suggestions which are anatomically impossible, yell things that are downright cruel.

I've tried to figure out how people who seem to be normal in everyday life, responsible citizens, can go so berserk at games. Often it's adults over whom the school has no control. They are an embarrassment to their community, school officials and students.

It's as if the person who is refereeing has no feelings. As if he or she was not a fellow human being just trying to do the best job possible. The referee is, after all, somebody's kid too.

And many people referee for nothing. Imagine, putting up with that kind of abuse when you're doing it for nothing!

I think one could paraphrase Shylock's speech in Shakespeare's Merchant of Venice and say, "I am a referee...Hath not a referee hands, organs, dimensions, senses, affections, passions? If you prick us, do we not bleed? If you tickle us, do we not laugh?"

The part I left out is "Hath not a referee eyes?" I thought that question might confuse the issue. The issue is that perfection is not a human attribute. And everybody knows somebody who referees. We know how hard they try.

Referees are a hearty breed. They tell me that they get used to the usual abuse and consider it comes with the job. In fact, tournament games, where emotions run the highest, are exciting challenges to them. Also, as noted in my poem, half of the people are usually with them.

But I've been at games when abuse gets ugly. And I wonder what kids learn from examples like that.

Perhaps if we take note herein of the hecklers who go beyond the bounds of civilized propriety, they might recognize themselves and make an effort to be only normally obnoxious. Unfortunately, according to the referees with whom I've visited, and I've visited with a few around the state, almost every community has one or two people who seem to be trying to break the obnoxious record.

Maybe we can't change that, **but maybe — just maybe — we can quit yelling long enough to remember how tough a job it is. We might even say thanks. Couldn't hurt.**

Juli's Head Figures In Double Play

June 1986

I got home from class the other afternoon and Kip said, "You'd better call your daughter. She was hit on the head with a softball and it knocked her out."

I was alarmed and called immediately. Perhaps she had a concussion. I would listen carefully to see if she sounded dizzy.

"It's not all bad, Mom," she said. **"The ball hit my head and bounced into the hands of the shortstop, so we got the batter out. Then the shortstop threw it to second base, so we got that man out. It was our first double play of the season.** John (her brother and fellow team mate) thinks we may have discovered an important new strategy." She sounded dizzy.

Compassionate soul that he is, John helped her to the bench after she was clobbered and gave her an enthusiastic account of the double play. She didn't remember what happened to the ball. She thought she had caught it. "I was lying on the ground and everyone was cheering," she said. "I thought I must have done something right." She had. She'd stopped the ball with her head.

Do you think just playing softball could addle the brain? This was not the first softball injury in my family. Our kids are supposedly mature, college-educated young people with post-graduate degrees. But even pain does not seem to dim their enthusiasm.

Isn't this supposed to be a gentle game? Don't they call it "softball?" I can't begin to remember the injuries sustained by the members of this family over the past twenty years. A sprained ankle here, a fractured arm there, and now, apparently, a mind-numbing concussion.

The team, "Class Acts" encompasses the whole Lincoln branch of the Burney family: Juli, son John and his wife, Lou Ann. Perfect grandchild Kate even goes to the games to lead the cheers.

If I thought the ball knocked some sense into Juli's head, I would think there might be hope. The fact that she went back in to play after she got knocked out seems an indication we're dealing with a hopeless case.

I'm going to have to get help for her and I know just where to go. I will round up Lyle George from Wayne and his "No Pitch Softball League" enthusiasts and take them down to deprogram the whole family. **The No Pitch League is for people who don't want to play softball. Lyle firmly believes that people who play softball get addicted and become incapable of rational thought.**

He rode to Lincoln with us to watch a dinner theater production by Juli's acting troupe and he confided to me that he was afraid Juli showed signs of being afflicted. The signs are subtle. Almost imperceptible calluses on the voice box from screaming at the referee and other teams. Bruises and bumps in odd places from violent contact with opposing team members while running around the bases. Limping.

I don't know what Lyle's deprogramming process is, but I suspect he can't start too soon. Hold on kids, help is coming.

After Six Golf Balls In The Lake "Can We Quit Having Fun?"

July 1987

An ugly grizzled little creature sits on my desk. He has bulging eyes, furrowed brow, hair wildly askew, clothes drooping and an expression of terminal weariness on his face.

A sign on his front says: "Why Me Lord?" He's a golf prize. Not one anyone in her right mind would want.

If you've never played in an out-of-town tournament and humiliated yourself by dunking six balls in the lake, or posted a score (on one hole!) of 23, don't talk to me about your troubles in golf.

In my wildest imaginations — in my worst nightmares — I could never have imagined such a terrible outcome for a day that started out to be "fun."

For many years while I slaved away in my classes, my friends have happily gone off to golf opens at surrounding towns. They always came merrily home carrying prizes and telling entertaining stories about what fun they had.

I envied my friends. I wanted to have "fun" in the worst way.

So this summer I decided that I owed it to myself. I would throw caution to the wind and go to a golf open...maybe even two.

I was excited. My first venture was to be at the Yankton Open. I prepared carefully. My golf socks with the little balls matched my golf outfit. Could anyone doubt I was a serious golfer? To further impress people, I took only bright and shiny new balls, including some I'd "borrowed" from Kip. There'd be no problem. I never lose a ball. I've played with my favorite orange pinnacle for two years. I don't hit that far.

That, it turned out, was to be my problem.

My orange pinnacle was the first to go. With a plunk and a splash it disappeared from view, never to be seen again. I mourned it briefly, and tried again. Another plunk, and splash. I won't take you through all the plunks and the splashes, but I dunked two more balls of my own, and three old beaters given to me by a compassionate Yankton golfer, name of Lou.

It was Lou and her partner Jo, both excellent golfers, who warned us about the water. I think it was on hole 13. Mercifully, I have blocked many of the details of this fiasco out of my mind. Anyway, Lou said, "Baby up to it and you'll get over with no problem."

I said to my friend Marge, who was riding in the cart with me, "I have a mental thing about water. I'd just as well go up there and throw all my balls in and be done with it." And we laughed merrily. But we babied up.

Six balls later, we were no longer merry or laughing. I can hit that far, you understand, but apparently not over water.

When I finally got a ball over the lake, to everyone's relief, it got hung up in the tall grass, took three to get on, and then I four putted.

Or something like that.

When I gave my score, Marge — kind person that she is — said, "I'm sure you didn't get that many strokes."

And I said, "After 20, it doesn't seem to make a lot of difference."

We'd started on the 12th hole, so this happened on the second hole we played. We had seven holes of fun-filled golf left to play.

Actually, we did have a good time. In fact, we laughed a lot. Bordered on hysteria, of course. But — it couldn't get any worse, could it?

Wrong. The last three holes it started to drizzle, and then began to rain, seriously. I was badly in need of a permanent so the curl went out of my hair, but the hair spray didn't and it was soon lacquered to my head. Our clothes were soaked through. Even the little balls on my matching socks dropped dejectedly.

In fact, when they gave me the dubious prize for most golf balls in the lake, I thought it looked familiar. And I realized I'd just seen that face in the bathroom mirror. It was me — especially the expression of terminal weariness.

I said to Marge, "Can we quit having 'fun' now?"

Positive Visualization Powerful Tool In Sports And Life

April 1986

Jack Nicklaus begins every golf shot by standing behind the ball and waiting until he "sees" in his mind's eye the exact flight of the ball that he wants. Only after he has "seen" the entire shot does he step up to the ball.

So it says in the latest Golf Digest. And Jack Nicklaus, older person that he is, won the Masters last week. Using that same method of visualization, this week I, a 121 handicap bowler, bowled games of 161 and 178. Can an appearance on Johnny Carson's show be far behind?

What do Jack Nicklaus, my bowling and Johnny Carson have in common? Mental imagery. A method available to anyone with a mind. It's a commonly accepted practice now in sports. And it's used with success by such diverse groups as weight control experts, doctors and brokers.

Our subconscious has a powerful effect on our actions. It can be a negative voice which says, "You're a dumb bowler, and you'll never pick up that spare!" or a positive one saying, "You can do it!" We have some control of that little voice. We can program it with positive mental imagery.

It's worked for me. It's not magic. It's simply using your mind to the fullest. You completely relax, and imagine whatever it is you want to happen as an accomplished fact. Just before I go to sleep at night, or wake completely up in the morning in that semi-sleepy stage, I visualize myself doing well whatever it is I have to do the next day. It could be writing a column, making a speech, bowling, taking a trip, or all four.

It takes a few minutes at best. After you've done it, your subconscious chews happily on these positive mental images while

216

you're asleep, or if you do it in the morning, your day has a pleasant start. Your subconscious can't tell the difference between your visualization and the actual event. So it becomes convinced, because you have visualized yourself performing well, that you can. And, by golly, within the limits of the realms of possibility, you do. It becomes your cheerleader. Go, Go, Go!

It's embarrassing to admit, but that's never stopped me before, so I'll tell you — sometimes I let my visualizations run rampant. I see myself, humble farmwife from Northeast Nebraska, having completed a wonderful book. Then I visualize that zenith of achievement for people who write wonderful books, an interview on Johnny Carson's show. I see myself coming through the curtain, looking thin (I'm always ten pounds lighter in my visualizations.) I'm no movie star, but I'm color coordinated and I'm cool.

I shake hands with Johnny (none of this kissing business) acknowledge Ed McMahon warmly (I have a close relationship with him because he's awarded me a million dollars in other visualizations) and I sit down with my knees together. When Johnny scoots out the little stool for short fat-legged people, I smile at him warmly. (Me and Dr. Ruth.)

He's tickled because I write for the Norfolk Daily News, his hometown paper. We establish instant rapport. Everybody buys my book and, at our house anyway, the farm crisis is over.

Now — to get the book written. And then, who knows?!! **If I can bowl 178** . . .